GOD
IS IN
CONTROL

Emmy's Story, Part 18

by
Kenneth Lee McGee

For Aunt Ann and Aunt Lorna

Thank you Tyler and Liz
for being part of our lives.

Thank you Teresa W. for your help

with the details about COVID-19.

May God keep you and all our healthcare workers safe.

Cover photo by Allen Taylor

Chapter One

"Are you kidding me? Tell me you are," Noemi Bertucci pleaded. "How is that even possible? She's too old."

"Apparently not. She told Zach and me at breakfast," Grace Randolph answered. "I have to call Natty and tell her."

"Should I call Heather and Isabella?" Noemi asked. "They will be so shocked. This is like a Christmas miracle."

"It's sure a surprise. Zach didn't say a word for almost a minute. That's got to be a record for him. He starts talking to his friends as soon as his eyes open."

"You're being sarcastic," Noemi said. "Your brother is the quietest kid in all of Bristol Ridge."

"True, but it's not his fault. With all your brothers and Kevin Michael around, Zach never has a chance to talk. I'll text you later if Mom tells me this has all been a nightmare, but I somehow think she was serious."

Noemi called Heather Colwell and told her the news.

"No way! Not possible!" Heather shouted. "This isn't funny, Noemi. It's not April Fool's Day. It's Christmas."

Isabella Colwell walked into her twin sister's room. "Why did you scream? Who are you talking to?"

"It's Noemi, and you are not going to believe what she told me."

"Let me talk to her."

Heather handed her phone to Isabella and Noemi repeated the news.

Isabella put a hand to her mouth. "Poor Gracie. How did she sound? Did she seem totally dazed?"

"I don't think she had a clue something like this was even possible. You never hear about this happening in real life."

"Tell me," Isabella said. "I'm going to tell Mom, and see what she has to say. Maybe it's all a dream or a false alarm."

"Probably, but Gracie sounded sincere. Talk to you later. I have to send a text to all my contacts," Noemi said.

Isabella handed the phone back to Heather. "Where's Mom?"

1

Heather shrugged and said, " Not sure. She said something about calling Grandma and Grandpa after we opened our presents."

"She's probably in the den. We have to tell her about this. I'm sure she would know if something this earth shattering has really happened."

The twins checked their parents' bedroom suite and didn't see anyone. They hurried downstairs and peeked around the corner into the family room.

"Not here," Heather said.

"Who left all the wrapping paper on the floor?" Isabella asked.

"Kevin Michael!" they shouted together.

"Let's try the den."

They turned to their right and scurried across the hallway to the den. Their mother, Emmy Colasanti-Colwell, was sitting in a recliner talking on her phone.

"Mom!" Heather hollered.

Emmy saw the girls and held up a finger.

"She's almost through talking to Grandma and Grandpa," Isabella said.

Emmy ended the call and motioned for the girls to enter.

They sat on the arms of the leather recliner.

"What's going on?" Emmy asked. "I heard you running around."

"Have you heard any weird news this morning?" Heather asked. "Anything that might appear like absolutely impossible but yet everyone swears is true?"

Emmy smiled.

"You have!" Isabella shouted. "Have you talked to Aunt Kristen?"

"She called me early this morning."

"How can it be possible?" Heather asked.

"It's entirely possible. Kristen is only forty, and forty's not that old."

"It seems old to us. We won't be fourteen until our birthday," Isabella said. "Do we even know anyone who had a baby at forty?"

2

"Wait!" Heather said tapping her mother's thigh. "If Aunt Kristen is... Could it happen to you?"

Heather and Isabella grinned.

"We're going to have a baby sister," Heather teased.

"Maybe a baby brother," Isabella replied."

Emmy shook her head. "Not possible."

"Why not?" Heather asked. "You're younger than her, and we know you and Daddy..."

"Hush! It's not possible because I had my tubes tied after your brother was born."

"So you can't get pregnant like Aunt Kristen?" Isabella asked.

"Not unless I get my tubes untied," Emmy answered with a grin.

"Can they do that?" Heather asked.

"That sounds weird. You make it sound like tying and untying your shoes," Isabella said.

The girls snuggled closer to Emmy as the news about Aunt Kristen's pregnancy set in.

"Mom," Isabella whispered.

"Yes, Isa."

"We know you used to call us your miracle babies."

"You are still my miracle babies," Emmy said.

"Then what is Kevin Michael?" Heather asked.

Emmy sighed and said, "He's your father's nightmare."

"He left a mess in the family room," Heather said.

"I saw it. I took one of his new DVDs away until he cleans it up."

"Has Daddy ever asked you to get your tubes untied?" Isabella asked.

Emmy grinned, then shook her head and answered, "No, he likes... never mind. Are you hungry? I can make more pancakes."

3

Chapter Two

"Are you sure they didn't cancel school?" Kevin asked. "It's snowing again, and there's still a lot left from the other day. There are drifts in the driveway up to my waist. Maybe my chest. I don't think we can even get out of the subdivision."

"That's why we have a Jeep," Emmy replied. "It will get through any snow."

"I think we'll get stuck and be stranded," Kevin said.

"I'm pretty sure the roads have been plowed."

"What if they aren't?"

Emmy smiled at him and tugged his stocking cap down over his eyes. "Then we'll call Tony, and he can come to our rescue in his big new truck. He loves to drive around in the snow."

"We're ready, Mom," Heather said.

"Have you heard anything about school being canceled, Heather?" Kevin asked taking off his stocking cap. "Did you text Noemi? Aunt Sloane would know because she teaches there."

"Why are you so determined not to go back to school?" Emmy asked. "You've been off for two weeks and had lots of time to play with Ben and all your friends. I really like the snow fort you made. Your father and I saw it when we took the snowmobile out. Did Tony help you?"

Kevin nodded. "He helped us make the snow into large blocks and stacked them up when the sides got too tall."

"I'll be right back," Emmy said. "I'm going to start the Jeep to let it warm up." She grabbed the keys and headed to the garage.

"Kevin, are you afraid to go back to school because of those eighth grade boys?" Isabella asked.

"No! And you better not tell anyone."

"You should tell someone."

"I'm not telling Mom or Dad," he insisted.

"You could tell Mrs. Toth. She's the principal," Isabella said.

"No way! I can't talk to her. She's a lady."

"You could tell Pastor Tyler or Pastor Wyatt," Heather suggested.

4

"Why? What can they do?"

"They could talk to those boys."

They heard the mudroom door open.

"Mom's coming. Don't say nothing," Kevin warned.

"It's time to go. Did everyone grab their lunch? Kevin, do you have your project?"

"In here," he answered. He picked up his backpack, put his stocking cap on and headed out the door. "Let's go. I might as well get this over with."

Emmy heard him, watched him walk away, looked at the twins and asked, "What is your brother talking about?"

Heather shrugged and said, "No idea."

"Isa, do you know?"

Isabella grabbed her lunch from the fridge, closed the door, picked up her backpack and put on her coat before answering, "He might be worried about his project. He has to stand in front of the whole class and talk about it."

Emmy watched the girls walk out. *He's never be shy about talking in front of anyone. Why do I have a feeling something's going on and no one is telling me?*

"See! I told you the Jeep would get through anything," Emmy said when they reached the end of the driveway. "We went right through that drift, and it wasn't five feet high like you said." She glanced at Kevin, who was staring out the window.

"Mom, will Aunt Kristen hire a nanny when she has the baby? If she needs one, can we apply for the job?" Isabella asked.

Emmy looked in the rearview mirror. "You are probably old enough to babysit, but not be a nanny."

"Did you start babysitting when you were fourteen?" Heather asked while texting her friends.

"I was thirteen, but it wasn't at night. Just a few hours at a time after school."

Emmy dropped the kids off and watched Kevin dragging his feet instead of running into school. *Something's bothering him. He didn't say a word on the way here.*

Heather and Isabella put their coats and backpacks into their lockers and looked for Noemi and Grace.

5

"There's Noemi, but I don't see Gracie," Heather said.

Noemi waved when she saw them. They rushed into the classroom and sat at their desks.

"Did Gracie say anything more about her mom?" Heather asked.

Noemi looked around to make sure no one was listening and said, "She's definitely going to have a baby. Grace said she went to the doctor with Wyatt, and they were smiling after they got back."

"Can you imagine having a baby when you're that old?" Heather said.

"It would be like Mrs. Kramer having a baby," Isabella said as their teacher wrote a poem on the whiteboard.

Mrs. Kramer taught English and was the homeroom teacher for one of the eighth grade classes.

"Do you think she's still in her forties?" Heather asked.

Noemi whispered, "Mom said she is older. Probably in her mid-fifties."

The girls watched as Mrs. Kramer smiled at some of the students entering the room.

"Hush!" Isabella said. "Here come those boys who keep sending us texts and asking us to eat lunch with them. They're so toxic."

"I think Seth is okay. He's not as gross as the other boys in our class," Heather said.

"You're only saying it because he said he liked hearing you sing," Isabella said.

Kevin sighed as he slumped into his desk. He glanced at Mr. Starks, who sat at his desk reading his Bible.

"Hey, Kevin! Did you hear Dad almost got the truck stuck on the way to school?" Ben asked taking his seat next to Kevin.

"No! Where?"

"In the driveway. He slid off the edge, and we had to dig it out of the snow. It was radical."

Kevin sighed and said, "Mom brought us in the Jeep. We didn't get stuck at all."

6

Grace and Natalie whispered as they took their seats at the front. Grace looked back at Ben and Kevin and smiled.

"Ben, what do you think about your aunt having another baby? Does your mom ever talk about having another one?"

"I think it's okay Aunt Kristen and Pastor Wyatt are going to have one, but Mom said she'd never want to have one because she's too old," Ben told Kevin.

"Is your mom older than Aunt Kristen?" Kevin asked.

"I heard Dotty ask Mama, and Mama said Mom is a month younger."

"My mom is a few months younger than Aunt Kristen, and she said she would have liked to have more babies, but she couldn't because... uh... it was something about tubes getting tied up."

"Your mom still looks young enough to have babies, but my mom looks too old. She has to color her hair because it will turn gray otherwise," Ben said.

"You mean like my grandma or Mama?"

Ben shrugged and said, "I guess."

Mr. Starks stood up to get the class's attention.

"I want to hide in the fort after school," Kevin said. "We need to use it before it melts."

"You mean play in it?" Ben asked.

"Yeah, what did I say?"

Ben looked at his friend and answered, "You said hide."

"How did it go last night?" Emmy asked as one of the other priests from St. John's drove Father James to St. Bart's.

He stared at his phone for a moment. "Seriously? How do you think it went? Once I started drinking that crap, I had to stay close to the bathroom."

"Sorry, I forgot about that. Kenny's father had to have a colonoscopy a few years ago."

"The worst part is having to drink so much liquid. The other part I could handle, but drinking all that stuff almost made me puke."

"Should I drop you off at the door, or can you walk?" Father Wieklaus asked as they approached St. Bart's.

"In my weakened condition I think you should drop me at the door. There's only one car in line."

Father Wieklaus turned into the horseshoe drive.

Emmy was still on the phone and said, "Your weakened condition, my butt. You're just too lazy to walk across the street."

"I would do the same for him. Besides, there is snow and ice around the sidewalk."

"Yeah, sure," Emmy said.

"One of these days you will be old and need a colonoscopy, too."

"I got a ways to go," she said with a laugh. "Is Father Wieklaus going to wait for you and take you home, or should I come and get you?"

"He is, but I had to promise to do mass for him for the next month."

"I bet. Call me when you get home. I want to know how it went."

"You were supposed to call me yesterday," Emmy said. "Why didn't you?"

"Because there was nothing to tell. I won't know the results until I see my doctor Monday," Father James answered.

"How did the procedure go?"

"I suppose it went well. I have no memory of it. I was on the gurney and they gave me something. The next thing I remember was a nurse talking to me in the recovery room."

"Did you have gas after it? Kenny's father did."

"They pump you full of some kind of gas to do the thing, so, yeah, I had gas."

"Call me back sometime. I want to know what the doctor says."

"Maybe I don't want you to know about my insides."

"Fine. Be that way. Talk to you later I have to work on songs for this week."

Chapter Three

"Measure me now, Daddy!" Isabella squealed with obvious delight. "I want to make sure I'm taller than Mommy, too."

Emmy rolled her eyes as Isabella pressed her shoulders against Emmy's. "You're taller, Isa. Everyone is taller than me now."

Heather grinned at Isabella, and put a hand on top of Emmy's head. "Quit trying to cheat, Mom. You're standing on your toes."

Kevin Michael walked into the kitchen, grabbed a donut from the island counter and took a bite. "What's going on?"

"Mom insisted she was still taller than us, so we are proving her wrong, and don't talk with your mouth full," Heather answered.

Kevin finished his bite and laughed. "Mom, you may be the shortest one in our family, since I'm like three inches taller than you, but I'm pretty sure you're still taller than Conor and Lily." He took another bite of his chocolate donut and picked up a chocolate glazed one.

"Hush!" Emmy said looking over her shoulder at her eleven-year-old son. "Lily is seven and Conor's only six and don't eat all the donuts. Someone else might want one."

Kenny patted Emmy's back and said, "It's official. Isabella is at least an inch taller than you."

"Doesn't matter," Emmy said as she stepped over to the island and snatched the last glazed donut. "I stopped growing when I turned fourteen, so the twins might not get any taller."

Kenny chuckled and said, "I wouldn't hold your breath, Em. It wouldn't surprise me if they grow another six or seven inches. I doubt they'll be as tall as me, but they're definitely going to be as tall as Diane."

"Don't worry, Little Mommy, we'll still respect you even if you're a shrimp," Kevin teased.

"Do we have to go to school today?" Heather asked. "It's our birthday. We should be allowed to stay home."

"I agree," Emmy said. "You may stay home."

"Really?" Heather asked. "Tell me you're not joking."

"Not in the least. I want you to stay home. I have a list of things to do. I need the upstairs dusted and all the windows cleaned. All the bathrooms need a thorough scrub, and the toilets need to be disinfected."

Heather grabbed her backpack. "Daddy, please take me to school. I have an English test I need to ace."

Kenny looked at Emmy.

"Works every time," Emmy said. "They may be taller than me, but I'm still smarter."

"I'm back," Kenny hollered when he returned from chauffeuring the kids to school.

"What are your plans for the day?" Emmy asked. "I'm going to write for a minimum of four hours each day this week. I want to have a first draft ready for Denise."

"I want to flesh out the songs I've been working on. We need to release a CD in the fall, and none of the guys have any new tunes. I might have to come up with all of them," he answered. "Em, you released two books last year. How many do you have planned for 2020?"

"Maybe one. This year is going to be busier than last year. You guys are touring in the summer, and we want to fit a vacation in somewhere."

"If we want to take the Jeep out West, we might have to do it during the spring."

"But we can't take the kids out of school," Emmy reminded him.

"The girls don't care about seeing Utah or Arizona. Kevin would just as soon stay home and build forts in the woods. It might only be the two of us. I'll be downstairs if you need me."

Emmy took a break from writing before noon and walked downstairs.

"I'm hungry. Are you?" Emmy asked.

"Sorta. Do we have any single serve pizzas left?" he asked while looking at his notebook and leaning back in his chair. "Those are the perfect size."

10

"I'll check. Have you made any progress?" she asked. "Did you record anything, or are you working on lyrics?"

He tossed the notebook on the mixing desk. "I haven't even booted it up. I've got a melody and part of a chorus for this idea, but I'm stuck on the verses. I have one kinda done, but the second verse is eluding me."

"I could help after we eat. I got more done this morning than I expected. I could see what you've got. Maybe my brain will function better than yours," she teased.

"Hey! My brain functions just fine," he replied pulling her onto his lap and kissing her.

She let the kiss linger and, when he stopped, said, "You better be careful or else I might end up like Krissy."

He tilted his head. "You said it's not possible."

"If you mean getting my tubes untied, Dr. Walsh said it's possible but if I was serious I shouldn't wait too much longer. He doesn't recommend the procedure for women over forty."

"If Kristen wasn't expecting, would you even be thinking about this?"

She pushed his hair away from his ear and got more comfortable on his lap. "I think about how many kids we could have had if my health had been different."

"I've never regretted not having more kids. I love the ones God gave us, and it was the best option for you at the time."

She grabbed his chin, pulled his face to hers and whispered, "I'll get my baby fix from holding the babies at church and giving them back to their mothers when they have a poopy diaper, but right now I need some attention." She kissed him and giggled when he stood up and carried her to the couch.

"Okay, what did your doctor say?" Emmy asked Father James that afternoon. "You were supposed to call me earlier. Why didn't you? Did your doctor give you bad news?"

"Sorry, I didn't call earlier. I was busy at St. Bart's. There were a dozen people admitted with the flu."

"So what did he say?"

"For the most part, it was good news."

"But not all, huh?"

"He said I have a mild form of colitis and evidence of diverticulitis."

"That sounds serious. Do you need surgery or anything?"

"No, he prescribed a couple medications, and said I have to have another colonoscopy in three years."

"Lucky you," Emmy said.

"It could be worse. He said I should be able to control it."

"Have you been having a lot of pain or blood in your poop?"

He sighed and answered, "Not that I've noticed. You have such a delicate manner. You should have been a doctor."

"I don't fool around. I ask the straight questions."

"Thanks for coming over," Kenny said to Will Consoli the next morning. "UPS delivered this earlier than I expected."

Will responded, "Not a problem. I did some research on how to install this new gear. It shouldn't be too difficult. Then you'll be able to livestream using state-of-the-art technology."

Will had been working for Steward Music as a studio engineer, producer and front of house mixer for Fridays At Five for over twenty years.

"I can't imagine using it very often, but I was curious. I've seen some videos posted on YouTube by independent artists. They sometimes do whole concerts without leaving their home."

"Think of how much you could save on travel expenses," Will said as he opened one of the boxes.

"Maybe, but it would be like doing TV shows where you're performing for a camera. I love getting feedback from a live audience."

An hour later the new gear was installed and tested.

"It's easier than I imagined," Will said. "I've never been involved in the video side of things, but I could handle it with this software program."

"I have no doubt, but we may never need to test it," Kenny said. "Do you want to come up for some coffee or something? Emmy was asking about your kids earlier."

12

"Thanks, but I should get back. I'm supposed to start mixing the project for the new band Mr. Kesson signed."

"I heard part of it. Sounds different," Kenny said.

"You can tell Emmy the kids are doing great, and I have three grandchildren now. Too bad they live in Idaho."

"I'll let her know," Kenny said. "It's none of our business, but Emmy was wondering how old you are. You've been with us for a long time."

"You can tell her I will turn sixty in February. I don't feel old, but my wife reminds me every once in a while."

Kenny laughed and said, "Emmy's always reminding me I'm older than her."

"Who was on the phone, Mom?" Isabella asked.

Emmy replaced the landline and smiled at Isabella. "It was Mrs. Osborne."

"Who's that?" Kevin asked as he opened the fridge and grabbed the chocolate pudding.

"Don't eat out of the container," Emmy said. "Use a bowl."

"Fine! But there isn't much left. It's only half full." He showed his mother. "Who is Mrs. Osborne? Is she the fat lady from church who's always trying to hug me?"

"No, that's Mrs. Springside and don't call her fat."

"But she is."

"That's beside the point." Emmy made a face at Kevin. "The Osbornes live next to Dr. Beggs-Jeffrey, and she needs a babysitter tonight. Would you and Heather be interested? I need to let her know."

"Would we actually get paid?" Isabella asked.

"Paid for what?" Heather asked. She held up a pink top. "The stain didn't come out. I only wore this twice and it's ruined. Such a waste."

"Mrs. Osborne wants a babysitter tonight. We would earn some money," Isabella explained.

"How many kids and how old are they?" Heather asked. She set the top on the island. "Can you work some magic on it, Mom?"

Emmy picked up the top and looked at the stain. "I might be able to fix this, and there are two kids. Milton is six and Mia is four. Are you interested?"

"How long?"

"She thought it would be three or four hours. They have to attend a company dinner in Newcastle, and their regular sitter is sick."

"Did she say how much she would pay us?"

"I don't think so, but no matter how much she offers, you should accept the offer. It would be good experience."

"And we can earn some spending money," Isabella said rubbing her fingers together.

"Okay, but if her kids are holy terrors, we might lock them in a closet," Heather said.

"Thank you so much for agreeing to babysit," Mrs. Osborne said opening the door for Heather and Isabella. "Please come in. I'm Merrill. Milton and Mia are still finishing their dinner."

Isabella waved at her father, and he drove away.

"I'm Heather and this is Isabella. Thank you for giving us the opportunity to care for your children. We will do our very best to look after them."

Isabella looked at her sister with a mixture of admiration and surprise.

"What?" Heather whispered as Mrs. Osborne turned around and walked away.

"What was that about?" Isabella asked.

"Mom told me to be nice, and I thought if I sounded intelligent and responsible she might pay us more."

"Good thinking."

They followed Mrs. Osborne to the kitchen and met Milton, Mia and Paxton Osborne.

"Hello, I'm Paxton Osborne." He stood up and adjusted his red bow tie.

The twins looked up and up because Mr. Osborne stood only an inch under seven feet tall.

14

"Our driver will be here within five minutes, and we should return sometime between ten and ten fifteen at the latest," he said checking his Rolex.

The twins smiled at Milton and Mia.

"They look adorable," Heather said.

Mia smiled at the girls and held up a stuffed giraffe. "This is Jerry."

Milton smiled and then threw some macaroni and cheese at Heather.

"We will be back before you know it," Mrs. Osborne said. She blew the children a kiss, and she and Mr. Osborne fled the scene.

As soon as the front door closed, Heather frowned at Milton. "You will pick that up this instant!"

"Make me," he said. He jumped down and dashed out of the kitchen with Heather in pursuit.

"That's a lovely giraffe," Isabella said.

"Mommy gave him to me on my birthday. I love giraffes, and I sleep with Jerry and lots of other animals every night. Do you want to see my room?"

"Yes, I would love to." Isabella picked up Mia and carried her to the stairs. "I will follow you."

"You can't catch me!" Milton hollered.

"Where did you go?" Heather asked as she opened another door in the long hallway. She heard a door slam behind her and caught a glimpse of Milton running out of the house. "Get back here, you little monster. This is going to be a long night," Heather said with a sigh.

"How did it go?" Kenny asked at ten minutes past ten. "Did you enjoy babysitting. Was it boring or an adventure?"

Heather slumped into the backseat of the Jeep. "I didn't have to chase the twerp all the way to Chicago, but it felt like it. He should be medicated. Severely medicated. Why would anyone ever name a kid Milton? That's a life sentence."

"How was it for you, Isa?" Kenny drove down the winding driveway.

"Peaceful would be the best word to describe it, I think," she answered.

"My night was the total opposite," Heather said.

"Mia showed me her room and all her stuffed animals and dolls. We had a tea party. I read to her, and she fell asleep at eight thirty. I was able to text Noemi and Grace the rest of the night."

"I never had a chance to use my phone. I was totally out of the loop," Heather said. "The world could have ended, and I would have been the only person not to know."

"Mrs. Osborne gave each of us fifty dollars. Easiest money I ever earned," Isabella said.

Heather stared at her sister. "Maybe for you. I never want to babysit for that child again. He was a holy terror. I had to chase him through the woods and after I caught him he kicked me." She rubbed her shin. "I think he broke my leg. It still hurts. When I finally got him back inside, he threw a magazine at me and then hid in the basement. I should have left him there and locked the door, but I didn't. He kept me going until five minutes before his parents got home. When they got back, he acted like he missed them so much and I almost puked."

"It sounds like you earned your money the hard way," Kenny said with a grin.

Isabella stuffed her money in her front pocket and said, "I told Mrs. Osborne to call me whenever she needs a sitter."

"Next time you have to watch Milton," Heather insisted.

"I would but Mia and I have bonded. She said I was her best friend ever, and loved how I read to her."

"If I have to watch that demon again, can I put handcuffs on him and shackle him to his bed?" Heather asked.

"Be serious, Heather," Isabella said.

"I am serious, Isa. Those are my terms. Mrs. Osborne can either accept them or find another guinea pig."

Chapter Four

"Hi, Mom. How are you? I was going to call later." Kenny set the acoustic guitar down next to the mixing board in the basement studio. "Are you enjoying the warm weather?"

"I took your father to the hospital this morning," Elly Colwell said.

Kenny straightened up in his chair. "What happened? Is he all right?"

"He was complaining about always feeling worn out, and he was having trouble breathing, so I took him to the ER."

"Has he seen a doctor yet?"

"Yes, his regular doctor came in about an hour ago to talk to us. He said your father's oxygen level is too low, and his red blood cell count is off. He spouted off a few numbers, and said something about platelets or something. I'm not sure what it means, but he's been admitted for observation."

"Should I fly down there? Is he going to be in the hospital long?"

"It depends on his blood, I suppose. They are doing tests to see why it's low. They put him on oxygen and he's breathing okay."

"But he's going to be there the rest of today, right?" Kenny asked.

"Yes, because the doctor said he wants to do another test in the morning."

"I'm going to fly down there."

"You don't need to. He might be able to come home tomorrow," she said.

"Doesn't matter, Mom," Kenny replied. "I'm not doing anything right now. I can come down there and help you take care of him. He's not a very cooperative patient."

"You do what you think is best, son."

Kenny put his guitar away, turned off the lights and headed upstairs. He turned the corner to check the den and saw Emmy.

"What's up?" Emmy asked. "I thought you were going to keep working on your songs."

"Mom called. Dad's in the hospital," he said then explained everything he knew. "Would you mind terribly if I fly to Florida in the morning?"

"Not at all. You should be there to help your mom," Emmy said. "The kids and I will be fine. I'm almost finished with the first draft."

"That was pretty quick."

"I had most of the story set in my mind. Should I check flights for you, or will you ask Mr. Robertson if you can use his plane?"

"I don't want to bother him. They're in Idaho, right?"

"They are, but his plane isn't. It's here in SoHam. I'll call him and see if it's okay for you to borrow it. I'm sure he won't mind. He probably has to pay the pilots anyway."

Emmy talked to Mona Robertson and told her what had happened.

"Bill is fishing somewhere. Ice fishing. Tell Kenny to use the plane. Bill won't mind. We won't need it for another week at least."

"Thanks, Mona. I'll let Kenny know."

"And I will call the pilots," Mona said. "I'm sure his father will be all right, dear."

After taking the kids to school, Emmy drove Kenny to the SoHam airport.

"I'll come home as soon as Dad is all right," Kenny said.

"Give me a kiss and tell your father to follow the doctor's orders," Emmy said.

Kenny boarded Mr. Robertson's Gulfstream III for the flight to Florida. Emmy waited until the plane was in the sky before heading home. She called Kristen at work.

"I am fine, Emmy. I haven't had morning sickness or anything. Did Kenny leave already?"

"The plane left ten minutes ago."

"I am sure his father will be fine. Daddy had the same problem a few years ago. His doctor put him on a special diet, but I think it was more for his blood pressure."

18

"Kenny's father won't like it if he has to go on a diet. Especially if he has to give up red meat."

Kenny landed in East Hastings, Florida, and picked up his rental car. He headed straight to the hospital, explained who he wanted to see and took the elevator to the fifth floor. After reversing his path, he found the right room.

"Anyone home?" he asked knocking on the door. He walked into the room and saw a nurse taking his father's vitals.

"You didn't have to fly all the way down here," Carter Colwell said.

Kenny shrugged and replied, "I thought about flying part of the way, but then I would have to shout really loud for you to hear me."

Elly Colwell shook her head then hugged her son. "I won't tell Emmy you're trying to be funny. Is everyone okay at home?"

"We are doing good. Kevin didn't want to go back to school, so that's on my mind. He usually loves school."

"We heard about Kristen. How is she feeling?"

"Okay, as far as I know. Em knows more. She calls Kristen every day."

The nurse finished and smiled at her patient. "Your numbers are getting better. We might be able to boot you out of here tomorrow."

"Good. No offense, but I'd rather not enjoy your hospitality any longer than I have to," Carter said with a grin.

"Carter! You better be nice to her. She's the one taking care of you," Elly said.

"It's all right, Mrs. Colwell. I'm use to dealing with patients like him," the nurse said. "He's not as bad as some of them. The man in 506 buzzes every twenty minutes to complain." She headed out the door. "I'll be back shortly after you fall asleep. I time my visits to cause the most interruptions possible."

Carter waved at the nurse and then said to his wife, "I was just trying to be funny. Everyone on the staff has been very nice except for that doctor who mentioned something about losing weight and going on a diet."

19

"It wouldn't hurt you to lose a few pounds."

"Are you saying I'm fat?"

"Kenny, will you tell your father I don't think he's fat, but he could lose a few pounds, and he needs to eat healthier."

"Dad, I agree with Mom. I've seen how you eat. I'm not saying you have to eat nothing but grapefruit and salad, but you could cut back on the fatty stuff."

Carter waved. "Ba! If it were up to your mother, I wouldn't be allowed to eat anything that tastes good."

"What time is the doctor going to get here? I'm ready to go home now," Carter said the following morning.

"Be patient, Mr. Colwell. He will be here soon. He wants to talk to you about your diet," a different nurse said.

Thirty minutes later Dr. Armaan Jhaveri walked briskly into the room. "How are you feeling today, Mr. Colwell?"

Carter stared at the doctor, who didn't appear older than his mid-thirties, before answering, "I told you I feel great. I never should have been forced to stay here."

Dr. Jhaveri checked Carter's chart on the computer. "Your numbers have improved, and I will discharge you. However, I would like to see you in my office in two weeks."

"We will make an appointment today," Elly said as Carter rolled his eyes.

Dr. Jhaveri handed Mr. Colwell a pamphlet. "I would like you to look at this. It lists several foods to avoid and others that would be beneficial for a man in your condition."

"What condition am I in exactly?" Carter asked. "I feel fine."

"You are typical of men your age. A few pounds overweight. Your cholesterol is high, and your heart is working too hard."

"I can shed a few pounds by exercising more. Why should I quit eating what I like?"

"I'm not saying you need to give up everything you enjoy, but you should use better judgment in how much you eat."

"I don't eat as much as I used to," Carter said.

"Maybe limit the trips to fast food restaurants. The food you make at home is usually healthier." Dr. Jhaveri shook hands with Mr. Colwell. "I will sign the paperwork and you can go home, but I expect to see you soon with some progress on your change of diet. Nice to see you, Mrs. Colwell." He smiled at her and left.

Carter rolled his eyes after the doctor left the room. "I know what you're going to say. You've been after me to eat better for years."

"It's not all your fault. I am guilty as well. I am often too lazy or busy to cook a proper meal, so we order out or run to the nearest fast food place. With a little effort on both our parts I'm sure your numbers will improve, and you might even fit into those pants I have stored in the cedar closet."

Kenny arrived at the hospital later that morning to find his father dressed, packed and anxious to leave.

The orderly made Mr. Colwell ride in a wheelchair and was flirting with one of the nurses aides as they headed to the elevator bank.

"What did your doctor say about your diet?" Kenny asked as he followed his father down the hall.

Carter looked over his shoulder. "Which side are you on?"

"This side," Kenny answered.

Carter looked over his other shoulder. "He gave me a pamphlet listing what food I can eat. I gave it to your mother. I don't know what all the fuss is about. I can lose five pounds without giving up what I enjoy eating."

"I think the doctor is talking about fifteen to twenty pounds, Dad."

Carter waved a hand. "He's crazy. Does he expect me to become nothing more than skin and bones like your uncle Parker? He's the skinny one in the family. Thomas and I are normal sized adults."

"Where is Mom?" Kenny asked.

"In the gift shop. She wanted to buy something nice for the nurses."

"Sounds like Mom."

"Heather, you should help Mrs. Osborne. She can't find anyone else to watch Milton," Emmy said.

"I can see why. He almost broke my leg Wednesday night, and it still hurts." She showed Emmy the bruise. "She can't pay me enough to watch him."

"Isabella can't watch both kids."

"Why not?" Heather asked. "Mia will fall asleep, and Isa can tie Milton to his bed."

Emmy asked, "Isa, will you babysit?"

She thought about the money and grinned. "I'll do it. I'm sure it won't be that hard."

Heather laughed.

Emmy picked up Isabella at nine. Heather rode along.

"How was it?" Emmy asked.

"Was it like the most horrible ordeal ever?" Heather asked.

"I don't know why you couldn't handle Milton. We had fun," Isabella answered.

"Did you chain him to the kitchen table, or did you sedate him? Horse tranquilizers might work."

"No. They were eating when I arrived. I did the dishes while the kids were watching *The Dragon Prince* on a laptop at the table. Then I read to them. Mia fell asleep early, and Milton and I played games on his Xbox. He went to bed around eight thirty, and I spent the rest of the night on my phone. Mrs. Osborne even gave me a tip for doing the dishes and folding some laundry."

"How much did you make?" Emmy asked.

"Sixty for three easy hours," Isabella answered showing the money to Heather.

"I hate you," Heather said.

"What time are you arriving?" Emmy asked Monday morning. "Will you need a ride home?"

"I should be back in SoHam around noon. I could get an Uber if you're busy."

"No, I'll pick you up. Uber rides cost money. I want to hear about your father."

22

Emmy watched the Gulfstream land shortly before noon and waved when Kenny disembarked.

"How is he?" Emmy asked after giving Kenny a kiss. "Is he going to be stubborn about following his doctor's orders?"

"You know my dad," Kenny said with a sigh. "He insists he can give up a couple burgers and fries and walk around the block and everything will be hunky dory. He needs to change his diet, and I know he will get mad at Mom if she forces him to cut out the junk food and snacks."

Emmy patted Kenny's stomach. "He's not the only one who should lose a pound or two."

"I will lose this without any trouble. I'll start running before the summer tour, and the pounds will disappear in no time."

"That may work for now," Emmy said opening the door to her BMW, "but it won't be as simple when you are your father's age. Better start eating healthier now."

"Are you saying we have to give up pizza or Darby's?"

"Who said anything about we? I'm talking about you, buster. It's in my genes to remain slim and tiny."

Kenny got in and buckled up. "Grandma Isabel and your mother were tall and slender, but Grandma Colasanti was as round as she was tall. Which one will you look like when you are sixty or seventy?"

"Will it matter when I'm that old? Grandma Isabel looked pretty good when she reached a hundred. If I look like a typical Italian grandma, will you trade me in for one who looks like a supermodel?"

He rubbed his jaw for a moment.

"Oh, stop it! You know you love me and can't live without me. By the time I'm seventy, you will have forgotten about sex."

Chapter Five

"Have you heard anything about this?" Emmy asked carrying her laptop into the family room.

"About what?" Kenny asked. He poked the logs in the fireplace and watched the orange flames.

"I was watching Greg Benton, and he's talking about some virus from China showing up here in the states." Emmy held out her laptop. "Do you know anything about it?"

"I read something about people in China getting sick."

"Apparently they're dying, and now it's spreading all over the globe. A couple days ago a man in Washington walked into a clinic with a fever and a cough. He had been in China visiting family or something."

"Does this illness have a name?" Kenny asked closing the fireplace doors.

Emmy listened for a moment. "He's calling it the Corona Virus."

"Like the typewriter," Kenny said with a grin.

Emmy stuck out her tongue. "Ha! Ha! This guy's making it sound pretty serious. Lots of people in China have died."

"Really?"

"Yes, but they all... or most of them lived in the same area."

"Is it like the flu?" he asked.

"According to the government doctor Benton interviewed, the symptoms are fever, sore throat, coughing and headaches. He didn't mention vomiting."

"Good to know. I hate getting sick to my stomach," Kenny said.

"Oh, and shortness of breath."

"Breathing can be important." Kenny kissed Emmy's forehead and grinned.

"I think not breathing might be more critical to one's health."

"Why are they making a fuss about this virus? The common flu affects more people than some virus in China."

"I don't know, but I'm not gonna worry. God has everything under control." She started to walk away, but then turned around. "Do you think it's possible your father has this virus?"

"I doubt it. He's never been to China."

"I know, but that doctor said it affects old people more than younger ones."

"You have such a tactful way about you, Em."

She made a face. "How should I put it?"

"Pastor Tyler refers to the older people in the church as seasoned citizens."

"Fine. I will be more tactful. I wouldn't want to hurt anyone's feelings. Have you talked to Fez lately? He's probably lonely living there all by himself."

Kenny sat down and answered, "I saw him the other day building a snowman in the front yard."

"For real?" Emmy asked then laughed.

"He said he wanted the kids in the neighborhood to see it, and I think he wanted there to be evidence of someone living in the house."

"Are you too busy to talk?" Mary Galves asked Emmy Thursday afternoon. "I could call later."

"Now is better. We have worship band rehearsal tonight, and I need to be there by six thirty," Emmy answered. "How have you been? The kids don't see you at school as often since their classes are on the second floor."

"I am feeling great and I have some news," Mary said with joy in her voice.

"Are you expecting?" Emmy asked.

Mary laughed and said, "How did you know?"

"I suppose it's because Kristen and Rebecca are expecting, so I've had babies on my mind. When are you due?"

"August 23, but it's still early. It could change by a few days."

Heather and Isabella came into the kitchen. Heather checked the stove, and Isabella opened the fridge looking for a snack.

"Mom, why are we having pasta again?" Heather asked.

"Hush! I'm talking to Mary," Emmy said. "Should I tell the girls, or would you like to tell them yourself?"

"Oh, please, let me tell them," Mary answered gleefully.

"I'll put you on speaker, and you can tell them both," Emmy said.

"Tell us what?" Isabella asked.

"Listen and you will find out." Emmy set her phone on the island.

Heather and Isabella stared at each other then at the phone.

"Hi, Mary, have you heard about Aunt Kristen?" Isabella asked.

"I have and I called to share some news. Jonah and I are going to have another baby."

"Really!?" Isabella exclaimed.

"When?" Heather asked.

"The middle of August."

"Are you having a girl? I think you should have a girl then Isa and I can be her nanny like you were our nanny," Heather said.

"Mom says we are too young to be nannies, but old enough to babysit," Isabella said.

"I agree with your mother about the babysitting. Jonah and I cannot afford a nanny."

Heather looked at Isabella, and they both said, "We could do it for free."

Mary laughed. "That's a very generous offer, but we can talk about babysitting when the time comes."

"We could watch Erin and Ewan now if you need a babysitter. We could do it together," Isabella said.

"Would you charge me double?" Mary asked.

"They shouldn't charge you anything after all the time you took care of them," Emmy said.

"I was very well compensated for my time as their nanny," Mary said.

"We wouldn't charge much," Isabella said. "We need the experience for when we try to get a real job."

"Have you heard anything about the worship team?" Emmy asked Saturday.

Kenny took a bite of his tuna salad sandwich and shook his head.

"Are you sure?" she asked. She scooped more of the kidney bean salad onto her plate. "This is pretty good. I don't think we've had it for years."

"Save some for me."

She pushed the plastic container across the table.

"Why are you asking about the worship team?" Kenny spooned out more of the kidney bean salad. "It's almost gone. Next time get as much as that." He pointed to the German potato salad.

"I would have if I knew we were going to eat it this fast."

"Are you worried the team will mutiny against you and Rebecca?" he asked with a grin.

"No, but our style of leadership is certainly different than the Schulenbergs." She scraped the last of the kidney bean salad off of her plate. "Mom used to make this when I was a kid, but I don't think I liked it back then."

"Our taste in food changes as we get older, Em. I never used to like hard-shell squash."

"You still don't like it. You refuse to eat it if someone makes it for a church potluck."

"Oh, I meant the other kind of squash."

"Are you referring to zucchini and yellow squash?" Emmy asked. She reached for the kidney bean salad container, but Kenny grabbed it before she could. "Hey! You've had two helpings."

"So have you."

"Fifty-fifty?"

"Okay."

"It went fast and you still don't like summer squash as much as other veggies."

He pointed his fork at her. "True, but now I will eat it. I wouldn't as a kid. It would make me gag."

"Be careful. You could stab me." She swatted his hand away. "Good to know. Would you tell me if you heard anything about the way Rebecca and I lead the team?"

"Maybe," he answered. "I haven't been a part of the worship team for a long time, and I didn't know Riordan and Sadie as well as you, but I think you and Rebecca are trying to get the team to focus more on spiritual growth. I always got the impression the Schulenbergs were more concerned about the... I hate to say it... the performance. They left the spirituality of the team to Pastor Tyler. I'm not saying they weren't spiritual or anything. He is the senior pastor of his church now."

Emmy finished the last of her lunch, took a long drink of water, then said, "Some of the members were so used to Riordan's way I think they might resent the changes Rebecca and I have made."

He laughed and asked, "Do you think it's harmful to learn more about the Bible?"

"Of course not, you goof."

"Will it hurt the team if they become closer and more caring of each other?"

She made a face as she shook her head.

"Will it be detrimental if they become more active and comfortable in their prayer life?"

"You've made your point, and I shouldn't worry as long as Rebecca and I are doing what the Holy Spirit tells us to."

"I've always loved how smart you are," he said. He grabbed her hand and kissed it. "Even when we were in school."

"Ha! Most boys in school didn't want a girlfriend who was smart. They wanted girls who were..."

"Mom! Is there any of the kidney bean stuff left? I didn't think I would like it, but I did," Kevin said.

"Sorry, Kevin, but your mother ate the last of it," Kenny answered. "She needs to learn to share."

"I'm going to stop at Rose Hill," Emmy said after church. "It's been two years now."

"Okay, should I grab lunch for us?" Kenny asked.

"If you want. I might not get back for a while."

Kenny kissed her and rounded up the kids. They stopped at a Nuclear Sub Station and picked up sandwiches and chips.

Emmy parked close to her parents' gravesite. She got out and wrapped her arms over her chest to fight the cold winter wind. She hurried to the site, placed an acrylic angel on the headstone, knelt and whispered to make sure no one would hear her.

"I can understand how difficult it must have been to raise me and Diane. My kids are so much better behaved then we were, and I still struggle at times to parent them. I'm doing the best I can, but sometimes I feel as though it's not making any difference..."

She talked to her parents for a few minutes before heading home.

"Mom, we got you a sandwich," Kevin said. "It's in the fridge. Did you go to the cemetery?"

"I did. I wanted to visit your grandparents' graves."

"Do you talk to them when you go?"

Emmy opened the fridge and took out her sandwich. "I do unless there are other people around. Does that sound weird?"

He shrugged and answered, "In a way, but I guess it's okay. Do you tell them about us?"

Emmy grinned and said, "I do because if there's a way they can hear me, I think they'd want to know how you're doing."

"Too bad you can't send them a text or an email, huh?" he said with a laugh.

"That would make things easier," Emmy replied. She sat at the island and unwrapped her sandwich. "What kind did you get me?"

"Dad was going to order a number five, the tuna sub, but we talked him into getting a number three. It's the Italian one with pepperoni, salami and ham. We added a bunch of veggies and the hot peppers. If you don't want the peppers, you can take them off."

"Thanks, Kevin. I might eat some of them, but if they're too hot, I'll give them to you."

Chapter Six

Kenny heard the door open and asked, "Who do you want to win? Kansas City or San Francisco?"

Emmy joined him in the media room. She sat in her recliner and took a sip of Dr Pepper. "Is the game finally going to start? I hate the eight hours of pregame stuff."

"Kickoff is next. Who are you pulling for?"

"I like the Kansas City quarterback."

"Patrick Meacham?"

"Is that his name? He's kinda cute," she said with a grin.

Kenny shook his head. "You're rooting for him, huh?"

"He's cuter than the 49ers quarterback," she teased.

"So, you root for the team with the hot quarterback."

"Why not?"

"Is that why you used to be such a Chicago Bear fan?"

"I never thought Bobby McMullen was cute when the Bears were in the Super Bowl, but there was this one player I kinda liked." She tapped a finger against her chin. "What was his name? I think he played middle linebacker."

Kenny shook his head. "I know you thought Tony was cute..."

"He wasn't cute as much as he was big and strong."

"If you like players who are big and strong why don't you pick out one of the lineman to cheer for?"

"The quarterbacks make more money," she said with a straight face. "If I wasn't married to a famous rock star who makes tons of money, I'd go for a quarterback. Is Meacham married?"

"I have no idea, and now I know you married me for my money."

She grinned and said, "I married you despite your funny looking ears."

He reached out, grabbed her arm and pulled her onto his lap. "Funny ears, huh?" He tickled her side until she kissed him.

"Stop it," she said as she settled onto his lap. "You might have funny ears, but I still like the way you kiss me."

30

"Are you still pulling for Kansas City?" Kenny asked. "It's the end of three quarters, and the 49ers are up by ten."

"Doesn't matter," she said.

"Doesn't matter who wins? I thought you wanted the Chiefs to win because of their hot quarterback."

"No, it doesn't matter how far ahead San Francisco is. Haven't you followed the playoffs this year? The Chiefs have been behind every game and come back to win. Wait and see."

"Care to make a small wager?" he asked while making his eyebrows go up and down.

"Such as?"

He smiled.

"That's not a bet. It's a sure thing."

As they watched the fourth quarter, Kenny became very quiet as Emmy got more and more excited.

"See! I told you they would win. They scored twenty-one points to zip for the 49ers. I told you Patrick Meacham was a hot quarterback."

"Fine. You win the bet. When do I have to pay up?"

"We could lock the door..."

"Emmy, are you busy? Can I stop by the house?" Bobby O'Connor asked Tuesday morning.

"Sure, I'm not going anywhere. I have too much laundry to do," she answered putting her phone on speaker. "Do you want to drop off a rent check?"

"No, Shay gave it to Kenny Sunday. Sorry it was late."

She folded a towel and said, "I don't care about that. How's Karissa doing?"

"Great! She's walking and I saw her reading a book last night."

"You're such a punk. She's two months old."

"Yes, but she has good genes."

"From Shay."

"Should I bring her with?"

Emmy laughed. "Do you have to ask? I'd much rather see Karissa than you."

31

"I'll bring her unless she's sleeping," Bobby said. "Be there in a minute."

"I'm in the laundry room folding clothes and slaving away. You can help if you want."

Bobby laughed.

"You're still a punk. The service door's unlocked."

Bobby, Shay and baby Karissa O'Connor lived in the guesthouse, and he could walk to the main house in a few minutes.

"In here," Emmy said when she heard the door to the garage open. "You better have Karissa with you."

"Sorry, but she was taking a nap, and Shay told me not to wake her."

Bobby walked into the laundry room and saw Emmy sorting clothes. "I brought this instead." He held out a CD.

Emmy grabbed it and smiled. "When did you get it?"

"Today's the official release. Do you like the cover?"

She inspected the cover, turned over the CD and smiled. "Clever title. Whoever thought of it must be a genius."

"We offered to pay you for coming up with it."

"I know, but I said you could pay me back by letting me spoil the baby." She looked at the cover again. "I like this picture. It makes a better cover than a shot of the band."

"Are you saying we're a bunch of ugly dudes?" Bobby asked knowing he was setting himself up to be dissed.

"Not at all," she answered.

"Really?"

"The rest of the band is rather handsome, but you look like a punk. Doesn't Shay want you to get a grownup haircut?"

"She likes my style."

"And does your style have a name other than a punk cut?" Emmy teased.

"Hey! I told the stylist to cut it evenly. She screwed up. It will grow back."

"Is this copy for me, or do you want it back?" she asked.

"It's yours. Do you want it autographed?"

"Absolutely! I want the rest of the guys to sign it."

"Not me?"

She tilted her head and asked, "Do you know how to write now?"

"Give it back." He grabbed for the CD, but she put it behind her back.

"It's mine," she said with a laugh. "You can't have it."

"I could get it back," he said reaching out.

"You could try, but it might hurt."

"Why?" he asked.

"Because I would smack you."

He backed away and held up his hands. "I surrender."

"I'm kidding. Take the plastic off and sign it for me. Did the logo for Kenny's record label turn out okay?"

He cut the plastic with a fingernail, opened the digipak and showed the disc to her.

"I like it. At first I thought Bristol Woods Records was so dorky, but the logo turned out nice."

"The picture was taken in your woods."

"I know. I was there when Brady took it."

"Does he still own that gallery?"

"He does, but his cousin runs it. Brady doesn't have much time to be there. He's doing all the traveling for Carson & Caden."

"How is his company doing? Is he gonna be as rich as his father?" Bobby asked while leaning against the counter.

"No, but he and Bennett are making tons of money. Bennett could quit working at Barclay Academy and never have to worry about money again."

"Did I tell you the Prater-Saylor Agency booked us in a couple places?"

"Really? How did they manage? Did they pay the venue to let you guys play there?"

"That's not how it works, Emmy."

"I know."

Bobby laughed and said, "You didn't when you were starting out. You thought you would have to pay the promoter."

"I was kidding, punk. I was part of Kenny's band in the beginning, so I knew how the business worked." She folded Kevin Michael's underwear while Bobby watched. "Where?"

33

"We're booked for a week at the Broken Horseshoe in Newcastle and a few gigs at Graffiti Gallery in the city."

"Those places are still open?"

"Yeah, they actually are."

"Fridays At Five played there back in the nineties."

"We're also booked at what used to be called Lights Out!. It's under new management and has a new name."

"Isn't Prater-Saylor working on a tour for you guys?"

"There's a good chance we're going to open for The Lyricon on their summer tour.

"It would be good exposure for the band."

"If all goes well, we could be headlining at small venues in the fall." He watched her folding some t-shirts. "Don't you iron those?"

"Never. Takes too long." She opened the washer and tossed in another load. "You should see if Kenny or Andy would let you use one of the trucks for your fall tour. They will be finished with their tour by then. You could use a couple of the buses, too."

"We did talk to Andy and Charles about it."

Andy Walker and Charles La Rosse owned Walker Management and had managed Fridays At Five for their entire career. The company also managed a few other artists including Emmy.

"Let me know if they give you a hard time. I'll straightened Andy out real fast."

Bobby laughed and said, "He's got such a reputation for being a hard case, but you know how to push his buttons. Is Charles back in the states?"

Emmy shrugged. "Who knows? He's been going back and forth between Tennessee and Germany. The last I knew he was booking tours for Mike Rowell and the 88s and the Reign in New Zealand and Australia."

"I've met him a few times, and he never travels with more than a backpack and a small carry-on case."

"He knows how to travel light," Emmy said. She handed Bobby a basket of clean clothes. "Carry that for me."

"Yes, boss," he replied.

She bumped his hip. "You better not let Shay hear you call me that."

He bumped her back, laughed and said, "I may be a punk, but I'm not stupid."

After returning home from church Wednesday night, Emmy sat in the family room and watched the news.

"Are they talking about the virus again?" Kenny asked.

"Yes, and they're saying it could be more widespread than what people reported last week."

"It's probably not anymore dangerous than the ordinary flu." Kenny sat beside her and put an arm around her waist. "Do you think you should talk to the kids about it? They might be hearing stuff at school. I'd rather they hear the truth than some rumors from other kids."

"Why me? You can talk to them just as easily."

"You know more about this thing. I've not paid much attention to the news."

"Have you heard them talking about it? I haven't, but they could be talking to their friends at school," Emmy said. "I'm going to talk to them." She got up, made her way upstairs and knocked on Heather's open door.

Heather turned around in her desk chair. "I'm finishing my homework, but it's not due until Friday."

"Good. I need to talk to all of you," Emmy said. "We can do it in here if you don't mind."

She asked Isabella and Kevin to join Heather in her room and then waited in the hallway for a moment.

"Dear Lord, please give me the wisdom to say the right thing to my children. I don't want to scare them because I know You have everything under control. I want to pray for the people who are getting sick because of this virus. I especially want to pray for the doctors and nurses who might be getting exposed to it every day."

Mom! We're waiting," Kevin said.

Emmy dried her eyes with her hands, took a deep breath and entered Heather's room again.

"We heard you praying, Mommy. Are you going to talk to us about the virus? Does Grandpa have it? Is that why he was in the hospital and Daddy had to fly to Florida?" Isabella asked. She sat next to Heather on the bed with her arms wrapped around her chest.

"I do want to talk about it, but as far as we know your grandfather doesn't have it."

"That's good," Heather said.

"Some of the kids were talking at school yesterday. They said all the old people who get the virus will die. Is that true?" Kevin asked. He sat on the floor in front of the bed looking up at his mother. "Is it worse than cancer? Jarrett's grandmother had cancer."

"That's not what the people in charge are saying," Emmy said. "It's true some people have died, but in China."

"So no one we know has died?" Isabella asked.

"No, and no one in this country has died from the virus so far."

"But someone could die, right?" Kevin asked.

"I suppose so, but we have to remember God has everything under control."

"Then why do some people get sick and die?" Kevin asked. "Why did Jennifer die? She was getting better then she got worse and died."

"I can't explain it, but I do know God has a reason."

"I wish it wasn't so hard to know why God lets things happen," Isabella said. "I know He loves all of us the same."

"He does, and there are some things we will never understand. We have to rely on our faith that everything happens for a reason."

"I will pray for the people who catch the virus," Kevin said.

"We should all pray for the people who get sick and the ones who have to take care of them."

36

Chapter Seven

"I don't care if nothing happened, Heather Rose!" Emmy yelled. "You are not allowed to have boys in the house when we aren't home."

"I'm sorry, Mrs. Colwell, but we were just watching a movie," Ian Plant said. "We weren't even sitting next to each other, and I didn't kiss her or anything."

"Trust me, Ian, you are not helping the situation. I think you need to go home." She pointed to the stairs leading up to the garage. "Heather will be grounded for the foreseeable future so she won't be able to see you."

"Mom!" Heather whined.

Emmy pointed at her. "You and I are gonna have a talk. You can go to your room. I will be there as soon as I finish unpacking the groceries."

"I'll text you later, Ian," Heather said.

"No you won't!" Emmy shouted. "You will not be using your phone until I give it back." Emmy held out a hand. "Hand it over now."

Heather slapped her phone in her mother's hand. "You are so mean to me. You treat me like a child. I'm fourteen. I should be allowed to have a life. I think it's illegal to treat your kids like this."

Ian waved to Heather and headed toward the door. Emmy watched until he left then faced Heather. "I can't even talk to you right now. I am so mad I could spit."

"Are you going to let me tell my side of the story? I'm pretty sure even criminals get a chance to talk in court," Heather said sarcastically.

"You will have a chance to talk, but it won't change my mind."

Heather stomped up the stairs and slammed the door hard enough to rattle the handrail in the stairwell.

Emmy sighed and closed her eyes. *Lord, give me the patience and control to deal with this without exploding.* She headed upstairs and saw Kenny in the kitchen.

"Was it Heather who stomped upstairs?" he asked. "She smacked the wall and then went upstairs." He pulled two cartons of eggs from a plastic bag. "Will we use these before they go out of code?"

"Yes, Kevin will eat most of them."

"Did you remember to send Carson a birthday card? He turns eighteen today."

"I sent a card, and I'll call him later." She put her elbows on the kitchen island and kicked at it.

"You're mad at Heather. What was she doing?"

Emmy straightened up, took a deep breath and answered, "She was watching a movie with Ian Plant."

"What movie?" Kenny asked while unpacking more groceries. Then he turned around quickly. "Did you say Ian Plant? The neighbor boy?"

"Do you know another Ian Plant who would be in the basement?"

"No, what were they doing?"

"Did you hear what I said?"

"Sorry, I was busy unpacking." He removed two bunches of bananas and placed them in the fruit bowl on the island.

"They were coming out of the media room when I walked into the basement from the garage. I went down there to put the furnace filters in the utility room. I can't be sure, but he might have been holding her hand."

"He's the boy she kissed..."

"Yes, and he's still two years older than her."

"Was Isabella with them?"

"No, she's helping Kristen and Grace clean the nursery."

Kenny scratched his ear. "So, she was alone with him, huh?"

Emmy shook her head. "Why do I even bother? Can you finish putting everything away?"

"Yes, I can handle it."

"And don't put the chicken breasts in the freezer. I want to split the package before I freeze them."

"Where are you going?"

"I told her to wait in her room until I talked to her."

Kenny removed three loaves of bread from a bag and set them on the island. "Have you calmed down enough to talk without losing your temper?"

"I don't have a temper," she said loudly.

He stared at her.

"Fine!" She stomped her foot. "My temper isn't close to what it used to be. I am calm enough to talk rationally and listen to her version of the story. Then I'll yell and scream and ground her for all eternity again."

Kenny grinned. "So far, I think she's grounded for three or four eternities."

Emmy made a face and walked away.

Kevin rushed into the kitchen, took off his coat and threw it on one of the barstools. "I saw Ian walking through the woods toward his house. Was he over here with Heather?"

"He was. Do you know anything about why he was here?"

"Not really, but before he got here, Heather told me to stay out of the basement. She told me to get lost in the woods for a couple hours." He grabbed one of the bananas. "Is she in trouble again?"

"Very possibly, and you shouldn't eat that one. It's too green."

Kevin chose a different one. "She was in the media room, and I saw her turn on the big TV. I thought we weren't supposed to use it unless you or Mom was here."

Kenny gathered all the plastic bags and put them in the pantry recycling bin. "You aren't supposed to without someone here to fire up the gear. Remember last year when you turned it on and the setting wasn't right, and Ben turned up the amp and about blew the speakers?"

"Yeah, I remember. I thought a bomb went off."

"That's why we don't want you to use it."

Kevin raced out of the room and galloped up the stairs.

"Hey! That's not where your coats belongs," Kenny said. He shook his head and put Kevin's coat in the mudroom.

Emmy knocked on Heather's door and walked in without waiting for an answer.

"Hey! I didn't say..."

"And I don't care," Emmy said sitting on the edge of the bed. "I am your mother and can come into your room whenever I like."

"I could lock it," Heather said from her desk. She closed her laptop before Emmy could see it and turned around.

"You do and I'll have the lock removed before you can... Were you using the laptop to talk to Ian?"

"No."

Emmy glared.

"I had to tell him something."

"I will take away all your electronic devices if I have to," Emmy said holding out her hand.

"I promise not to communicate with the outside world for the duration of my sentence," Heather said too sarcastically.

"You aren't making good choices right now." Emmy withdrew her hand.

"Sorry, I didn't intend to sound so disrespectful."

"Whose idea was it to watch a movie? Yours or Ian's?"

"He suggested it. I told him he should wait until you and Dad got back, but he said he had plans for later."

"That's no excuse."

"I didn't think it would matter."

"You know the rules about boys, and you aren't supposed to use the media room unless your father's here."

"Ian knew how to turn everything on, and we didn't turn it up real loud." Heather stood up and closed her bathroom door. She walked up to her bed and sat on the opposite side from her mother. "You don't say anything if Carson or Caden come over."

"They are family."

"What about Peter and Zach and Ben? They come over sometimes, and they aren't real family."

"They are family for all intents and purposes, and quit changing the subject. What movie were you watching? Not that it makes any difference. You still broke the rules."

"Then why should I tell you since I'm going to have to live the rest of my life locked in this room? Maybe I'll grow my hair real long and escape out the window like Elsa."

"You need to tell me because I asked. What movie was it?"

"It was a new one Ian brought over," Heather answered.

"Which one?"

Heather took a deep breath and then walked back to her desk. "Clara's Eyes."

"I've never heard of it. What was it about?"

Heather shrugged and mumbled, "It's about two strangers who meet and fall in love."

"What was it rated?"

"Not sure."

"I can look it up, Heather," Emmy said.

"It was rated R, but so what. You watch R rated movies once in a while."

"Not very often, and I am an adult. Those ratings are for a reason. Why was this one rated R? Was there a lot of swearing? It doesn't sound like there'd be much violence."

"There was some swearing."

"Why do I get the feeling you're holding back on me?"

"It was only a movie, Mom," Heather replied.

"Tell me more about the plot."

Heather gave Emmy a brief summation.

"So, this older boy charms the new girl in school, huh?"

"She likes him and he's pretty hot. He doesn't wear a shirt in some scenes."

"What?" Emmy asked.

"I've seen boys without their shirts on."

Emmy stared at Heather for a moment. "Was there a sex scene? Tell me the truth, and I may reduce your sentence to ninety-nine years instead of life."

"Fine! There was a brief scene, but you could hardly see anything. It only lasted a minute or so."

"That's a minute too long," Emmy said.

"Oh, Mom, it was so sweet." Heather sighed and wrapped her arms around her chest. "They kissed so tenderly."

41

Emmy got off the bed and walked to the door. "I don't care how tender and romantic it was. Sex is not for young teenagers, and you're grounded for five eternities. No chance of parole until you're a grandmother."

"How can I ever become a grandmother if I'm confined to my prison cell forever?"

"You know what I mean," Emmy said and walked away.

"You weren't perfect when you were a teenager. I've heard stories about you and Uncle Rory," Heather said before slamming her door closed.

"That was delicious, Emmy. Can I help with the dishes?" Rochelle said after Sunday's lunch.

"Thank you, but it was simply homemade leek and potato soup. The kids used to think it sounded gross, but you saw how much Kevin ate. That's why I make it in a large pot, and the dishes can go in the dishwasher."

Rochelle helped load the dishwasher and then talked about the house she and Rory purchased the previous year.

"I never would have thought Rory would buy his old house. It was in rather bad shape," Emmy said.

"It was lucky for us it stayed on the market so long. The price kept dropping until he couldn't pass it up. The timing was perfect. We moved back to SoHam and after a few months of hard work, the place looks better than ever."

"I hate to say it, but when we were kids, the place needed work, and neither Rory nor Owen had any interest in maintaining it. All Rory would do was mow the yard."

Kevin raced into the kitchen and said, "Thanks for lunch, Mom. Is it okay if I run over to Ben's house? We want to play football."

"Yes, but make sure you dress warm."

"I didn't know he liked football," Rochelle said.

"He likes it now because Ben likes it."

Kenny and Rory came upstairs and walked into the kitchen.

"I was showing Rory the new gear in the studio. Do you need help with cleaning up?" Kenny asked.

42

"No, you timed it right. Everything is done. Let's sit in the family room. I want to ask Rory something," Emmy said.

They sat on the couches in front of the fireplace. Kenny added more wood and sat beside Emmy.

"I heard you had to discipline Heather again," Rory said.

"How did you hear about it?" Emmy asked. "Did she complain about how evil I am?"

"Kenny told me. Something about a movie with tons of sex and nudity, right?" Rory asked hoping to embarrass Emmy.

"How much is too much for a fourteen-year-old girl?"

"Point taken," Rory said.

"After I talked to her she hollered something about me hanging out with you. I ignored it at the time, but now it's bothering me. I don't know what she's heard, or who might have told her, but I got the impression she thinks we did more than... you know."

"Have you told her about all the times you snuck out late at night and we'd go to wild parties?" Rory asked.

"Very funny! I only snuck out a few times, and it was not to go to parties."

Kenny looked at Emmy.

She shrugged and said, "Not parties like kids have now."

"Would you like me to talk to her and straighten out her misconceptions?" Rory asked.

"No! You'll tell her lies about us doing things."

Kenny laughed and Emmy poked him in the side.

Rochelle smiled at Rory then looked at Emmy. "He's told me everything you guys did. The only thing even remotely wild was when you would play football with the boys."

"Where is Isa, and why didn't Heather come down for lunch?" Kenny asked.

"Are you finally realizing she skipped lunch?"

"I knew it before."

"I told her what we were having, and she said she would rather starve. Isa, is in her room finishing some homework. She ate lunch with us."

"I know she did. I sat across from her," Kenny said.

43

"This might be a crazy idea, but I could talk to her," Rory suggested. "I have some experience dealing with teenage girls."

Emmy stared at him.

"I didn't mean it like that, Em. I have two nieces who are still teenagers. Well, Jane is twenty now, but I used to talk to her and Melissa when I first came back to SoHam, and I didn't screw up their lives."

"It's hard to picture Amy's girls in college," Emmy said. "I haven't seen them since her funeral."

"That was almost ten years ago, Em," Rory said. "Doesn't seem possible but it was."

Emmy grabbed a throw pillow and held it to her chest. "I've been knocking heads with Heather kinda like your mother did with Amy when she was about their age. A little older but close enough. I am almost desperate enough to accept your offer."

"Thanks for the vote of confidence," Rory said with a laugh.

"If I talk to her, she ignores me," Kenny said.

"I'm willing to put my advanced education to the test," Rory said.

Emmy rolled her eyes. "I knew you'd lord it over us. Just because you're a *doctor* doesn't mean you know it all."

"What harm can it do?" Kenny asked Emmy.

Emmy raised her eyebrows and pointed to Rory. "You know that is Rory Porter. The boy who..."

"What?"

Emmy sighed, took a deep breath and said, "Never mind. If you want to try, be my guest."

Rory headed upstairs and knocked on Heather's door.

"Go away, Mom! I'm not hungry," Heather hollered.

"It's Uncle Rory. Can I come in?"

Heather bounced off of her bed, ran to the door and opened it. "When did you get here?"

"We were invited for lunch. You missed it. The soup was delicious." He walked into the room. "I like how you've decorated it. It looks like a young lady's room now."

"Thanks."

"Your mother is an excellent cook, Heather."

"I know the soup is good, but I didn't want Mom to know I like it. Please don't tell her, but Kevin brought me up a sandwich."

Rory zipped his lips. "Our secret. I heard what happened. Care to talk about it?"

"Will you be honest if I ask some questions about you and Mom?"

"I would never lie to you."

"Okay, but this has to be in strictest confidence. Like I was confessing to Uncle James."

Rory laughed and put an arm around her shoulders. "When did you get so tall?"

"Promise, Uncle Rory?"

"Absolute confidence," he replied. "Can we go downstairs to talk. We could use the library. No one ever goes in there."

"Okay, but I don't want a lecture about how times were different back in the nineties."

"I will be straight with you."

She followed Rory to the library and sat on the couch facing him with her legs tucked under her.

"Tell me about Ian and the movie."

Heather told him about the plot, the coarse language and the sex scene.

"I didn't see anything I haven't seen before," Heather said. "Mom made it out to be a big deal."

"Sorry, but I have to agree with her, and let me tell you why," he said without sounding preachy. "Back in the old days when your mother was your age, she didn't have access to everything you have available. Sure, if you looked for it you could find porn and drugs and whatever kind of vice you wanted to experience."

Heather's eyes opened wide and she held her breath as Rory talked frankly to her.

"I wish I could say I resisted those temptations but I can't. I did my share of experimenting with alcohol, but I never did drugs."

45

"Really?"

"Maybe a little pot, but nothing hard. Your mother and father never did any drugs. As far as I know neither one has ever smoked anything. Not even a cigarette."

"Aunt Diane did."

Rory sighed before nodding. "She was more open to things."

"I know she was pregnant when she got married. I can do the math, and babies aren't born in five months," Heather said.

"Do you think your mother behaved like her sister?" he asked.

"Did she? I know she wasn't pregnant like Aunt Diane."

"You mother wasn't totally ignorant about boys. She liked to kiss your father after she got a little older."

"Did she ever kiss you?" Heather asked with a grin. "You have to tell the truth."

"That's easy. I never kissed your mother," he said slowly. "I might have wanted to because she was as pretty as you and Isabella, but I never did. We were friends. We did do something she would kill me for telling you..."

"What did you do?" Heather asked sitting up higher.

"We stole some of your grandfather's beer."

Heather's shoulders slumped. "Isa and I know all about that. Mom told us how she used to steal a beer when she was younger than us. She offered to let us try it, but I can't stand the smell. Uncle James doesn't even keep any in the garage anymore."

"How did you feel when the sex scene came on and this boy was with you?"

She hesitated for a moment.

Rory waved a hand. "You don't have to answer if it makes you feel uncomfortable."

She stared at the ceiling for a second. "It's not that. I feel I can tell you more than Daddy. He gets embarrassed whenever anything about sex or female stuff is mentioned."

"He always has," Rory said and then chuckled.

"Ian didn't say anything, but I know he knew it was there. It was his movie."

"Do you think he expected you to do anything?"

"He never said so, and I would have smacked him if he tried to kiss me. I kissed him a couple times when I was ten, but I wouldn't kiss him now. He doesn't go to church like ever."

"Good. You should tell your mother."

"I will but not until she stops getting on my case about everything I do. I'm not going to be like Aunt Diane, and if I'm totally honest, I was embarrassed by the scene. It wasn't much compared to other movies, but it was enough."

"Your mother loves you and Isabella so much."

"And Kevin?"

Rory laughed. "Even your brother. She is concerned about the pressures teens face today."

"I guess I can't blame her. I hear stories about the crap kids in public school face. At least we have good Christian teachers at our school."

"I know you and Isa well enough to know you are smart enough to make good choices, and the way you and your mother clash reminds me of your grandmother and Diane. They used to fight all the time."

"Did Mommy fight with her, too?"

"Not like Diane, but she disliked being treated like a kid. I was gone by then, but I heard she and your grandmother fought about her moving out. She was only seventeen at the time."

"She doesn't have to worry about me wanting to move out. I might live here even after I get married."

Rory laughed and said. "You could almost fit their old house in this room."

"Do I have to apologize to her?" Heather asked.

"That's your decision," he said with a shrug. "But I would hate to see you two fighting all the time."

Heather took a deep breath. "I shouldn't have let Ian come over."

Rory stood up and walked toward the door. "Don't tell me. Tell your mother."

"Ughhh!" Heather groaned. "I hate it when grownups are right."

47

Chapter Eight

"Mom, why are you coming to the party?" Heather asked. "It's supposed to be for Noemi's friends."

"Sloane asked if I would help chaperone since Kristen doesn't feel well."

"Is Aunt Kristen sick because of the baby?" Isabella asked.

"I think she feels tired. Get your coats on and don't forget Noemi's presents."

Emmy drove across the road since the light snow of early morning had turned into heavy flakes that were now sticking to the pavement.

"I love how snow turns everything into a Christmas card," Isabella said.

"What do you mean?" Heather asked without pausing in her texting.

"If you'd get your eyes off your phone for a second, you would see how everything is covered in snow and looks so refreshing," Isabella said.

Emmy drove up Tony's driveway and parked behind several other cars. *I'm glad I drove the Jeep. If it keeps snowing this hard, the driveway will be drifted over.*

"Mom! Do we have to walk through the snow? I'm wearing a good pair of shoes, and I'd rather not ruin them."

Emmy looked over her shoulder. "Should I send Tony out to carry you, Heather?"

"No, but if these shoes are ruined, you have to buy me another pair. They are Connie Clarks, and they weren't cheap."

"Where did you get them? I didn't buy them for you," Emmy said. She opened the door and stepped into snow almost up to her knees.

"I used my gift card and bought them myself." Heather opened her door, took a look at the drift, sighed and jumped out. "We should have used the snowmobile."

"Step where I do, and maybe your fancy shoes won't be ruined," Emmy said.

They made it inside the garage and knocked on the door.

48

"Mom, I think we can go right in. Aunt Sloane is expecting us," Heather said.

"Take off your shoes before you track snow everywhere," Emmy said as Tony opened the door.

"Yes? May I help you?"

"Hush, and let us in. Is your snowblower broke? I almost had to dig a tunnel to make it to the garage."

"I did clear the front sidewalk, brat."

Heather rolled her eyes. "Great! My shoes are ruined for nothing."

"Well, the driveway in front of the garage is drifting over."

"I would use the snowblower, but there are too many cars in the way, and it wasn't snowing hard earlier."

"You may have to plow it with your truck if it keeps blowing like this. How many kids are here? I thought it was just a small party for Noemi's closest friends."

"She has a lot of close friends, I guess. I don't interfere. I sign the checks and pay the bills," Tony said.

"Is Mama here? I need to talk to her." She removed her coat and handed it to Tony. "You may take our wraps," she said snootily then giggled.

Tony took the coats from the girls and walked into his mother's section of the house. He set them down on the couch in the sitting room.

"Where is she?" Emmy asked again.

"At Kristen's house."

"Why didn't you tell me before?"

"You didn't give me a chance."

"Fine. I will talk to her later. I'm supposed to help Sloane control this rowdy bunch."

"They're in the basement." He pointed toward the door leading downstairs. "Pardon me if I don't show you the way, madam, but I have to stay up here with the boys."

"Didn't Noemi invite any boys?" Heather asked. "I thought she would."

"She did, but she doesn't want her younger brothers to ruin her party."

Heather raced down the stairs. Isabella and Emmy followed at a leisurely pace without making a ruckus.

"From what you told me, I expected total chaos," Emmy told Sloane. "This is almost peaceful."

"I keep telling them to keep the music down, but someone keeps turning up the volume."

Emmy looked around the room. "I'm guessing none of the boys want to dance, huh?"

"They're too shy," Sloane said.

Later, Sloane, Dotty and Emmy served the cake and ice cream.

"I'll take the ice cream upstairs before it melts," Emmy said. She was heading to the stairs when she heard Noemi's voice around the corner.

"I said no, Phillip, and I mean it," Noemi said sternly.

"Come on, Noemi, you know you will like it."

"You will like it. I don't think I will."

"Are you mad because I was teasing you before? All I said was you can't dance as good as Heather or the other girls."

"I don't like to be teased," Noemi said smacking his hand.

Emmy walked around the corner. "What's going on? Are you okay, Noemi?" She frowned at the boy standing too close to her.

He let go of Noemi's arm.

"I'm fine, but he wants to kiss me, and I said no."

Emmy handed the ice cream to Phillip. "She said no and that means no! Take this upstairs and give it to Noemi's father."

"Yes, Mrs. Colwell. Are you going to tell Mr. Bertucci?"

"Maybe."

Phillip gulped and raced up the stairs. He tripped on a step and bumped his shin.

"Are you all right, sweetie?" Emmy asked. "Do you want to tell me what happened?"

"I was talking to him, and maybe I was flirting a little, but I don't like him enough to kiss him. He's kinda strange."

"Sometimes boys take things the wrong way. They don't have the social skills to deal with these situations."

50

"He has no skills whatsoever," Noemi said.

"Was he teasing you? Does he do that often?"

"Yes, and Dotty said it means he likes me, but I don't like him that way."

"You don't have to."

"Are you going to tell Mom or Dad?"

"Not if you don't want me to."

"Please don't say anything now. I don't want him to get in trouble."

Emmy hugged Noemi, who was even taller than Heather and Isabella, and whispered, "You should tell your mother later. She would want to know, and you can always talk to her about stuff."

"It's hard to talk to her about boys. If I need to, I usually talk to Dotty."

"That's good, but Dotty doesn't have all the answers. Your mother has more experience."

"I'll tell her after the party." Noemi grinned and added, "I wish I could see Phillip's face when he gives the ice cream to Daddy. He looked like he was going to cry when you told him to take it upstairs."

"Emmy, we have a small problem," Rebecca said Sunday morning.

Emmy took off her coat, hung it up and asked, "What's wrong?"

"I got a text from Perry Johnstone this morning. He has to work, and Shaun called a minute ago. He's sick. We don't have anyone to play guitar."

"Have you tried Bryce Croft?" Emmy grabbed a glazed donut and took a bite.

"I texted him but haven't heard back."

Emmy could see the concern in Rebecca's eyes. "Well, it won't be the first time we haven't had a guitar player." She saw Fez Rivera standing in the back of the room eating a donut. *You mentioned you played bass guitar occasionally. I wonder how you'd feel about filling in at the last minute.*

51

"Emmy, what are you thinking?" Rebecca asked.

She turned back to Rebecca. "Sorry, my mind was elsewhere." She looked over her shoulder at Fez. *I don't want to place you in an awkward position. Besides, if I ask you to play bass, the tech team will be shorthanded.*

"Should we ask Zeke to play acoustic instead of bass?" Rebecca asked.

Emmy thought for a moment. "No, I'd rather have a bass player." She patted Rebecca's arm. "It will be all right."

"What about the second service?" *Should I ask Tommy Joseph or Nathan Kellett to play? They're usually here every week."*

"I know someone who will be here for Sunday School. I could ask him. He's so-so as a player, but he might be willing to play a few simple chords."

"Who?"

Emmy grinned and said, "Kenny."

Rebecca giggled and said, "You're kidding, right? Would he really play with the worship team?"

"He used to, but you have to realize he isn't that good. He knows how to play rock songs, but usually only plays two chords."

"You're teasing because all the guys know he's like the most amazing guitarist in the country."

Emmy waved a finger at Rebecca. "Don't believe that for a second, and don't ever repeat what you just said. His ego will inflate to the size of Jupiter."

The first service went without a hitch. No one appeared concerned about the lack of a guitar on the platform.

As soon as Kenny arrived with the kids, Emmy recruited him to play.

"Really?" he asked.

"Yeah, we're desperate. I get it. You're not that good, but maybe you could play a few basic chords and not screw things up too much."

"I'll give it a shot. Can I look at the music for a second. I know most of the songs, but I could use a refresher."

Emmy showed him the chord sheets.

With the exception of Emmy, none of the worship team had ever been on stage with Kenny. For most of the service he played rhythm guitar, but added a few riffs here and there.

"Did I do all right?" he asked Emmy when the worship team left the platform. He followed Emmy to the music suite across the hall. "Well, did I?"

"For the most part, you were all right. You didn't screw up too bad except when you missed my signal to play the chorus of 'Do It Again' one more time."

"Sorry about that."

"We have one more song after Tyler's message. Maybe you can get it right."

Pastor Tyler saw Kenny talking to Malcolm Starks, Kevin's sixth grade teacher, after the service. When Mr. Starks moved on, Tyler chuckled and said, "Thanks for filling in. Did you even have a chance to rehearse with the team?"

"Not really, but I did look at the music briefly. Em got on my case for missing the extra chorus on 'Do It Again.'"

"I doubt if anyone noticed. Thanks again."

Kenny asked Kevin about his schoolwork as they prepared to head home.

"I've done most of it," Kevin said.

"Mr. Starks said you didn't turn in much last week."

"It's too boring."

Emmy put on her coat and stared at him. "You need to finish it today before you even think about doing anything with Ben or Taylor."

"Aw, Mom," he whined.

Tuesday afternoon Emmy made the kids sit at the breakfast nook table to finish their assignments.

"Why are we even bothering with this?" Heather asked. She held up a paper about the city government. "I mean, who really cares if Mayor Trumbetti wants another high school. I certainly don't."

"Mayor Trombone," Kevin said. "That's funny."

"That's not his name, Kevin Michael," Emmy scolded. "It's important because your teacher said so," Emmy replied to Heather. "Does he really want another high school. We already have four if you count St. Raymond's."

"Five." Isabella held up a hand. "You're forgetting about the Barclay Academy."

"Speaking of the Barclay Academy, do we really have to go there?" Heather asked.

"We haven't decided," Emmy said.

"Do we get any say in the matter? It is our education."

"We will discuss it later, Heather. Kevin, get back here! You aren't finished," Emmy hollered looking at his papers.

"Mom! None of the other kids are doing this stuff. It's a waste of time. He gives us stupid homework because he doesn't want us to have fun."

"How many times do I need to tell you not to use that word?"

"Sorry, Mom, but it's a total waste."

"It is not, and I don't care if no one else is doing their homework. You are doing what Mr. Starks wants."

Kevin grumbled but he finished the work.

"Now can I have some fun?"

"One of these days you will realize life is not all about having fun, young man."

Chapter Nine

After the first service Sunday morning, Emmy saw Bernice Abraham heading her way with a huge smile showing her pearly white teeth as she waddled along.

"Let me give you a hug, child." Mrs. Abraham smothered Emmy to her chest. "I know those girls of yours are so talented, but until today I didn't remember how much they sound like you when you first came to the church."

Emmy tried to escape, but Mrs. Abraham held her tight.

"They look so much like you except they are bigger," Mrs. Abraham said then released Emmy. "You must be so proud of them, and I love it when the young folks lead the service. I get so excited I could almost burst. If I was going to the Baptist church close to where I live, I would be shouting and carrying on. I thought about waving my hanky today, but I didn't."

"You shouldn't feel embarrassed or inhibited about how you worship, Mrs. Abraham."

"Child, you need to call me Bernice. I remember the day we got baptized. I went before you, and I thought I was going to get stuck on the stairs."

"I remember that day," Emmy said with a smile. *You told everyone you weighed over three hundred pounds.*

"I'm even fatter now, but I guess the Lord don't mind. You tell those precious girls what I said, okay?"

"I will tell them, Bernice." Emmy watched her waddle away and grinned. *If you weighed three hundred pounds then, I bet you're close to four hundred now.*

"What are you thinking about, Emmy? You're grinning like a cat stalking a canary," Sloane said. "I saw you talking to Mrs. Abraham. I was afraid she would smother you if she hugged you any harder."

"She reminded me of the day we got baptized and... never mind. She told me she liked how the teens led the service."

"They did a great job. I know Isabella is usually more shy than Heather, but she really took charge today."

"She did, didn't she? I'm so proud of her."

"She has gained confidence and it shows. I love how you and Rebecca let them do the service on their own. When Riordan was on the platform with the teens, he would do all the talking. He didn't allow them to do anything other than sing and play their instruments." Sloane waved at one of her teacher friends. "I better shut up before I run out of breath. Oh, and thank you for handling the situation at Noemi's party. I didn't hear about it until later that night."

"No problem, Sloane. I didn't want to make it into a big deal."

During the second service Emmy listened more closely to Heather and Isabella. *I guess you do sound like me from the recordings I remember, but I think you sound better because you blend so well.* She smiled later as Armon Perez prayed to close the team's part of the service. She and Rebecca moved from their places in the front row on opposite sides of the sanctuary, and joined their husbands.

"Heather and Isa sounded pretty amazing," Kenny said as he held Emmy's hand.

"Do they remind you of me when I used to sing with the band?" she whispered.

He whispered back, "Are you referring to when you were their age or later?"

"Their age."

"You sounded better."

She let go of his hand. "You're only saying that because you want a kiss."

Kenny looked around. "Not in here, Em."

"Where are the girls?" Tony asked in the foyer after church.

"Somewhere. Why?" Emmy asked.

"I wanted to tell them they did a great job. I thought Isabella handled the transitions like a pro."

"Did you like how they sounded on the last song?"

"The one where it was only them singing?"

56

"Yes, you doofus. How did they sound?"

Tony shrugged. "I'm not an expert, Em. I thought they sounded real good. I couldn't tell you what key they sang in or any of the technical stuff."

"Did they sound like I used to when I was their age?" Emmy handed Tony her purse and put on her coat.

Tony smiled at two of his friends before realizing he was holding Emmy's purse. He quickly handed it back to her. "How would I know? I didn't know you until you were a senior at Roosevelt. Except for when we were little kids, I mean."

"Didn't you ever hear me sing with the band in the early days?"

"You're confusing me with Derrick and Kristen. They were the ones who went to that first concert, not me. I spent all my time playing football."

"So, you never heard Fridays At Five in the old days, huh?"

"I went with you to the show in Chicago."

Emmy sighed. "The one I dragged you to. It was the first time I had seen Kenny in over a year."

"Yeah, and it was pretty obvious how much you missed him."

"I felt so bad on the way home. Guilty bad, I mean. I really screwed up our relationship, didn't I?"

"You were meant to be with Kenny, and I am so glad God arranged it. Otherwise, I might have been stuck with you."

Emmy put her hands on his chest, looked up, giggled and said, "We both know that would have been a disaster. We were meant to be good friends and nothing more."

"Who says we're friends? You're the pesty neighbor who lives across the road and hangs out with my wife."

She stuck out her tongue and walked away.

"Uncle Tony, did you hear Heather and Isa singing?" Kevin asked a moment later as he raced up to Tony. "I thought they sounded amazing, but you can't tell them I said so. I'm going to be the drummer for the teen band when I get old enough."

"It will be our secret, Kevin."

"Have you seen Mom or Dad?"

Tony pointed to Emmy.

"Thanks," Kevin said. He dodged through the mass of people still socializing after church, tugged on Emmy's coat but knew to wait until she finished talking to the older lady.

"... I remember when you first came to church and started singing with Pastor Hillman. You were such a tiny thing but you had a beautiful voice. You danced around too much, but you don't anymore. Now I can see who you gave your voice to. Those girls of yours are so talented."

"Thank you, Mrs. Thompkins." *You used to complain about my dancing all the time. I see you haven't forgotten about it.*

"Mom, can I see if Ben and Taylor can come over after lunch? We want to play outside."

"If Tony and Sloane agree, it's okay with me."

"Cool! Don't tell them, but I heard some of my friends saying how good Heather and Isa sounded, and one of them said they were cute."

"Thank you for participating so much in our devotions," Emmy told the worship team Thursday evening. "I don't want it to turn into me talking and you having to listen. I much prefer to facilitate the discussion and let everyone else talk."

Rebecca added, "I believe it's a good idea to share the responsibility of leading devotions. I think it's Shaun's turn next."

The team moved from the music suite to the platform in the sanctuary. Emmy looked up at the lights as the tech team ran through the light cues. *You like to push the boundaries, Josh, but like your father, you know when enough is enough.*

They were running through the third song when Emmy stopped singing, backed away from her microphone and listened.

"Why did you stop?" Regina Collins asked. "You were singing the melody."

"I wanted to hear you guys. You are amazing, and you don't need me to sing with you."

"Emmy, you're the leader," Ryan Deighton said. "The rest of us follow you."

"You didn't stop when I did. You kept going," Emmy said.

58

"Yes, but we kinda lost the melody."

"Emmy, you need to sing," Rebecca said from the piano.

After rehearsing the final song for several minutes, Emmy waved her hands. "Everyone stop. This song needs a male voice leading it. It doesn't sound right with me singing about loving the church as much as I love my wife. It sounds weird." She looked at Ryan. "You should sing the verses, and we could join you on the chorus and bridge."

"I can't sing a solo. My voice is too weak."

"Nonsense! You've got a good voice," Emmy said. "Try it for me and Rebecca."

He agreed to try after Rebecca persuaded him.

"Now that sounded much better than me singing it," Emmy said after they made it through the song. "Thank you, Ryan, for volunteering."

He looked at Emmy then Rebecca and shook his head. "I didn't volunteer. You guys roped me into singing lead." He placed the wireless microphone back in its stand and walked to the drum cage. "You should sing it," he told Robby Collins. "Your voice is stronger and you sing with more confidence."

Robby smiled and said through the Plexiglas, "I didn't have any confidence the first time I sang." He pointed at Emmy. "She made me sing, and then told me how great I sounded. She was lying through her teeth, but it gave me enough confidence to keep going. You sound good, and you will get even better. Trust me, I know."

Emmy was putting on her coat when she saw Fez, Robby and Regina walking out of the sanctuary.

"Fez, wait up, I need to ask you something." She raced after them.

Fez stopped but Robby and Regina kept going.

"We'll talk to you later, Fez," Robby said. "Good work on the computer tonight."

"Thanks," he answered softly then faced Emmy. "Did I mess something up?"

"No. You did great, but can I ask you something?"

"Sure," he answered with a shrug.

"Did I hear you play bass and can sing?"

He chuckled and answered, "I came from a small church, and we didn't have many musicians. I learned enough to play simple bass lines, and I sang because no one else would."

"Would you be interested in doing more for the worship team than working in the tech department?"

"You have plenty of volunteers, and I'm not an official member of the church."

"Would you like to be?"

"Yes, and I plan to talk to Pastor Tyler about becoming a member and getting baptized."

"Great. It's kinda a rule that to be on the platform as part of the worship team, you need to be a member," she said.

They started walking toward the foyer. Fez opened the door for her.

"I don't think I could play the bass well enough to be on the team, but I'm willing to learn. I can pick stuff up by watching how the other guys play," he said.

"What about singing?"

"I can sing harmony, but I wouldn't want to sing lead."

"I'll keep that in mind. Talk to you later, Fez."

"Mrs. Osborne called again," Emmy told the twins. "She is desperate. She has tried to find someone to watch Milton, but I've heard he can be a handful."

"A handful! Mom, he needs serious help," Heather said without looking up from her book.

"He was fine for me," Isabella reminded her sister. "I'll watch the kids."

Heather thought about the cash and weighed that against the bruise on her shin. "I'll help, but if Milton causes any trouble, you have to take care of him, Isa."

Emmy drove the girls to the Osborne home at six. She stared at Mr. Osborne. *You have to be the tallest person I've ever met. I love your bow tie. I should get one for Kenny since he's such a dork.*

60

"Thank you for bringing the girls over, Mrs. Colwell."

"They are always willing to help," Emmy said.

"I didn't know what I would do tonight."

"It's not a problem and please call me Emmy."

"You can call me Merrill. Paxton and I should be home by nine. He's taking me to Ciao Bella for our anniversary."

"I love that place. I've been going there since I was a little girl," Emmy said.

"Oh, I didn't know it has been there so long. I thought it was a new restaurant," Merrill said.

Emmy smiled. *How old do you think I am? You are in your thirties, but you look as old as me.*

"The girls have my cell number if they need to reach us, but I don't think they will have any trouble. Mia loves Isabella already, and Milton has been talking about the fun he had with Heather."

Heather stared at Milton as he made faces.

"I'm sure they will be angels," Emmy said. She left and the Osbornes followed after kissing the children.

"Where are you, Milton?" Heather asked peeking around the corner. She was rewarded with a tennis ball to the face. "I'll get you, you little twerp. Isa! Help me catch that creep."

"Sorry, Heather, but Mia and I are going to a winter ball. Play a game with Milton and you'll be fine."

"You can't catch me," Milton said. He ran up behind Heather and hit her with a plastic sword.

Heather touched her backside and clenched her jaw. "You are dead meat when I catch you, Milton," she said making his name into something vulgar. "I'll teach you to hit my butt."

Milton raced away and Heather slipped on the hardwood floor and bumped her shin in the same spot he had kicked her.

"Heather, you should ask Milton to join us. He might have fun going to a dance," Isabella said.

Heather rubbed her leg. "The only place he's going is to jail if he tries to hit me again. I wonder if his mother has any Xanax. Three of those should calm him down."

"You can't give him drugs. How do you know the name?"

"I know I can't drug him, and Aunt Diane uses Xanax."

"I'm sure he will calm down if you don't encourage him. Try playing a game with him."

"The only game I'm going to play with that twerp is Hangman, and I'm using a real rope."

The Osbornes returned home at nine thirty.

"We are back," Mrs. Osborne said walking into the kitchen. She put two Styrofoam containers in the fridge. "I am sorry we stayed out later than we planned. How were the children? Did they behave like perfect angels?"

Heather started to answer, but Isabella poked her in the side.

"They were delightful," Isabella said. "We pretended to go to a winter ball and had a marvelous time."

"I don't know what I would do without you." Mrs. Osborne hugged Isabella.

Heather walked up to Mr. Osborne and tilted her head.

He noticed the look on her face and reached for his wallet. "Thank you again." He pulled out two fifties. "Sorry, but I don't have anything smaller."

Heather took the cash without saying a word.

"Please call us anytime," Isabella said. "We love the kids, and they are so easy to watch."

"Should I run you home?" Mrs. Osborne asked. "Or Paxton could while I check on my babies."

"Thanks, but we can walk. It's snowing and I love to feel the flakes on my face," Isabella said.

The girls put on their coats and left.

"If that creep ever tries to sit on my lap again, I'm going to strangle him," Heather said while texting Noemi. "He hit my butt with his stupid sword one too many times."

"What did you do?" Isabella asked.

Heather put her phone away, laughed and said, "I grabbed it from him and broke it in half. Then I told him that's what I would do to him if he ever tried to swat me again."

"He doesn't know any better, Heather. He's a kid."

"He's a monster," Heather said.

Isabella stuck out her tongue to let snowflakes land on it. She danced in a circle. "Isn't this a wonderful night."

Heather slipped on the ice and landed with a thud. Isabella helped her up.

"If I keep babysitting much longer, I will be bruised from head to shin."

"We did make more money than sitting at home texting our friends."

Heather reached into her back pocket and pulled out her cell phone. "Great! It's cracked from landing on my butt. What else can go wrong tonight?"

"You could get grounded for texting Ian Plant again."

"Mom doesn't know about it, and you better not tell her," Heather warned.

"I won't, but you better be careful around him. I heard he tried to kiss Melany Lashley and watch out going down the hill. The street is slick."

"I don't care who he kisses." Heather slid down the hill but stayed on her feet this time.

Chapter Ten

"Thank you for calling, Donna," Mama Bertucci said. "I am so sorry for your loss."

"He was your brother, Maria," Donna Lombardi said. "I called Carmen, but could you call Karla for me?"

"Of course. I will call her right away. Were your sons able to make it to the hospital in time?"

"No, but they promised to be here for the memorial service. They would not have been allowed to see him because of the virus. I was the only one who got to see him."

Mama sighed and said, "I hope they keep their promise. Where are they living now? I've lost track."

"They are both in Oregon. I don't know why they live so far away. It rains there all the time," Donna said and then sobbed.

""It's all right to cry, Donna. I cried for days when Peter passed. Don't be afraid to take time to grieve. It's a healing process," Mama said.

"I'm sorry. Sometimes I forget you had to go through this when your children were young."

"Do you need help planning the service? I can call the funeral home for you."

Donna dried her eyes and wiped her nose. "There's no need, Maria. Vincent and I made our arrangements several years ago after his heart attack. Everything has been paid for, I think. I didn't know we would be doing this so soon. The doctor said people with existing health issues are more vulnerable to this virus. Vincent had trouble breathing the last year or so."

After Mama directed the conversation to pleasant memories for several minutes, Donna revealed the plans for the memorial service.

"I'm sure he would approve of your plans," Mama said.

"I hope you are able to be here, but I understand if it's not possible," Donna said.

"I will be there and Karla will want to come, too. I will have Tony make our arrangements."

Mama called Karla, the youngest of the Lombardi siblings.

"I didn't even know he was sick. Donna should have called me. We don't live far away. I could have come to the hospital to see him," Karla said. "I will tell Derrick. He's golfing with his father. He came to visit, but Amber is taking care of her parents."

Karla and her husband, Daniel Keasling, spent their winters in Florida like her older brothers Carmen and Vincent.

"She probably didn't want to bother you. If it makes you feel better, she didn't call me either."

"Why is she like that, Maria? She treats us like outsiders when she's the one who married into the family. I don't understand her attitude."

"It's the way she was raised, I suppose."

"You've always made excuses for her, and Vincent let her get away with it. He could have stood his ground," Karla said. "Can you imagine Carmen letting Sharon boss him around?" Karla's voice grew more agitated. "Why weren't his sons there? You'd think they would want to pay their respects to their father."

"Oregon is a long way away," Mama said. "Maybe they couldn't take time away from work."

"Please!" Karla said. "Don't make excuses for them. I would kill Derrick and Kristen if they didn't come to my funeral."

"Thanks for driving us to the airport, Kenny," Tony said Tuesday morning. "We could have taken an Uber."

"No problem. I can pick you up tomorrow. Text me when you're scheduled to arrive," Kenny said. He helped Mama get out of the car. "I am sorry about your brother, Mama."

She patted his arm. "I know you are and thank you for telling Emmy. I didn't want to hear her cry."

"She promised to attend the service at the cemetery," Kenny said.

Tony, Kristen and Mama boarded Mr. Robertson's Gulfstream III for the flight to Lake Delray, Florida.

"Should we call Donna and let her know we arrived?" Mama asked as they boarded a taxi.

65

"We can call her after we check in to the hotel," Kristen said. "I texted Mom to let her know where we are staying. She and Daddy are close. Maybe an hour away. Derrick is with them."

"I hope they make it in time," Mama said. "The service is supposed to start at eleven."

"They will make it," Kristen said with a grin. "Mom is driving and she drives like Emmy. They will arrive early."

After checking in and getting the keys to the two rooms, Tony carried the luggage down the hall.

"We have these rooms," Kristen said. "Yours is there, and Mama and I have this one."

"What did you put in here, Kristen? It weighs a ton," Tony complained.

"Just the usual bricks and small boulders," she replied.

"It feels like it."

"Are you getting weak? Do you need my help?"

"I can manage, but I might need a break before we head to the funeral home."

They arrived at the Plessner Funeral Home with twenty minutes to spare. Tony straightened his tie, checked his suit coat and opened the door for Mama and Kristen. They were directed to a large room on the right. Kristen saw her parents and brother talking to her uncle Carmen and his wife, Sharon.

Carmen saw Mama and smiled. The three surviving Lombardi siblings gathered for a hug.

"It's good to see you, Maria," Carmen said.

"You look better than you have in years," Mama replied. "Have you lost weight?"

"I'll take that as a compliment," he answered. "I have cut back on how much I eat, but not necessarily what I eat, and I take walks every day. I don't use a golf cart, so that helps."

"I see Bobby, but did Brian make it?" Mama asked.

"He couldn't take time away from the store," Carmen said without further elaboration about his younger son.

Tony shook hands with Carmen. "Marco couldn't get away from Johns Hopkins. He's a full professor now."

"Does he still have a bushy beard?" Carmen asked.

"As far as I know, and he's lost more hair on top."

Karla whispered to Mama, "I talked to Donna briefly, but I haven't seen her sons."

"I'm sure they are coming. They might be stuck in traffic," Mama said.

"Maria, there is no traffic in this town. Stop making excuses for them."

"I need to speak to Donna and offer my condolences."

Mama sat beside Donna and patted her hand.

"Thank you for coming, Maria," Donna said. "I didn't expect many people because of the virus situation."

Two men in dark suits rushed to the front of the room. They stopped in front of their mother and helped her to her feet.

"Are those Vincent's sons?" Kristen asked in a whisper. "I wouldn't have recognized them."

Derrick answered, "I kinda recognize them, but maybe because I was expecting to see them. I can't remember the last time I saw them. It might have been at Grandpa's funeral in 1998."

"We should talk to them after the service," Kristen said.

After the short service, Tony, Derrick and Kristen approached Vincent's sons.

"Which one is which?" she asked.

"The taller one is Edward, I think. He's the oldest, and that makes the other one Joseph."

"I hope you are right," Kristen said.

She smacked Tony's arm a few minutes later.

"Sorry, I thought the taller one was older. I didn't mean to embarrass you."

"It's all right. I should have waited for someone else to say his name."

"He could have been more tactful correcting you," Tony said. "It's not our fault they don't make an effort to be a part of the family."

"None of the Lombardi cousins make an effort to socialize with the rest of us," Kristen said looking at her brother.

"I email you once in a while," Derrick replied.

She made a face at him. "Just because we don't share the Lombardi name doesn't mean we are not members of the family."

"I still associate with you even though you're a Pearson now," Tony teased. "It's too bad Wyatt couldn't be here. He would have enjoyed meeting everyone."

"Quit being sarcastic. He had to stay for the funeral. Mrs. Whiteside requested he participate."

"Don't tell Mama or your mother, but I would have rather gone to Mr. Whiteside's service. He was something special in the church."

"He almost made it to a hundred."

"I think he was ninety-eight. Emmy told me stories how in the early days of the church he would sing in the choir and get excited and start walking around the sanctuary shaking hands and stuff. She said he called it *getting happy*."

"I'm glad people don't do that now. It would scare me."

"I get a kick out of some of the older people who say *amen* all the time."

Derrick listened to the conversation then replied, "I don't have a clue who you're talking about. Amber and I are isolated in Arizona."

"You could actually use your fancy phone to call me," Kristen said. "I talk to Amber once a week, or I try to."

Derrick put an arm around Kristen's shoulders. "I promise to call you more often, and we might come to SoHam for a visit after your have the baby. I can teach Wyatt how to play tennis."

"Did you talk to Vincent's sons?" Mama asked. "I don't think I would have recognized them if I met them elsewhere."

Tony grinned and told Mama what Kristen did.

"It's not your fault, dear," Mama said putting an arm around Kristen's waist. "How are you feeling?"

"Good, and the baby is getting bigger."

"We can tell," Tony teased.

"We have an appointment on the nineteenth. Hopefully, we will learn what we are having."

A much smaller crowd gathered at Rose Hill cemetery two days later as Vincent Lombardi was laid to rest close to his parents.

"Maybe I shouldn't have been here," Emmy whispered to Kristen after the graveside service. "I'm the only non-family person here."

"Don't be silly. You are more a part of the family than my cousins," Kristen said. "Derrick was at the service, but he had to go back to work yesterday."

"I haven't seen Derrick or Amber in ages."

"I got after him and told him he was becoming like Uncle Vincent's sons."

"Have I ever met them before?" Emmy asked.

"They were at Grandpa Lombardi's service, but you probably didn't actually meet them. You would not leave Tony's side because you were so shy."

"I was a kid, and your uncles were so intimidating," Emmy whispered.

"You are not a child now. Talk to them."

Emmy moved behind Kristen. "No chance. The taller one looks like a gangster."

"You are a goof. That is Joseph, and he works for the Oregon government."

"Is he a spy? Kevin Michael would like that."

Kristen rolled her eyes. "He is not a spy. I don't think state governments have espionage departments."

"What are you chatting about?" Tony asked.

"Emmy thinks Joseph is a spy or a gangster," Kristen answered.

"Do not." Emmy poked Kristen's arm.

"Actually, Joseph and Edward are both secret agents. They are currently working undercover attempting to infiltrate the infamous Colasanti crime family."

Emmy glared at Tony. "Hush! Or else I'll put a contract out on you."

Chapter Eleven

Emmy felt warmed by the sunlight streaming through the tall windows in the spacious foyer of the Crest Ridge United Nazarene Church. She listened as many of the people talked about the virus and what might happen in the coming days. She grinned as two older ladies claimed it was a sign of the last days.

"Are you waiting for Kenny and the kids?" Tony asked.

Emmy nodded and searched the crowd. "I thought he was going to meet me here. We drove separately because of rehearsal. Have you seen him?"

"Yes. Have you checked your phone?"

"Not lately. Did he text me?" She pulled her phone out of her purse.

Tony pointed to it. "Only one way to know."

"Hush. You're a dork." She read Kenny's text. "The kids wanted food from Darby's, so he's taking them there. I hope he brings me something."

"Have you been listening to all the gossip?" Tony asked. "Everyone's talking about the virus and what might happen. Do you know much about it?"

"Not really. What do you know?" She watched small groups of people huddling together and whispering.

"Only what Sloane has told me. I don't watch the news anymore. In fact, I rarely turn on my TV. I don't think I've watched it since the Super Bowl. I should cancel our cable and only keep the Internet service."

"I heard one of the board members say it's possible the government will shut down schools and churches and places where lots of people get together," Emmy said. She backed up to allow a family to pass. "Can they do that?"

Tony shrugged. "How would I know, but it would feel weird if we couldn't go to church."

"It would be chaos if the schools close."

"Pastor Milhuff said three of our church members in nursing homes have tested positive already and it could get worse real fast."

"I hope he's staying safe. He's the one who does all the visits to the senior citizens, and he's pretty old himself."

"I'm sure he's exercising caution and using sound judgment."

Emmy laughed and poked him in the arm. "What would you know about making sound judgments? You bought an expensive truck and a fifth wheel you hardly ever use."

"We're going to use it often this summer," he said then tried to grab her nose.

Tyler and Wyatt walked out of the church office an hour after the second service ended.

"Pastor Tyler, could I talk to you for a second?" Fez asked.

"Sure. Why are you still here?" Tyler asked.

"I wanted to ask you something, but you were kinda busy earlier," Fez answered.

Tyler turned to Wyatt. "I can lock up if you want to go. I've got my keys."

"Kristen is making a surprise for lunch," Wyatt said. "She wouldn't tell me what."

Tyler chuckled and said, "Emmy teases her about her culinary skills, but I'm sure she is a better cook than when she and Emmy were housemates."

"She's not bad. She keeps it simple." Wyatt shook hands with Fez. "Good to see you. I heard you joined the worship team."

Fez shifted his weight from foot to foot. "I was on the team in high school at my home church."

"I heard you can sing and play a little bass," Tyler said as he turned off the lights in the coffee shop.

"I can sing okay, but my bass playing needs to improve before I fill in."

"Talk to you tomorrow," Wyatt said as he left.

"What's on your mind, Fez? How are things going at Darby's and the carriage house?"

"Darby's is great. I'm working all the shifts Mr. Darby can give me, and the carriage house is amazing. It's bigger than I expected."

"Do you know when the Colwells are coming home?"

Fez shrugged. "Not sure, but I've been keeping an eye on the big house."

Tyler sat at one of the round tables. "Have a seat and tell me what's on your mind."

"I would like to be baptized and join the church. How do I do that?"

Tyler grinned. "As it happens, we are having a baptism service next Sunday. All I need to add you to the list is a short recording of your testimony. Joining the church takes longer. There is a membership class to go through."

"I was a member of my church in Wisconsin," Fez said.

"A Nazarene church?" Tyler asked.

"Yes, I joined when I was fifteen."

"That makes it simple. You can become a member by transfer."

"Cool!"

"I can get in contact with your pastor and work out the details." Tyler offered a fist and Fez laughed then bumped it.

The next day, Monday, March 16, the Illinois governor held a press conference. He shut down all restaurants and non-essential businesses.

"Does he mean we can't go out to eat?" Emmy asked Kenny.

"I think restaurants with drive-in windows can stay open."

"Does it mean Darby's will have to close?"

"Could be."

"That sucks. How will they stay in business?"

"I'm sure this won't last long. I don't think the government will close everything down. It would wreck the economy."

Emmy closed the dishwasher and started the cycle. "I suppose the stock market will go berserk."

"I hadn't thought of that, but our investments are ultra conservative. We should be okay."

"I could always get a job."

72

"Do I have to go to school today? It's my birthday. I should be allowed to stay home," Kevin said. "I think I might have a fever, so I should stay home." He touched his forehead and sighed. "I'm burning up."

"You don't have a fever," Emmy said after checking his forehead. "School has been canceled."

Kevin looked out the window. "Why? There's no snow."

"All schools in the state are closed because of the virus," Emmy said.

"Really?" Kevin asked with a smile. "For real, Mom?"

"Yes."

He suddenly felt much better. "This is great! I gotta call Ben and tell him. We can play all day and not have to do any homework."

"Before you get too excited, there is more news."

"What? What could be better than no school?"

"You can't play with Ben. Everyone is supposed to stay in their own homes and limit contact with other people," Emmy said.

"We can play without touching each other, Mom. We're not weird."

"I know that, but until the virus thing is under control, we have to stay inside and not see anyone."

"What about my birthday party? I invited a bunch of friends over after school."

"I can still bake a cake, but it will only be us for the party," Emmy explained.

He looked at her and frowned. "You're kidding, right?"

"No, Kevin. I'm sorry."

He shook his head and glanced at the ceiling before stomping out of the room.

"What do you mean we're having school?" Kevin asked the next morning. He poured extra maple syrup on his pancakes. "I thought you said school was closed because of the virus."

"We might like some syrup, too," Heather said. She turned to her mother and asked, "Does this stay-at-home thing mean we can't babysit for Mrs. Osborne?"

"Not until something changes," Emmy answered. "I thought you hated babysitting for her."

"I like the money."

"What about school?" Kevin asked.

"The school building is closed, but they have figured out a way to hold school online. For right now, your teacher will assign homework and go over your lessons using the computer."

"Do Heather and Isa have to go to computer school?" he asked.

"Yes, they will have assignments, too." Emmy chose two pancakes and spread butter on them. "We are fortunate your school is able to use computers and different programs."

"Good!" He made a face at his sisters. "I don't want to be the only one to suffer because of this stupid virus."

Emmy frowned. "Don't say that, Kevin Michael. Tony and Kristen's uncle died from the virus. It might affect lots of people before it can be controlled."

"I'm sorry he died, but I think it's silly to have school if we can't go to school. Why can't we wait until next week? We could have like an extra spring vacation."

"You need to understand this is not something the authorities know much about. Some people are saying this quarantine could last several months."

Kevin thought about this for a moment. "So, it's possible we might not have school the rest of the year, huh?"

"It's a possibility."

"That kinda sucks. I don't hate school. I like seeing my friends, and I like to do science experiments. I don't like having homework."

"I'm with you there. I tried to get all my work done at school, so when I got home I could play," Emmy said. "We have to be patient and remember God is still in control even though some people don't think He is."

Chapter Twelve

"Are we ready to start?" the ultrasound tech asked. "This might feel a little cold."

Kristen looked up at Wyatt and smiled. "I've been through it before."

"Do you want to know the sex?" the technician asked later. "Some couples do, but others want to be surprised."

Wyatt squeezed Kristen's hand and nodded.

"We want to know," Kristen answered.

"You don't have to worry about picking out a name for a boy. You're having a girl."

Kristen looked at Wyatt. "You are beaming as brightly as a full moon."

"I'm so happy right now."

"I will have to tell Emmy, or else she will pester me to death. She has probably tried calling a dozen times. That is why I left my phone in the car."

Wyatt smiled and said, "I feel satisfied. We accomplished something amazing today,"

"What might that be?"

"We eliminated half of the possible names."

Kristen checked her phone as soon as she got in the car. "Only four texts. I am surprised."

"She might be waiting at the house," Wyatt said. He pulled out of the lot and asked, "Are you hungry?"

"I have a craving for a hot dog and three pickles."

"Really?" Wyatt asked as he glided to a stop at the light. "Darby's isn't open, but there are other places."

"No, it would have to be Darby's," Kristen said and then laughed. "I bet she texted the hospital."

Wyatt pulled into the garage, and they made it inside before Kristen's phone rang.

"Yes, how may I help you?" Kristen asked very seriously.

"Cut the crap, Kristen. Tell me right now," Emmy insisted.

"The technician could not tell for sure."

Wyatt shook his head at Kristen.

"I don't buy it for a second. If you won't tell me, give the phone to Wyatt."

"Relax, Em, I will tell you," Kristen said and then paused.

"Now would be a good time, Krissy," Emmy said.

"We have eliminated fifty percent of the names."

"Don't make me come over there. You won't like it if I have to come out in the rain."

"Do you really want to know?" Kristen asked and then put her hand over the phone.

"You're enjoying this, aren't you?" Wyatt said.

"Okay, your wish is coming true. We are having a girl... or a boy..."

"It's a girl," Wyatt shouted. "You can get after Kristen later."

"A girl? Are you kidding me?"

"We are having a girl. I haven't had a chance to tell Zach or Gracie yet."

"You can tell them after I end this call," Emmy said. "What names are you considering?"

"I'm hanging up now, Em. I will talk to you later."

Tony carried his laptop into the family room where Sloane was working on lesson plans.

"Pastor Tyler sent an email," Tony said as he sat beside Sloane. "He met with the staff to discuss options and now he wants to know how we feel about the virus thing. Specifically about closing the church for right now."

"Didn't the governor say something about not having more than fifty people in a meeting?"

"I think so. Some of the other board members have responded. Most are in favor of following the guidelines set up, but a couple want to keep meeting. One suggested we use different rooms and use the TVs and cameras to hold services."

"Can we do that?" Sloane asked without taking her attention away from her laptop.

"Pastor Jonah said we have the technology, and we're also able to send the livestream out to everyone."

"Then what's the issue?"

"We've been recording the service for the website, but we have a license to go live."

"How are you going to vote?"

"I think we need to follow the guidelines. Can you imagine how terrible everyone would feel if we keep having church like normal, and people get sick and die because of it. I sure wouldn't want to feel responsible for spreading the virus to some older people."

"I wouldn't want that on my conscience. Do you know how your uncle Vincent caught it?" She closed her laptop and set it on the coffee table.

"They can't say for sure, but it was probably at a restaurant or maybe the clubs he belonged to. Who knows? How can they ever figure it out? He might have even caught it at his doctor's office."

Sloane looked at him. "It kinda puts the board in a difficult situation."

"Maybe, but Tyler has the final word."

"What about the district office. Surely, they must have some input."

"I'll ask him, but for now I'm going to say we close until told to reopen."

"If he closes the church, will everyone have to use the online giving app?"

"Some people mail in checks." He stood up and headed to the kitchen. "Can we have pizza tonight?"

"We would have to order it. There's only one left in the freezer."

"Let's order a couple. Who knows how long it might be before we have another one?"

"Kenny! Check your email!" Emmy shouted as she stood at the top of the basement stairs. "Kenny! Did you hear me?"

He appeared at the bottom of the stairs a moment later.

"Took you long enough."

"Did you need me? We still have an intercom system, Em."

"Sorry, but Pastor Tyler just sent an email. The church is closed until further notice. Everything is canceled. Church services, small group meetings and the kids' athletics program. Jonah won't have anything to do."

Kenny hustled up the stairs. "I'm sure Tyler and the staff will figure out a way to have church. It might have to be online for now, but the church is more than the building. We already have small groups meeting almost every night."

"Yes, but they meet somewhere. Some of them at the church and others at people's homes. Now we can't do either."

He pointed at her laptop. "We have the technology to fix it."

"Are you trying to sound like the six-million-dollar man?"

"What?"

"Never mind. I suppose he will let us know what to do before Sunday morning."

Emmy used the intercom system later to tell Kenny she was going out for a while.

"Are the kids doing their schoolwork?" he asked.

"They are. I'll be back soon."

She drove to Darby's, pulled into the lot and noticed a closed sign on the front door and in the window. *This sucks. Danny has to be concerned about how long this will last.*

She returned home and saw Kenny standing in front of the open fridge. "I'm home."

He grabbed the container of kidney bean salad and closed the door. "Where did you go?"

"I had to see if Darby's was open."

"Was it?" He opened a cupboard and grabbed a plate.

"No, there were signs saying closed. The whole area was completely deserted. Actually, there wasn't much traffic at all. I didn't see any other cars until I got to Raynor Street." She waved her hands. "I got a really weird feeling like I was on a set in a zombie apocalypse movie."

"Exactly what I was thinking," he teased.

Chapter Thirteen

"This is a new experience for me as well as all of you," Pastor Tyler Hammond said with a chuckle. He glanced around the room, looked at the camera and continued, "Because of modern technology and Pastor Jonah's knowledge of how to use it, I am coming to you this morning via livestream from the production office and not in the sanctuary as it might appear." He pointed behind him. "The picture or hologram or whatever this is, is not the sanctuary. Well, it is, but I'm not in there." He laughed and said, "I know this is live, but let me try it again. I am in the production office..."

"Is that where Mom is?" Kevin asked as he, his sisters and father sat in the family room Sunday morning.

"Yes, she is there with Pastor Tyler, Pastor Rebecca and Ryan," Kenny answered. "They are going to play some songs, but it won't be the whole worship team."

"Mom said Pastor Tyler learned how to play guitar in only a few days. Is that possible?" Isabella asked.

"It's possible to learn how to play enough chords, but he won't be as good as me," Kenny joked. "I've been playing guitar for more than thirty years."

Heather grinned and said, "Mom says you only know four chords and just turn the amps up real high."

"She is teasing you... and me. Let's listen to Pastor Tyler."

"I don't know how long we will be holding church in this manner, but this is how the church is going to function for the next few weeks. Please remember the church is not this building. You are the church. Hopefully, we will improve as we gain a better understanding of how to use this platform. We had some glitches earlier, but I think Pastor Jonah has straightened them out. We are going to sing some songs, using a much smaller worship team, but we have to limit the number of people involved. Please join in from your homes and sing along... "

"That was pretty cool," Kevin said after the service. "I could hear Mom singing, but it was harder to hear the others."

"They will work on it for the future. I don't think they were using more than one or two microphones. I know they weren't using a mixer. Maybe next week they can use one of the small mixers from the teen room or something."

"Do you think Pastor Tyler felt weird preaching to a camera and not real people?" Heather asked.

Kevin answered, "If you were listening, you would know. He said it felt weird. You should pay more attention to what he says and stop texting your friends."

"I was listening. I didn't hear that part."

"It takes getting used to that's for sure," Kenny said. "I remember the early days of the band. I recall the first time we taped a TV show, and we had to play without an audience. It was different."

"Did they really have TV when Fridays At Five started?" Kevin asked.

"Of course, I'm not that old."

"Gotcha! I was kidding, Dad. I know there was TV when you were a teenager."

"Mom, did you bring any lunch home?" Kevin asked as soon as Emmy walked into the house. "Dad said he would make sandwiches, but we wanted burgers and fries and real food."

Emmy dropped her purse and keys on the desk and set four bags on the island. "I brought food home. That's why I'm late."

Kenny opened one of the bags. "Is this from Darby's? How did you get it? They're closed."

"Danny figured out a way to do curbside delivery. You call in your order, and they get it ready. You pull up by the entrance when you get there, call them again and they bring it out. You don't even get out of your car."

"Who brings it out?" Kevin asked.

"Danny delivered the food. He said there's only three other people in the building. Two cooks, one taking orders, and he delivers them."

"I got dibs on a chili cheese dog," Kevin hollered.

"I knew you and your father would want those. I got hamburgers for everyone else, and enough fries to share."

"There are three slices of chocolate cake in here, Em," Kenny said.

"I didn't ask for cake. Danny must have thrown those in."

"Good. They have the best chocolate cake in the whole world!" Kevin exclaimed grabbing one of the slices.

"I need to call James," Emmy said after lunch. "He's still doing his chaplain job at St. Bart's even though I told him to stop."

Kenny laughed. "Did you really expect him to stop simply because you want him to?"

"Maybe not stop, but he could cut back. He could catch the virus as easily as anyone."

"Make sure you order him to stop when you call him," Kenny teased.

Emmy stuck out her tongue and headed to the den.

"I'm in my room. Where did you expect me to be?" Father James answered Emmy's question. "I have spent the last four hours praying for my flock."

Emmy tried to decide if he was being serious or simply his usual self. "Really?" she asked after several seconds.

"Maybe it wasn't four hours, but I did pray for the sick and needy..."

"And the widows and orphans?"

"Them, too. What's on your mind this glorious Sunday afternoon? How did your livestream go?"

"A few minor technical difficulties, but overall, I think it went well. The church website crashed because so many people were using it. Did you have a service?"

"We haven't figured out how it's going to work yet. We have to wait for the big guy to issue a proclamation or something. It takes time."

"You better be careful. He might ex-communicate you."

"Then I might have to switch churches. Could I become a Nazarene?"

Emmy laughed and said, "I don't know. We have pretty strict rules about how we conduct our lives. I'm not sure an ex-communicated Catholic priest would be allowed in the building."

"Then I will have to seek forgiveness elsewhere."

"Seriously, are you gonna cut back? Better yet stay home like you should."

"I have a job to do like the doctors and nurses and everyone else at St. Bart's."

"Are you wearing a mask and washing your hands more often?" Emmy asked. "The CDC said masks aren't necessary, but other officials are saying it would help."

"I always wore one if I visited someone who was contagious, and not from the corona thing. Now St. Bart's requires me to wear a mask at all times. They are being ultra cautious."

"Are there any Coronavirus cases in the hospital?"

"I don't have all the information. There are laws about patient privacy."

"But have you heard anything through the grapevine?"

"I do not participate in gossip..."

"Yeah! Yeah! What have you heard?"

"No confirmed cases, but not everyone has been tested."

"Well, promise me you'll stay away from anyone who is admitted and tests positive."

"Yes, dear sister, I will abandon my calling if it puts my life in jeopardy. Heaven forbid the sick and dying receive the comfort they need."

"You can be such a... I don't know what... but you can be so aggravating at times. Use caution and wear a mask."

"Could I borrow one of Kevin's Halloween masks. I like the one..."

"No! Goodbye and stay safe. Wash your hands."

"Oh no!" Emmy sobbed as she read an email the next morning.

"What is it?" Kenny asked pouring another cup of coffee. He sat next to her in the breakfast nook and took a bite of her toast. "Bad news?"

"Lillian Palczewski passed away yesterday afternoon. Do you remember her?"

"She's the lady who used to take attendance on Wednesday night for the kids. She would sit at her table, talk to them and hand out treats. That's sad. The kids will miss her."

"I wonder if they even remember her. She's been in the nursing home for over a year, I think. Pastor Tyler said she might have been a victim of the virus."

"If that's true, she would be the first, right? From the church, I mean."

"I think so. I haven't heard of anyone else."

Kenny rubbed his jaw. "What will her family do? They can't hold a funeral in the church right now."

"No idea. Pastor Tyler will have to figure out something."

"I suppose they could go ahead and bury her and have a memorial service later after this thing has blown over. Remember when Richard Cornejo had a memorial service for his mother a few years ago?"

"I kinda remember it. Why?"

"She wasn't there."

"You can be so gross at times," Emmy said. "Can't you be more respectful of the dead?"

"I didn't mean any disrespect. I was merely pointing out you can have a memorial service without the body."

"If I die during this virus thing, would you bury me and maybe have a funeral later when you happen to think about it?"

"You aren't going to die for a long time, Em." He put an arm around her waist. "Why are you so emotional all of a sudden?"

"I'm heartbroken for the family. I know they've had difficulties and now Lillian dies at the worst possible time."

He rubbed her back and held her close. "We have to remember God is in control. The virus cannot defeat God."

"We know, but it seems like too many people are going crazy over this thing."

"The media is playing this for all it's worth. The common flu kills lots of people every year."

Emmy poked his side. "That makes it all better, huh?"

Chapter Fourteen

"What is this book about, Mom? What happens to Claire and Ruby this time? Are they still in high school?" Isabella asked after UPS delivered a box of Emmy's new book. She looked at the cover. "Is this really about basketball?"

Kevin grabbed one of the books, saw the cover and hollered, "About time you wrote one for us guys. All the other books are for girls."

"Boys can read the other books, Kevin," Heather said. "Well, some boys. Others are too stupid to know how to read."

"That's not nice, Heather. Please find a different word to use," Emmy said.

"Why did you decide on the title 'The Winning Basket', Mom? Is it a true story?"

"It's based on a true story like the other books."

"What happened?" Kevin asked.

"When I was in high school, the Roosevelt basketball team won the state championship."

"For real?" Kevin asked.

"Yes. I think it was the only time they won in basketball. They used to win football championships more often. Tony played on a team that won the championship. I remember being at the game with Kristen. It was like a blizzard, and the team won easily. I remember these boys throwing snowballs at me."

"Mom! What does that have to do with the book?" Heather asked.

"Nothing really. I was reminiscing. Anyway, the basketball team won the championship, and Mace Franklin was the best player on the team."

"Who's he?" Isabella asked. "Do we know him?"

Emmy shook her head. "Not really. He and Annie O'Dell are good friends."

"We know her. She writes good books," Heather teased.

"I try to write good books," Emmy said. "Are my books boring?"

"No, Mom, but they can be a little... I don't know..."

"You need to add zombies and dragons to your books, Mom," Kevin said.

Heather poked his arm. "They aren't fantasy books. They're like real life except they sound old-fashioned at times."

"Really?" Emmy asked. "I try to use language kids use today. I listen to how you talk to your friends."

"Yeah, but you don't quite get it, Mom. No offense, but some of the slang you use is so last century. It can be pretty lame."

"I did put some sex in the last book," Emmy said.

The girls laughed.

"What?"

"Mom, you didn't write about sex. You told us what Ruby did without describing how it happened," Heather said.

"I wasn't going to go into great detail about it. The point was she made a choice that will stay with her the rest of her life."

"Can I read the basketball book?" Kevin asked. "I might like it even if there aren't any zombies or sex."

"You don't know anything about sex," Heather said. "You're afraid to kiss a girl."

"I'm not afraid!" Kevin insisted. "I don't want to waste my time kissing girls when I could be doing stuff with the guys. I'd rather do cool stuff like build forts and ride mountain bikes through the woods."

"It doesn't matter," Emmy said. "Yes, you can read the book, and next time I promise to mention zombies."

"Mom! How can you say that? You know you won't write about stuff kids really like," Heather said.

"What was the letter about, Em? I saw it was from Tyndale-Norton Publishing. The envelope looked pretty official," Kenny asked later that afternoon.

"Nothing," she answered while sitting at the kitchen desk going over bills.

"Em, it must have been something. It wasn't junk mail."

"Fine. It was an offer to publish my books. No, only an offer to negotiate a contract really. I think Denise must have had something to do with it."

"Wow! An offer from a traditional publisher. That's cool. How much did they offer?"

"No specifics about money. It was simply an invitation to meet. They probably made the offer because you are still kinda famous in some people's minds. Not sane people, but you know..."

"You are as well known as me now."

"Not even close, but thanks."

"Are you going to think about it. Traditional publishers don't usually make offers like that."

"I might think about it, but if I went that way, I would lose control over the stories. Those kind of companies want to make money. They want material that will sell tons of books. What if they ask me to change the stories to fit the real world?"

"The real world? You write about reality. None of your books are about zombies and walking dead people or wizards and dragons, Em."

"Kevin wants me to include zombies in the next one."

"There are enough books like that already. I love how your stories are... not exactly real, but they're based on things that really happen."

"The girls think they're boring. Heather wants to read about sex."

Kenny's eyebrows lifted. "Tell me you're joking."

Emmy waved a hand. "No matter."

"Should I talk to our attorney?"

"About Heather?" Emmy asked.

Kenny laughed. "No, I was referring to the publishing offer. I doubt our attorneys would be interested in Heather's curiosity about sex."

"I certainly hope not."

"You could at least meet and hear what they're offering. I know you sell more books than the average self-publisher, but you could sell even more with traditional publishing."

"I'll think about it. Did you see how much the Com Ed bill is?"

"Should we start using candles?"

86

"Are we going to join the Zoom meeting?" Kenny asked Wednesday evening. "The kids are already meeting with Daryl and Brenda. How many different Zoom things are there?"

Emmy brought her laptop into the den. "Are you gonna hook it up to the TV? I want to watch in here."

Kenny connected the laptop to the large TV on the wall and made sure it would work.

"Tyler is doing a meeting, and I think there are two or three others. I know there is one for the older people. At least the ones who have computers and stuff."

"Are we still studying the Book of Isaiah, or did we finish it?"

"We finished it. I think tonight is going to be more informal. Tyler wants to see how this will work."

"Is there a limit to how many people can join a Zoom meeting?" Kenny asked. He sat next to Emmy on the couch. "Can they see if I kiss you?"

"Not yet, but they can after we join the meeting."

"Too bad."

"Behave! You wouldn't kiss me if we were at the church."

"I might." He kissed her until she made him stop.

"Stop it. The meeting's about to start."

"You didn't answer my question."

"What was it?"

"How many people..."

"Oh, that one. Tyler said it depends on the license or whatever it's called. I think the church can have up to 300 people on one meeting."

"Is there a time limit? I've never used Zoom."

She shrugged. "Like I have. I guess we'll find out. If the meeting stops in the middle of someone talking, then we'll know there's a time limit."

"Haven't you and Rebecca practiced using Zoom? You have a worship team meeting tomorrow night."

"Tyler said we could use his meeting room tomorrow night."

"His meeting room?"

"I think that's what Zoom calls them. Anyway, he will help us get started, and Rebecca and I will take it from there." She pointed to the TV and made the proper connections on her wireless keyboard. "Now behave because everyone can see and hear us."

Liz laughed and asked, "What were you guys doing, Em?"

"He threatened to kiss me in front of everyone."

Tyler shook his head.

"I thought Kristen and Wyatt were the newlyweds," Tony said.

"They are," Emmy answered. She stared at the screen. "Where are you, Tony?"

"In the family room. Why?"

"Then why does it look like the church logo is behind you?"

"It's a trick I learned from Peter. He showed me how to..."

"Hey! Sloane's head disappeared!" Emmy shouted.

"I chopped it off," Tony replied.

"Now she's back," Emmy said.

"I see we have over fifty people who have joined us so far," Tyler said. "We will wait a few more minutes before we begin. I'd like to discuss our options for the coming weeks. I'm sure we might encounter some bugs, but we will make this work." He paused then laughed. "Emmy, you don't need to raise your hand to talk. You can say something whenever you feel the need."

"I didn't want to interrupt. This is kinda like being in school and you're the teacher."

"Pastor Tyler, can you mute her?" Andy Walker asked. "It might be a long meeting if she's allowed to talk."

Emmy stuck out her tongue at the TV.

"Em, they can see that," Kenny said.

"Sorry everyone. I promise to behave now."

"Thank you, Emmy," Tyler said. "We have close to a hundred now in the room so to speak."

"Why are the boxes so small?" Emmy pointed at the TV.

"It's because there are so many people in the meeting. I can change it to this if you want." He changed a setting and Pastor Tyler's face appeared.

"That's better."

An hour later Tyler said, "I will pray to end the meeting, and next week we will begin discussing the Book of Romans."

"Are you ready to start?" Pastor Tyler asked Emmy and Rebecca the next evening.

"I'm ready," Rebecca answered.

"Give me a minute," Emmy said. "I need to catch my breath. I was upstairs using the bathroom."

Tyler laughed.

"Shoot! I shouldn't have shared that," Emmy said. "Did everyone hear me?"

"Just Pastor Tyler and me," Rebecca said with a laugh.

"Good. I'm ready now."

Tyler opened the worship team meeting and soon twenty-one members of the team were in the online meeting room.

"I will pray to open the meeting," Rebecca said. She prayed for the group and some of the needs expressed earlier. "It's so good to see you. I wish it was at the church, but until that can happen again, we have this." She waved her arms and giggled.

"How are we going to rehearse if we're all in different places?" Bobby O'Connor asked with a grin.

"You can figure it out on your own," Emmy said. "For those of you who have recently joined the team I want to welcome you. I can see some new faces and some who have been on the team almost as long as me." She paused and then said, "I can't believe I've been part of this team for almost twenty years. It doesn't feel like it was that long ago. Anyway, now I'm helping Rebecca lead the team..."

"I'm helping you, Emmy," Rebecca said.

"I'd like to say something if I may," Fez Rivera said.

"Go ahead, Fez, and welcome to the team," Rebecca replied.

"I talked to Pastor Tyler the last Sunday we met at church about baptism. He said he was planning to have a baptism service the next week. Then all the crazy stuff happened. Anyway, he baptized me and three other people this afternoon."

"That's great!" Emmy said.

"We recorded videos of our testimony, and they should be on the website later. I transferred my membership, too. I'm now an official member of Crest Ridge United Nazarene."

"Yes!" Emmy high-fived Fez's image. "Now you can sing with us."

Thirty minutes later Emmy said, "Since we can't meet normally for now, We will use this time to have a short devotional and stay in touch. Would anyone like to volunteer to lead next week's meeting?"

After no one volunteered, Rebecca said, "I will lead next week to get us started."

"Do we need to buy a book to study?" Julia Weishar asked.

Emmy smiled at the tall, slender woman in her early twenties who had joined the teen team in 2015. "We can start with the Bible. If this goes on long enough, maybe we can consider purchasing a book to use."

"Any other questions before we close?" Rebecca asked. She waited and then closed the session with a prayer.

Emmy immediately called Rebecca.

"How do you think it went?" Emmy asked.

Rebecca made a clicking sound then answered, "I was pleased with the turnout. I really want to find a way for the team to stay connected through this."

"So do I," Emmy said. "I loved the way some of the younger people expressed themselves. They have grown so much spiritually, and I would hate for this social distancing to retard their growth."

"I would love to have a cookout or something when this is all over."

Emmy laughed and responded, "I suppose you want to have it at our house."

"Ryan and I live in an apartment. I don't think everyone would fit."

Chapter Fifteen

"Should we wear masks if we're going to meet for rehearsals?" Ryan Deighton asked Saturday morning.

Rebecca laughed at him. "Why? The government hasn't said we need to."

"I'm serious," he replied. "What if one of us is exposed to the virus? I wouldn't want to spread it to you guys."

Tyler entered the church's production studio. "I heard part of your conversation."

"What is your opinion about masks?" Ryan asked.

"I don't feel you need to wear one, but if Emmy is afraid to be in the room with us, maybe we should."

"Should what?" Emmy asked as she rushed into the rectangular room located off the main music suite.

"I was asking if we should wear masks," Ryan replied.

Emmy answered, "You guys aren't that ugly. Maybe if Tony was on the team, I'd make him wear one."

"I'll let him know," Tyler said with a chuckle. "What songs have you chosen for this week?"

Rebecca answered and the small team rehearsed for close to an hour.

"Kenny wondered if we should use a mixer."

"I thought about it, but it would mean more people involved," Tyler said. "We need to draw the line somewhere, and unless the sound is atrocious, I would rather not expand our group."

"The feedback I heard was positive for the most part," Rebecca said. "Other than one of the older members who emailed us and said Ryan was banging on whatever contraption he was sitting on much too hard. His words not mine."

"I'll try to bang more softly tomorrow," Ryan replied.

March 29 was the second Sunday of the forced closure of churches. Pastor Tyler, Ryan, Rebecca and Emmy again used the production studio to livestream the morning service. Pastor Jonah joined the team to keep an eye on the technical aspects.

Ten minutes after Pastor Tyler started, the livestream froze.

"Can you tell what happened," Tyler asked.

"Not for sure," Jonah answered. "It's possible we have too many viewers or the equipment we're using isn't powerful enough." He shrugged and said, "I don't know what to say."

"Could we start over?" Tyler asked. "Would you guys mind?"

No one objected, so they started from the beginning. This time they made it through the music with only a couple glitches.

Pastor Tyler moved to a stool in front of the camera. "Thank you for hanging with us. As I said before, we are trying to figure this out as we go. This morning Phoebe asked me if I was going to be on TV again. She's six, so she thinks it's cool to see me on the computer."

"Dad! It froze up again," Heather hollered from the family room. "Do we have to sit here if it's not working?"

Kenny closed the door to the half bath at the end of the hall and rejoined the kids. "What happened?"

Kevin pointed to the TV. "It's been like that for a whole minute or more."

"Let's try using Facebook instead of YouTube. It might make a difference."

The switch to Facebook worked, and they were able to watch the rest of the livestream without any issues.

"When can we start having church like normal?" Kevin asked. "This kinda sucks."

"Kevin! It does not," Isabella said. "You might have to get used to this. I talked to Noreen yesterday, and her mom thinks it might last for several months. She works at St. Bart's, so she knows things."

"Are you going to make lunch, or will Mom bring something home?" Heather asked.

"Yeah! Darby's," Kevin hollered.

"No Darby's today. It's too far away. I'll call and see if she has plans."

He called her cell phone and asked about lunch.

92

"I could stop, but I thought we could make a taco salad."

He asked the kids about taco salad.

"I heard them. If you brown the hamburger, that will help."

"Em, I do know how to make taco salad. I even know the correct order to add the ingredients unlike someone I know," he said knowing the kids would laugh.

"Go ahead if you want. I'll be home in thirty minutes or so. How did it go today? I know we had some glitches."

"We ended up using Facebook..."

"YouTube broke," Kevin hollered.

"We will get it straightened out. I'll be home as soon as I can."

"Would you like to help me this morning, Em?" Kenny asked after breakfast Monday morning."

"What are you going to do?" she asked.

"I want to start recording demos of my new songs, and I thought you could play keyboards for me. Nothing fancy, but something to fill out the sound."

"I can do it after I take a shower."

"Do you want someone to play the drums?" Kevin asked. "I could help."

Heather laughed. "Since when do you know how to play the drums?"

"I can play a little bit. Enough to keep the rhythm," he said.

A while later Kenny, Emmy and Kevin were in the studio. Kevin sat behind the drum kit and played a simple pattern.

"That will work," Kenny said. "Keep playing that through the verses."

Kevin adjusted his headphones. "Am I playing too loud?"

"It doesn't matter. I will make adjustments from here if I need to. Can you hear okay, Em?"

Emmy sat behind the keyboards in the main recording area. Kevin was on the other side of the room and Kenny was in the control room. He would play guitar and sing a guide vocal from there so he could start and stop the recording.

"I can hear you and Kevin, but I need more of your guitar."

93

Kenny made an adjustment and played a few chords."

Emmy gave him a thumbs up. "That's better."

"Are we all ready?" Kenny asked. He could see everyone through the window and they nodded. "Count it off, Kevin."

Emmy rolled her eyes.

Thirty minutes later Kenny stopped recording. "Wow! Kevin, you did a great job keeping time. If you keep practicing, you'll be better than Dave."

"Dad, all I did was play the same pattern over and over and add a few cymbal crashes."

"Yes, but every great drummer has to start somewhere."

"Kevin Michael, come here. I need to talk to you," Emmy hollered from the den.

Kevin walked out of the family room, across the hall and into the den. "What?"

"I got an email from Mr. Starks. Do you know why?"

Kevin shrugged. "I turned in my homework."

"It's not about homework. Before school closed were there some older boys bothering you?"

"No! Why would you ask me that? No one was bothering me."

"Why would Mr. Starks think so?"

"Because he's weird. Can I go now?"

"Okay, but you can tell me if someone is bullying you."

"No one was bullying me, Mom. Geez! Let it go."

"Maybe I should call Mr. Starks. He might have sent this to the wrong parent. It could be some other boy in your class is being bullied, and that boy's parents should know about it."

"Mom! Don't call him. He's probably busy grading all the stupid homework we have to do."

"Are you sure there's nothing you want to talk about?"

"I am sure."

"Did I ever tell you about the time Rory stood up for me when these older boys were pestering me?" She patted the arm of her recliner. "Come and sit by me. I'll tell you what happened to me, and how Rory handled the situation."

Kevin's shoulders slumped, but he sat next to his mother.

She put an arm around his waist. "I remember when I was nine-years-old. I was playing at the park by the school. I was having fun, and these two older boys appeared out of nowhere. I didn't pay any attention to them at first, but they walked over to me and started asking questions. They wanted to know where I lived, my name and stuff like that. I told them my name, but not where I lived. They were quite a bit bigger than me, and I was scared of them. I thought about running home, but one of the boys grabbed my arm. He squeezed it hard enough to hurt and pulled me over to a bench on the opposite side of the park away from the little kids. The taller boy began to talk about some stuff I didn't understand. You get the picture?"

"Are you talking about... sex stuff?"

"Yes. I remember wrapping my arms around my knees on the bench. I closed my eyes and felt a hand on me. I think I started crying, and then I heard someone yell. I opened my eyes in time to see Rory Porter yanking both boys off the bench. I will never forget the look on his face as he pounded those boys with his fists and he kicked them. Within a few seconds those boys ran away like rabbits. Rory sat beside me and used his shirt to dry my face. We really didn't say anything to each other, but we sat there for a few minutes. He finally asked if I was okay. Then he took my hand and walked me home."

"I'm sorry those boys were bothering you, Mom, but I'm glad Uncle Rory was there to protect you. Can I go now?"

"Are you sure no one was bothering you at school?"

"Are you going to keep pestering me until I tell you?"

"No, but it might help if you talk about it."

He put a hand to his mouth. "I kinda blew it, huh?"

Emmy nodded.

"I'll tell you, but it wasn't anything like what happened to you."

"I'm listening."

"I'm not going to tell you their names, but they're eighth graders."

"You don't have to mention names."

95

"They would call me names and push me in the hall when the teachers weren't watching."

"Did you mention it to Mr. Starks?"

"No, because they would have picked on me even more."

"What kind of names did they call you?"

"Just stuff like dork and twerp and jerk. They didn't swear at me."

"They shouldn't call people names."

"You and Uncle Tony call each other dork and brat and stuff."

Emmy grinned and said, "We do, but it's our way of being nice to each other."

"Yeah, sure. Anyway, I got mad at them one day because they said Dad was in a stupid band and the band sucked big time. I wanted to hit them, but I figured that's what they wanted so they could pound on me. I told them to shut up and walked away. They said I was too scared to defend Dad, but I remembered how Jesus told people not to fight. They stopped bothered me so much after that. How did Mr. Starks find out?"

"He didn't say, but I suspect he might have heard them bullying you or another boy. I'm proud you didn't fight back, but I would still love you if you did."

"I got mad when they called Fridays At Five a lousy band, but after I thought about it for a while, I laughed."

"Why did you laugh?"

"Because that showed me how stupid they were. Everyone knows Fridays At Five is like the coolest band in the world."

"Cooler than my band?" Emmy asked.

"Maybe a little because they play louder."

Chapter Sixteen

"Kenny, I'm going to run over and see Diane. It's Caden's birthday, and I have a card for him," Emmy said Tuesday afternoon. "I won't be gone long."

"How old is he?"

"Fourteen. He's the same age as the girls. You know that."

"Right. I was thinking about Carson. Tell him happy birthday from me."

"Did you call your mother back? She wants to talk to you," Emmy said. "I told her you would call today."

"I'll call her after I finish the lyrics to this tune. I'm on a roll and don't want to stop."

"Don't forget."

Emmy decided to drive since the temperature had dropped ten degrees from earlier in the day. She knocked on the door and Caden let her in.

"Happy birthday, Caden. I have a card for you." Emmy handed it to him. "Where's your mother?"

Caden hooked a thumb over his shoulder. "In the kitchen talking to Dad. She's mad because he promised to be back today." He opened the card, read it quickly and held up the cash. "Thanks, Aunt Emmy. I promise not to spend it foolishly."

Emmy patted his arm. "It's a hundred bucks and you can spend it anyway you want. Just don't tell your mother."

"Tell me what?" Diane asked.

"Nothing. I gave Caden a card and a couple bucks for his birthday." She smiled at him and asked, "When did you get taller than me?"

He shrugged and headed upstairs.

Diane laughed and said, "Em, everyone is taller than you."

"Not Lily and Conor," Emmy replied. "Are you mad at Brady?"

Diane sighed and headed back to the kitchen. "Come and sit. I made coffee."

"Thanks, but I'm not thirsty."

"Then watch me drink it. Talk to me."

Emmy joined Diane at the kitchen table.

"He promised Caden he would get back last night. Then he called and said there was an issue and would need to stay."

"Where is he?"

"Houston. Some aerospace company down there. I don't remember the name." Diane waved then took a long sip of coffee. "I'm glad he started the company because he was going nuts without something to challenge him, but I never thought after seven plus years he would travel this often. He was gone most of February and part of March. He should make Bennett quit his job at Barclay Academy and help out. He makes more money from their company than from the Academy."

"You might get your wish sooner than you think. Kenny said the government might restrict airline travel to those in essential jobs."

Diane snorted. "Won't help me. Brady's company is considered extremely essential by those yahoos in Washington."

"He's not a spy, is he?" Emmy asked with a grin.

"Yeah, he's James Bond in disguise. Are you gonna make him a character in your books?"

"Maybe. The girls say they're boring and need more action."

"How are the kids coping with the school being closed?" Diane asked. She got up and refreshed her coffee. "I'm smart enough to keep Lily and Conor interested in their work, but Caden is acting like he doesn't need to do anything since he's in eighth grade."

"What about Carson? It must be hard to be so close to graduating and then have the school close. Do you know if they will have a prom?" Emmy asked.

"I don't have a clue. He asked Lauren to the prom before school closed."

"Is he serious about her?"

"Serious enough to spend some cash. Speaking of cash, how much did you give Caden?"

"Too much, but it's okay."

"You shouldn't spoil him."

"He said he would spend it wisely," Emmy said. "It's about time Carson got serious about a girl. Have you met her parents? They sell real estate, right?"

"They own Garvey Realty, and I've met them. They appear nice if a little snobbish."

"What about Lauren. I've seen her with Carson, but I haven't talked to her much."

"She's sweet. She's a junior and plans to attend North Park."

"Does Carson still want to go there? If he does, make him live in a dorm and not commute from home."

Diane drained her coffee. "But it's cheaper to commute," she said mocking Emmy.

"If I could do it over, I'd live in a dorm."

"Yeah, so you could party with the hot college guys."

"That is a benefit of living on campus," Emmy said and then giggled.

"It's a good thing you didn't. Hey! Caden told me Kevin was playing the drums in the studio. What's that all about?"

Emmy waved a hand. "Kenny was recording demos for the next CD. Kevin and I helped him."

"So, Kevin was really playing the drums, huh? I assumed he was bragging to Caden and Ben about goofing around in the studio."

"He was playing simple patterns and rhythms, but he does have some talent. I guess he gets it from me," Emmy flipped her hair back and batted her eyes.

"Most definitely, Em. I'm sure Kenny's talent played no part in it."

"Gotta run. Oh, did I mention the church is live streaming the services now? You can watch them without having to set foot in an actual church."

"I come to your church."

"Yeah, you're a regular CEO."

"What does that mean?"

"Christmas, Easter and occasionally. See you later."

99

"Em, It's time to Zoom," Kenny hollered from the family room. "Are you coming?"

"Give me a second. I'm loading the dishwasher. Did you connect to the meeting?" She put the last of the plates into the dishwasher and closed the door. *I'll wait to run you later.* She raced down the hall and plopped onto the couch next to Kenny.

"Nice to have you join us, Emmy," Pastor Tyler said. "Does anyone have any prayer requests?"

Several people did.

Tyler finished praying and smiled. "I see a few more faces tonight. If this continues to grow, we will have to add more meetings. In order to lessen the confusion about who is speaking, I am going to mute everyone. If you wish to comment, raise your hand like Emmy did last week. With this many people in the meeting it could become rather chaotic."

Emmy raised a hand.

"You aren't muted yet, Emmy. Go ahead."

"At our worship team meeting we had everyone recite a memory verse, and it was so garbled no one could understand a word."

"Then we need to try something different tonight."

Tyler's new approach worked out. Although the discussion took more time, everyone could understand what was said.

After closing the meeting with a prayer, Tyler said, "Same time next week and think of more topics to discuss. Email them to me during the week, and I will give you some choices."

"Hello, everyone," Emmy waved to the TV in the family room. "It's good to see so many beautiful faces, and yours too, Bobby," she teased to open the Zoom meeting.

"How can you tell, Emmy? I'm wearing a mask," Bobby said.

"You are such a punk," Emmy said with a laugh.

Bobby took the mask off and several people groaned.

"Put it back on!" Robby said.

"Okay, enough of this goofing around," Emmy said a moment later. "We need to get serious."

100

Emmy led the devotional study and was pleasantly surprised by the group's participation. She would ask a question, and they would respond. An hour later, the meeting was coming to a close.

"Before we go I would like to ask for prayers for me and the baby. I am due in less than two weeks, and my blood pressure has been going up and down. My doctor might admit me to Mercy if it doesn't stabilize."

"Why didn't you tell us earlier?" Emmy asked.

"I didn't want to be a bother," Rebecca said.

"It's not a bother," Liz said. "You should have said something. Emmy, I think we need to spend a few minutes praying for Rebecca and the baby."

"I agree," Emmy said. "If you have to leave because it's getting late, please go ahead. Those who can stay connected will pray."

No one left the meeting. Emmy and several others prayed for Rebecca. Liz was the last to pray.

"Thank you everyone. I feel so much love from you all," Rebecca said.

Emmy dried her tears and replied, "We are here for you, Ryan and Isaiah. Don't hesitate to call if you need anything. Anytime. Day or night."

"Thank you, Emmy. I will."

"Mom! You have to do something about Kevin Michael," Heather said as she and Isabella stood in the doorway of the den Saturday night."

Emmy set her laptop down. "What did he do now?"

"It's not what he did," Heather said. She looked at Isabella.

"What is it then?"

"Mom, he's making us sick," Isabella said.

"How? I haven't heard him coughing or anything," Emmy said.

"Mom, he stinks to high heaven. I heard Grandma use that expression before and never knew what she meant. Now we know. He smells so gross it's making us sick."

101

"I almost puked," Heather said. "He was playing all day, and now he stinks. We asked him to take a shower and he said he wasn't going to until school starts again. Make him shower before the smell kills everyone in the house."

"I will tell your father to have a talk with him," Emmy said.

"No!" the girls screamed together.

"Daddy won't do anything. You have to do it, Mom. Drag him into the shower if you have to, but, please, for our sake make him shower tonight."

"He's bigger than me. I can't force him to shower." Emmy saw the serious looks on the girls. She got up and nodded. "I will talk to him right now. Where is he?"

"In his room. We came downstairs because the stench was suffocating," Heather said.

"It can't be that bad," Emmy replied.

Isabella pinched her nose and pointed up. "See for yourself, Mom."

"Smell for yourself," Heather added.

Emmy headed upstairs and knocked on Kevin's door.

"Go away, Heather."

"It's your mother and I'm coming in."

"Mom, I told them I would shower when we go back to school."

Emmy held her nose and shook her head. "You aren't waiting until then. I don't know what you guys were doing all day, but you are getting into the shower right now." She pointed to his bathroom.

"Mom!"

"Now, and I'm going to stay right here until you get in the shower."

"Mom!"

"Go! Now!"

He stomped into the bathroom and slammed the door. "I hate taking showers."

"Throw those clothes out here. I'll toss them in the washer."

She heard the water running, and a minute later he tossed the clothes out.

"Use lots of soap and scrub everywhere," Emmy said. She picked up the clothes and held them at arms length. She threw them in the upstairs washer and added a packet of detergent. She turned on the machine and added another packet. She walked back into his room and knocked on the bathroom door. "Are you using soap?"

"Yes, Mom. Go away."

"I'm staying here until you're done."

Three minutes later he turned off the water.

She knocked and asked, "Did you wash your hair?"

"Yes!"

"I want to check," Emmy said.

"Mom!" he yelled. "I'm getting dried. Go away!"

"Cover up because I'm coming in."

He barely had time to wrap the towel around his waist.

"Did you use lots of soap?"

"Yes."

"I know you don't like to shower, but you're getting to the age where you need to more often. Did you scrub your face?"

"Yes."

"Good because it will prevent acne if you keep your face clean."

"I don't have any pimples, Mom. Are you going to tell anyone about this?"

"Of course not. Why would I?"

"Will Heather or Isa?"

"No. They are your sisters, and they love you. I'm sure they won't try to embarrass you."

"They better not, or I'll tell everyone they started their periods."

"That's not a secret, Kevin. It happens to all girls their age."

"They better not tell anyone."

"I promise they won't."

"Can you go away now so I can get dressed?"

Emmy grinned and said, "I did change your diapers..."

"Mom!" he yelled and she giggled and left.

Chapter Seventeen

"Good morning, sleepyhead," Kenny said. He turned on his side, placed a hand on Emmy's stomach and kissed her cheek. "Do you know what today is?"

She brushed his hair out of her eyes. "It's Sunday and why are you trying to wake me up so early. I don't have to be at the church until nine thirty. I can sleep late today." She turned onto her side away from him.

He moved his hand lower. "It's more than just Sunday. It's a very special day, Em."

"Ummmm. That feels good, but you better stop."

"Why?" He kissed her again. "Don't you remember what today is?"

She swatted his hand away and turned onto her back. "I do believe it's April 5th. Why?"

"April 5th. Doesn't that ring a bell?"

She shook her head while stifling a grin. "Is it income tax day?"

He touched her side exactly where he knew she was ticklish. "You're being a stinker. You know what day it is."

She laughed and tried to push his hand away without any success.

"It's our anniversary, Em. Do you remember how many years we've been married?"

"From the way you're acting, I would guess it's only been one year."

"Can I help it if I still find my wife sexy and adorable?"

"I still have to be at church by nine thirty," she whispered.

"I'll make sure you get there on time."

"Mom, we watched the livestream and there weren't any problems. It was smooth as glass," Kevin said making a flat motion with his hand. "Did you bring anything home for lunch?"

"I brought chicken and mashed potatoes home, but I left it in the car. Would you get them for me, please?"

"Okay, and guess what?"

104

"What?" Emmy asked as she let Kenny kiss her.

"I took another shower."

Heather and Isabella came into the kitchen in time to hear his remark. They rolled their eyes.

After lunch Emmy was putting the leftover chicken in the fridge when her phone rang.

"Did you watch the livestream, Diane?"

"Hello to you, too, Emmy. As a matter of fact, we all watched."

"Even Brady?" Emmy asked closing the refrigerator with a kick.

"Yes, he got home last night.

"Did you like the service? Did Brady say anything?"

"I enjoyed it. Brady said you should dance more."

Emmy laughed and said, "The production room is too small. Before I forget, did you and Brady talk about his traveling?"

"He promised to hire or promote two account managers. They will do much of the traveling. I understand there will be times he has to take care of matters himself, but he can send someone to handle more routine issues."

"I'm glad to hear it." Emmy spooned out the last bit of mashed potatoes and ate it.

"Happy anniversary. How many years has it been?"

"If I went by the way Kenny was all over me this morning, I would say we're still newlyweds."

"TMI, Em."

"Don't tell me Brady wasn't happy to see you last night."

"He might have been, but I'm not going to tell you about it. Did you tell everyone at church what you guys did?"

"No!" Emmy said.

"Emmy," Diane drew out her name. "Tell the truth."

"Liz was there for a little while with Phoebe and David and I told her."

"You are such a goof. How many years for real?"

"Seventeen! Can you believe it? Sometimes I feel like we just got married..."

"Yeah, you told me about this morning."

"Other times, too. Not only when we're having sex."

Kevin heard Emmy's part of the conversation as he was walking into the kitchen. He shrugged and quickly headed back to the family room.

"Lately he's been more attentive. Just little things. The other day he made the bed."

"Were you still in it?" Diane asked.

"No, and he's done the dishes a few times. He carried some dirty laundry downstairs. I even saw him weeding the flower beds."

"Don't you have a crew to take care of the landscaping? We do."

"Yes, but he was working with them. I think he's bored because of the virus thing. He's been working on new songs, but it's not looking good for a summer tour."

"This thing has to be over before summer," Diane said. "Schools have to reopen soon, and everything will get back to normal."

"I don't know. I heard news reports saying it could last longer than a year."

"You need to stop listening to those news shows. You're worse than Andy Walker when it comes to politics. None of those so-called experts know a lick about what will happen and how long this will take."

"I keep hearing different opinions all the time. I should know we have to trust God is in control of the whole thing, and we don't need to worry."

"That's what you always tell me."

"What politician are you going to complain about now?" Emmy asked when Andy called five minutes later.

"All of them, but why didn't you wear a mask for the livestream? Haven't you heard what the CDC mandated?"

"It might be difficult to sing while wearing a mask and what is the CDC?"

"The Center for Disease Control. They flipped again."

"What? Are they gymnasts?"

"Ha! Ha! They've been saying masks weren't necessary, but the other day they switched. They are now recommending everyone wear a mask outdoors." His voice grew more animated. "Can you imagine the whole world walking around in masks? Who's going to pay for them? Do you have a supply of masks at home? I don't. I am sick and tired of the politics of this crap..."

Emmy listened as he ranted for several minutes.

"...if you ask me, they are all idiots." He finally paused to take a breath.

"Are you finished?"

"Yes, but I will not be wearing a mask anytime soon."

Emmy laughed and said, "I can't see anyone forcing you to wear one, but I might just to follow the guidelines." *That will push your button.*

He roared, "It's people like that who blindly follow everything the politicians say who will be the downfall of this country."

"I gotta go, Andy. Call me later."

He was still ranting when she ended the call.

"Em, come to bed," Kenny said patting her side of the bed.

"Why? I'm not sleepy yet."

"I want to see your present."

"You saw it when you wrapped it. I could tell you did it yourself because none of the corners were straight."

"I was going to have Isa do it, but she would have wanted to see what I bought you."

Emmy walked out of the bathroom wearing a robe.

"Hey! You aren't supposed to wear that."

"Why not?" she asked holding the robe closed.

"Because I want to see how your present looks on you."

She giggled and said, "It doesn't keep me warm enough, and why are you calling it my present. You bought it for yourself."

"That I did," he said with a wicked grin. "Now take off that flannel robe and let me see you."

She held onto the robe. "You've seen me for thirty years."

107

"Not the way you look in my present." He rubbed his hands together. "My hands are nice and warm. If you come to bed, I'll make sure you stay hot."

"You are insatiable," she whispered removing the robe. She stood at the side of the bed and modeled his present. "Happy now?"

He reached for her and pulled her onto the bed. "Very happy, Em, and the day isn't over. It is still our anniversary."

"Did you cancel those reservations we had in Wisconsin?" Diane asked Monday morning. She warmed her coffee and sat at the kitchen table.

"What reservations?" Emmy asked putting her cell phone on speaker.

Diane rolled her eyes. "Remember we made reservations to get away for three days back in February?"

"Shoot! I forgot all about those. Do you think we can get a refund?"

Diane took a long sip of coffee and said, "I don't know, but I don't want to waste money on a hotel we can't use. I'll call and find out. Maybe with this quarantine, they will be more lenient in their cancellation policy."

"Are you sure we still can't use them? We could say we're quarantining ourselves because your kids are sick."

"You mean we should lie to them, Em?" Diane asked with a laugh.

Emmy sighed. "No, we can't lie. Why didn't you remind me about the reservations? I totally forgot about them."

"So did I. It's a good thing Brady mentioned staying home with the kids. Sorry, I totally blew it."

Emmy checked the calendar next to the desk. "Call the hotel and see what you can do. Call me back."

Diane called thirty minutes later.

"So? Did they give us a refund?" Emmy asked.

"I had to sweet talk the manager and promise we would reschedule our visit after this is over."

"Did you lie to him, Diane?"

"Better me than you. You were never any good at hiding the truth."

Emmy didn't respond for several seconds.

"Are you still there?"

"Yes, and I just thought of something."

"What?"

"The Robertsons are still in Idaho, right?"

"Yes," Diane answered. "Why does that matter? We can't fly to Idaho."

"No, but their house is empty, and since Brady was already planning to watch the kids..."

"I see where you're going. You get Kenny to watch your kids, and Brady will watch ours and we can vacation next door. Not exactly a vacation in the Caribbean, but better than nothing."

"Yeah, but how will we convince the kids to leave us alone? Now that I'm thinking about what we planned, I'm realizing I really could use the time to recharge my batteries."

"I thought Kenny recharged your batteries yesterday," Diane teased.

"Hush! I could use a day to be totally lazy. I don't want to deal with homework, or Kevin smelling so bad, or the girls fighting because they feel all cramped up..."

"As much as I love you, Em, I don't want to hear every detail about the kids."

"I'll ask Kenny and if he agrees, we can stay there."

"Before you pack and rush out the door, I do need to call Mona and ask her."

"Right. I'm sure she will agree. We can use the guestroom next to their master suite."

Diane laughed and said, "No way will I share a room or a bed with you. I remember how you used to kick me when we were kids. I like my legs to be bruise free."

"They have plenty of rooms. We don't have to share one. Call her and see what she says."

"Okay, give me a chance, Em. Learn to be patient. Geez, you are worse than Lily sometimes."

"I have some bad news, Em," Diane said two hours later.

"Aw! Can't we use the house?"

"Yes, we can use the house, but Mona said Mr. Robertson tested positive for the virus."

"Oh, no! That sucks!" Emmy replied.

Diane replied, "Tell me."

Emmy put a hand to her mouth. "He's old. Will he be okay?"

"Mona said he's not in any real danger, but he has to stay in Idaho for now. He can't go anywhere, and they have to sleep in different rooms."

"How terrible!"

"Em, they're in their seventies. I don't think it matters as much as if you and Kenny had to sleep in different beds."

"Very funny. How long will he be quarantined?"

"Two weeks at least. Would you mind if we don't go until Wednesday? I have some things to do before I leave Brady to fend for himself."

"Wednesday will work for me. I can get all the laundry done, and plan the meals, and make sure..."

"Bye, Em," Diane said shaking her head.

Chapter Eighteen

"I hate to agree, but it's the right thing to do," Dave Persching said over the phone Tuesday morning as Fridays At Five discussed business via a conference call. "We've never had to cancel an entire tour before, but the President is closing everything down."

"We need to think about how many employees this will affect," Jeremy Lenhart said. "The people on salary will continue to be paid, and I think most of the other employees can collect unemployment."

"Stephanie should handle the press release this morning. She's already been in contact with the promoters. One good thing is we were doing three nights in each venue instead of one-nighters. Less promoters to deal with."

"And tickets have only been sold for the first two weeks. Whoever made the decision to hold off selling them was a genius," P.J. said.

"I think it was my idea," Jeff said with a laugh.

"Now that we've got our whole summer free, it's a shame we can't go anywhere," Kenny said.

"Wait a minute," Jeremy said. "This thing could change in a month. That might not give us time to reinstate the summer tour, but maybe we could travel with our families this summer and do a fall tour."

"There's no use trying to plan anything at this point," Andy Walker said. "Right now we're all stuck at home."

"I have an idea," Dave said.

"Go ahead," someone said.

"Kenny bought new gear to do video and streaming, right? What if we could figure out a way to do virtual concerts from his studio? We wouldn't have to travel, and we could still perform for the fans. We could release it on the website."

"We couldn't sell tickets, could we?" Jeremy asked.

P.J. asked, "Wouldn't that violate the stay-at-home policy?"

They discussed this for several minutes.

"Okay, I'll talk to Will and Stuart," Kenny said. "They will know if this is feasible."

"I should talk to the attorney," Andy said.

"It could work, and I would be able to play," Jeff said. "My doctor cleared me for playing my bass. He said I shouldn't tour because of the stress, but didn't forbid it."

"I will only be gone until tomorrow night," Emmy said Wednesday morning. "You don't need me to constantly tell you what to do, and your father will be here."

"Where are you going?" Kevin asked. "What if something happens? What if I fall out of a tree and break my arm?"

"Don't climb any trees," Heather said.

"Can you tell us where you're going?" Isabella asked.

Emmy looked at Kenny. He shrugged.

"I'm not supposed to tell you because Aunt Diane wants it to be a secret, but we are going to stay at Bill and Mona's house."

"Why?" Kevin asked. "They aren't home. You said they are in Idaho because of the virus. You won't have any fun."

"Your aunt Diane and I need a little time to recharge our batteries. Sometimes adults get so busy doing things, and they don't take the time to unwind and take it easy."

"You mean you need a break from us, right?" Heather asked. "Go ahead. We can get by without you." Heather got up and rushed away.

"She's mad at you," Kevin said. "I'll miss you, and if you want I can stop by to make sure you're okay."

"That will not be necessary, Kevin," Kenny said. "I can take care of you."

By ten o'clock the members of Fridays At Five were in Kenny's basement studio, Will Consoli and Stuart Lederer sat behind the mixing desk adjusting various levels.

"If this doesn't sound as close to a real concert as we can make it, I want to scrap the idea," Dave said. "I don't want it to come across as amateurish."

"I think we all agree with that," Kenny said.

The guys arranged the gear to allow them to all be in the video. They did a soundcheck and then jammed for an hour. Will and Stuart recorded the jam session in case something useful was produced. The guys moved to the control room and listened to the recording.

"If we can sound that good, I say let's set up a virtual concert," Dave said. "We could send out an email and promote it on the website and social media."

"We should set a date," Jeff suggested.

"I suggest we get Randy Lemmert here to handle the video. Stuart and I have enough on our hands to get the mix right."

"Good idea," Dave said. "It would mean nine of us here. That's still under the ten person limit."

"I think we should do the first livestream as soon as possible," Kenny said. "We might not have many people tuning it, but we can gauge how much interest there might be."

After talking to Randy, the guys agreed to set up the first Fridays At Five virtual concert for Saturday at three o'clock.

"How did you sleep last night, Em?" Diane asked. "You look rather haggard this morning."

Emmy sat down at the breakfast table in the Robertsons' house. "I didn't get more than two hours of sleep. I tossed and turned all night."

"You missed Kenny, huh?" Diane asked. "I got a few hours of sleep, but not as much as at home. There's something about sleeping in your own bed."

"Can you make some coffee?" Emmy asked. "I need a jolt of caffeine to jump-start my morning."

"I can make more if you want," Diane said. She looked at Emmy and laughed. "I remember you used to wake up like this when we were in high school. Mom and Dad would be at work, and you would drag yourself out of bed and want me to make breakfast. Most of the time I would snap at you and tell you to make your own."

"What's your point?" Emmy asked without looking up. "Coffee. Now."

"Nothing, I guess. Maybe I should have been nicer to you. I treated you pretty much like crap at times because I didn't want you hanging around me and my friends."

Emmy raised her head. "I remember a few times when Mom made you drag me along on one of your dates. I don't know what she hoped to accomplish. All it did was make both of us feel uncomfortable. You certainly didn't want me around, and I would have rather been with Kenny or Rory."

"We had some rough times, but I think we're pretty close now."

"That's true, Diane." Emmy paused and added, "We would be closer if you felt the same way about Christ."

"Don't go there, Em. I know you and Kristen and Liz are really close." Diane waved a hand. "That doesn't bother me. Friends are different than family. You get to choose friends."

"I would choose you as my sister even if I could change it. Do you understand what I'm trying to say?"

"I think so." Diane poured coffee for Emmy and sat down.

"I know they wear me out at times, but I missed the kids all day yesterday."

Diane laughed and said, "Me, too."

"Do you think they would mind if we came home early?"

"I'm already packed," Diane said.

Emmy dropped Diane off next door and headed down the street to home. She pulled into the garage and sat there for a moment. *Lord, this must be your way of reminding me how much I love the kids. Thank you for making last night miserable.* She got out of the car, walked up the steps to the mudroom, took off her coat, set her overnight bag down and listened to the kids jabbering in the kitchen. *That sounds like heaven to me.*

"I get the last cinnamon roll. I claimed dibs last night. You can eat the crummy old soda bread," Kevin yelled.

Heather hollered back, "First come, first served. You eat the soda bread."

Emmy grinned, opened the door and entered the kitchen. "What's all this ruckus about? I can make more cinnamon rolls if someone takes my bag upstairs."

114

"Mom! You're home!" Kevin shouted. He rushed to his mother and almost knocked her down as he hugged her. "I'll take it upstairs."

Heather and Isabella looked at Emmy without saying a word.

"Did you miss me?" Emmy asked.

"I did," Kevin said. "Dad doesn't know how to make pancakes unless he uses the box stuff, and we ran out."

Emmy looked at the girls. "Did you miss me?"

They didn't answer.

"Why are you ignoring me?"

Isabella looked at Heather then at their mother. "We don't want to be a bother."

"I'm sorry. I kinda gave you that impression, didn't I?" Emmy said.

"You made us feel like we're a burden," Heather answered.

"I made a mistake," Emmy admitted. "I was tired and not feeling well, and I took it out on you. I am really sorry. If it makes you feel any better, I didn't get any sleep last night. I was thinking about you and your brother and your father." Emmy held out two fingers. "I came this close to coming home, but I didn't want Diane to think I was a baby."

"We're sorry if we were getting on your nerves, Mom," Isabella said. "Sometimes we forget you go through stuff like us."

Kevin returned, opened the fridge and pulled out the frozen cinnamon rolls. "Can I have three of them?"

Chapter Nineteen

"Emmy, what are you doing out here?" Bobby O'Connor asked.

"I needed some fresh air. Why are you clearing out the woods? You know we have a landscaping crew."

"Yeah, but I like working in the yard." He removed a work glove and wiped sweat off his forehead.

She laughed. "You know this isn't exactly the yard, right?"

"It's close."

"How are Shay and Karissa? I haven't seen them for a while." Emmy picked up a branch and tossed it out of the way.

"They are doing great. Karissa will be five months in a couple days. She's getting so big and she has three teeth already."

"I told you the summer tour was canceled, right?"

"Yeah, I heard. What a shame. We had to cancel all our shows. We were going to open for The Lyricon this summer."

"That would have been good exposure for you guys," Emmy said. "I don't mean to be nosy, but are you guys okay financially?"

"We still have some income, and we have savings set aside for a rainy day." He looked at the sky. "I guess it might be raining soon."

"Let us know if things get bad. We can always help with the rent."

Bobby grinned and said, "You mean you'll raise it, right?"

"Sure, but just for you. We want Shay and Karissa to stay, but you have to move out."

"Liz, I'm sorry to call so at the last minute, but could you do the Good Friday service for me? I'm feeling yucky."

"I can fill in, Emmy. Is there anything I can do to help you feel better?" Liz asked.

"No, I need to go to bed. Thanks, Liz."

"No problem. Get some rest so you feel better."

Tyler heard the conversation. "Who is going to watch the kids? You were going to do that."

116

"We need to figure it out," Liz said.

"Natty and Grayson could watch David in the nursery and Phoebe would be all right with them, but someone has to watch Isaiah. Rebecca is due any minute. It could end up only me and Ryan trying to do the music."

"We could ask Isaac Ladlow or Jared Brodie to play the keyboard."

"True," Tyler said. "But it would mean getting more people involved. I'd rather limit the number of people who come to the church."

Liz grinned and said, "Well, Rebecca can still fit behind the keyboard, so you will have to pray the baby doesn't decide to come in the middle of the service."

"That was a nice service," Kenny said that night. He and Emmy watched it from their bedroom on his laptop.

"I feel terrible for calling Liz at the last minute."

"I know, but everyone is supposed to stay home if they feel sick." He wiped her nose with a tissue. "You definitely have a cold or something, Em."

"I wonder who watched the kids?"

"You'll have to ask Liz."

"I'll call and ask," Emmy said. "Could you grab my phone for me, please?"

Kenny saw her phone on the dresser and handed it to her.

"Liz, you guys did a great job. I'm sorry I had to bail at the last minute."

"It's okay. It all worked out in the end. Are you feeling better?" Liz asked.

"Better, but my nose is running a marathon. Kenny keeps handing me tissues."

"It's probably best you stayed home."

"I feel bad because you usually watch the kids. Who did it tonight?"

"I brought our kids to the church, and Dany came over to help." Liz laughed and said, "Rebecca is ready to pop. I wouldn't be surprised if we get a call anytime in the next day or two."

"I'm glad everything worked out, and I should be all right for Easter Sunday," Emmy said.

"I pray you are, but just in case, we will make the necessary adjustments."

"Kevin, you need to stay upstairs and not pester Daddy and the band," Isabella said. "You should watch the concert with us, and make sure Mommy has enough tissues."

"How soon is it supposed to start?" he asked.

"Three o'clock," Emmy answered and then sneezed. "We are already signed in. As soon as they go live, we will see it on the screen. Watch the timer."

Kevin handed her a tissue and then sat on the floor in front of the TV. "Will we be able to hear them playing downstairs?"

"Maybe, but we can turn the TV up higher than normal," Emmy answered.

In the basement Fridays At Five prepared to start their first virtual concert. The soundcheck was completed, and Randy Lemmert made sure the video was working properly.

"Five minutes to go," Kevin said. "I think I can hear Dave playing his drums. Maybe I should see if he needs someone to hand him a stick if he breaks one."

"You stay right here, young man," Emmy ordered.

The video appeared at exactly three o'clock.

"Welcome to the first virtual Fridays At Five show," Kenny said. "We are going to play some old tunes and maybe a new one during the next hour. I hope you are safe wherever you are."

Dave counted off the song, and the guys started playing 'Too Bad' their first single from back in June of 1996.

"That was like a real concert except nothing exploded," Kevin commented after the band signed off an hour later.

"We couldn't let Daddy blow up the basement," Heather said. "It was pretty good, but they need to stop talking so much and play the songs."

"I will pass along your critique," Emmy said. "Anything else?"

"He needs new material," Kevin said.

118

"I've been telling him for years to stop using the same old jokes."

The band joined the tech guys in the control room.

"How did it turn out?" Dave asked.

Jeff sat heavily on the couch. "Sorry I blew the bridge to 'Whiskey Fire' but I thought we were going to play it four times."

"No problem," Jeremy said. "I think we all messed up a little. It was harder than playing in front of people. We're so used to the feedback from a live crowd."

"I can play it back if you want to hear it," Will said.

"I have a question," Kenny said. "Did we send it in stereo or mono?"

"Good question," Stuart replied. "We recorded using... " He checked the board. "Thirty or so channels. We mixed it down to stereo and recorded it, but the feed we used on Facebook was mono because they don't support stereo."

"Yeah, we researched it yesterday, and even if we send a stereo source, it gets combined into a mono signal, so we adjusted the mix to sound better in mono. Does that makes any sense?"

"Sure. Glad Kenny asked," Jeremy joked.

They watched and listened to the recording in its entirety.

"Not bad for a first try," Dave said. "We could schedule more if you guys are willing."

"Sure," Kenny said. "Maybe we could do one show a week. We could play some of the songs we rarely play live."

Jeff got up. "Let me know. I need to get back. Don't want the quarantine police to arrest me for leaving the house."

"We could get used to doing shows this way and never have to leave SoHam again," Adam said.

"Are you ready to worship?" Pastor Tyler asked to start the Easter service. "I know I ask all the time, and it feels a little weird to be asking the camera, but are you ready? You can answer in the comment section. Let me begin the service with a prayer."

Kevin sat on the couch with his father and pointed to the TV. "It looks better today. The lights are different."

"Hush," Heather said. "Pastor Tyler is praying."

119

"Close your eyes," Isabella said.

"Why? Does it say anywhere in the Bible we have to close our eyes when we pray? I bet Jesus kept his eyes open."

"Let's get started with some songs, and I'm glad Emmy is well enough to join us today. Please sing along unless it makes you feel awkward," Tyler said and then chuckled.

"I thought it went rather well," Ryan Deighton said after the service. "We only had a little hiccup with the music. I wonder how many people were watching?"

"I can tell you in a second," Pastor Tyler said. He checked and smiled. "Over 1,000 people watched part of the service. I wish we could tell how long they watched. I'm sure some of them only tuned in for a short time."

"Mom! You did a great job today," Kevin said as Emmy hung her keys on the rack.

"Did your father tell you to say that?" Emmy asked.

"Maybe," Kevin admitted. "Why?"

"Because my voice sounded like I had a sore throat."

"You don't have the corona, do you?" he asked.

She shook her head. "I don't think so. I haven't been around anyone who has it."

"I took the ham out of the oven ten minutes ago," Kenny said. "Should I slice it now or wait until the sweet potatoes are done?"

"You can slice it now. I'm going to change clothes and be right back."

By the time Emmy came downstairs, the ham was sliced, the sweet potatoes were cooling on the island, the green bean casserole topped with onion rings was on the table and the rolls were browning in the oven.

"It looks like you've done an excellent job of making our Easter dinner," Emmy said. "Someone has even set the table."

"I would have made mashed potatoes, but I didn't want to mess them up. We have a package of Sainsbury's potatoes with garlic in the fridge. I could pop it in the microwave."

"I'd like mashed potatoes even though we have the sweet potatoes," Emmy said.

"What do you want to drink, Mom? We have iced tea, water or pop."

"Tea, please."

Everything was soon ready, and they sat down to eat. Kenny prayed a little too long for Kevin's comfort. His stomach growled loud enough to be heard around the table.

"This is the first Easter in a long time we haven't had family over to share the meal," Emmy said.

"We're family, Mom," Kevin reminded her.

"I think your mother meant additional family," Kenny said taking a scoop of the green beans.

"Uncle James called and said he was eating with the other priests at their house," Heather said. "I told him to come and see us, and he said he might if he's not too tired after stuffing his belly."

The kids helped their father clear the table, put the leftovers away and even loaded the dishwasher.

"Thank you for helping," Emmy said. "I'm feeling tired. Would you mind if I take a little nap?"

"Go ahead, Mom." Kevin said. "We'll be quiet so you can sleep. Should we wake you up if Uncle James comes over?"

"Yes, please do." She went upstairs and didn't wake up until a few minutes after six. She came downstairs and found everyone, including Father James, sitting in the breakfast nook eating the leftovers.

"Why didn't anyone wake me?" she asked.

"I tried," Kenny said. "I talked to you and rubbed your... arm, but you moaned and turned over. I thought you needed to sleep more than see us."

"I feel better now."

Kevin tapped Father James on the arm. "We think Mom has the corona."

Chapter Twenty

"You should call Rory or Rochelle and ask if you need to get tested, Em. It's possible you might have caught the virus from someone," Kenny said the next morning.

"I don't want to bother them. Rochelle is working a lot of overtime, and I don't want Rory to know."

"You should learn more about how to get tested."

"I could call Terry from church. She works in the ER at Mercy. She would know what we should do."

"We? What do you mean by we?"

"If I have to get tested, you should, too. I'll call her."

Emmy called Terry's cell phone and got her voicemail. She left a message and Terry called back an hour later.

"I hate to bother you, but..." Emmy told Terry the details.

"If you were having chest pains or trouble breathing, I would tell you to go to St. Bart's or come here, but since your symptoms are rather mild, I suggest you either call your doctor and ask him where you should go, or else you could call the county health department."

"There's a Coventry Shield Healthcare clinic not far away. Would they be able to test us?"

"Yes, but you might have to wait for the results. They are working on a new test where you get the results right away, but they aren't ready yet."

"Thanks, Terry. I'll see if Coventry can test us."

"Is your husband sick?"

Emmy laughed. "No, he's never sick, but I thought if I have to get checked he might as well get tested, too."

"Was that Terry on the phone?" Kenny asked.

"Yes, and she told me what to do." Emmy explained everything to him.

Later that morning they were tested.

"We have to wait five days for the results," Kenny said on the way home.

"It took longer than an hour, too," Emmy said.

122

Kenny checked the clock in the Jeep. "I suppose it could have been worse."

Emmy nodded as she read the list of things to do on the information sheet given out by the clinic.

"Did you hear me?" Kenny asked.

"Yes. Five days. Sorry, I was reading about all this stuff we need to do at home. We need to disinfect the whole house."

"The whole house?" Kenny asked.

"Anything we touch. Door handles, the fridge, remotes, phones. Lots of work to do."

"Better to be safe than positive," Kenny said with a laugh.

"We might have to sleep in different rooms if one of us is positive."

"That would suck, but I don't think it's likely."

"Hi, Liz, what's up?" Emmy asked the next afternoon. "I've been disinfecting the house."

"Rebecca had the baby about an hour ago," Liz said.

Emmy stopped wiping the countertop. "She did! Is everyone all right? I remember when baby Maggie was born and had trouble breathing."

"Ryan called. Rebecca and Hannah are both doing great."

"Did they name her Hannah Ruth like they were planning?" Emmy asked.

"Yes, and she weighed seven pounds and four ounces. Ryan said she has dark hair and is already nursing."

"I'm assuming she has the right number of toes, fingers and stuff."

Liz laughed and answered, "It's hard to tell in the photos, but I think Ryan might have mentioned if she had an extra foot or something."

"I'm so happy for them," Emmy said.

"This means you are officially in charge of the worship team now, Emmy. What there is of it."

"Right. I'll have to get something together for the Zoom meeting. Thanks for reminding me, Liz. I'll talk to you later."

"We had quite a drop in participation tonight," Tyler told Liz after the Wednesday's Family Night Zoom meeting.

"How many? I would have joined, but David wasn't feeling good and needed cuddles."

"Less than forty. I wonder if the newness is wearing off, and people are finding other things to do."

"We will have to keep track, I guess."

"I think everyone I talked to is here," Emmy said. "I will pray and we can get started."

"Emmy, you should ask for requests," Regina Collins said.

"Oh, I'm sorry. I was going to do that after I prayed, but I guess it make sense to ask first. Do you have one?"

"Robby's great-grandmother tested positive. She's in a nursing home in Salem, Georgia, and recently turned ninety-three."

"Any others?" Emmy asked. She wrote the information down.

"Dad lost his job," Zeke Mehta said. "He drives a truck, and his company let all the drivers go."

"I'm sorry to hear that, Zeke," Emmy said to the young man from Turkey who played bass and guitar for the team.

Shaun Runyon added, "My little sister is scheduled for another operation next Monday. The doctors are going to replace the pins in her leg."

Emmy wrote it down and smiled at Shaun. Shaun's parents pastored a church in East St. Louis while raising ten adopted children. Shaun being the oldest.

"I have a praise if that's okay," Josh Belanger, who played bass for the teen group, said.

"Of course," Emmy told him.

"My father and my uncle work for Fridays At Five and they're still getting paid even though the band can't tour because of the virus. They could have laid off all the employees to save money, but they didn't. I want to thank them for that."

"On behalf of the guys, you are welcome, Josh. Dan and Noah joined the crew too many years ago to remember. They were among the first employees."

"My mom works in the ER at Mercy," Jared Brodie said. He ran a hand through his long blonde hair and added, "She is exposed to sick people all day and I worry about her."

"I'm sure she takes all the precautions she can," Julia Weishar said. "My mom works in the ER, too, and I pray for all the nurses and doctors at Mercy and St. Bart's."

When no one else had a request, Emmy said, "I'll pray first and could someone close?"

"I will," Zeke said.

After the prayers, Emmy read a short devotional, and then asked if anyone had suggestions for the group to do in the coming weeks.

"I'd like to see us study a book of the Bible, or maybe a book like the Men's Group did," Regina Collins said. "Robby enjoyed the Robert Galt books."

"Kenny read those, and he enjoyed them, but I thought they were more for the guys." She noticed someone else wanting to join the meeting, grinned and let them into the 'room'.

As soon as everyone saw and heard Rebecca, they began talking simultaneously which resulted in a garbled mishmash of noise. Emmy muted everyone to clear up the noise. Rebecca smiled as she held her sleeping daughter.

"I'm going to let Rebecca talk for a moment before I unmute everyone. Please try not to talk over each other because we know how that sounds. Go ahead, Rebecca. Hi, Hannah! You are too cute."

"Thank you for the cards and prayers. Hannah and I thank you," Rebecca said then giggled. "We got home around four, and she's been sleeping most of the time. She's eating well and Isaiah loves his baby sister." Rebecca sighed and added, "It's so good to see everyone, and I hope we can be together in person real soon."

Emmy unmuted everyone and this time the chaos was more manageable as people talked to the baby.

"Now that everyone has talked to Hannah, we need to come up with a plan for the coming month."

"I read this book called *The Insanity of Obedience* and I loved it," Pastor Rebecca said.

"Could we study the book Pastor Rebecca suggested?" Julia asked.

"We could. It sounds interesting," Emmy said.

After a short discussion, the team voted to follow Rebecca's suggestion.

"I will send out an email so you can either purchase the electronic version or the physical copy. It might take longer to get the actual book, but I know some of you prefer physical copies."

"Let's start the study in two weeks," Emmy suggested. "That should give everyone time to acquire a copy. Would someone like to pray to close us?"

Rebecca volunteered after no one else did.

"See you next week at the same time," Emmy said closing the meeting.

"Mom!" Heather hollered from the family room. "Did you know Rebecca and Hannah would join us?"

"I knew she was coming home today, but I was surprised she could join us. She looked so happy and not tired like me."

"Were the schools ever closed this long when you were a student?" Isabella asked.

"No, the most we ever had were a few snow days. Nothing even remotely like this," Emmy answered.

"I bet you were thrilled when school was canceled."

"I suppose I was, but it was different."

Heather grunted and muttered, "That's what adults always say when they don't have a real answer."

"I am just your mother. I don't have answers to everything life throws at us, but I do know school is important."

"What will happen to graduation if the schools don't open soon?" Isabella asked.

Emmy bit her lip then said, "I wish I knew, Isa."

Kenny picked up his parents Friday morning at the SoHam airport. He loaded their luggage into the back of the Jeep and headed to Raynor Park.

"How do you like driving this?" his father asked.

126

"It's great if you're off-roading, but it handles weird on the highway. I think it has to do with the way the steering is designed. Overall, I give it up a thumbs up."

He brought the luggage inside and sat with his parents in the living room.

"How was Florida?"

"Much warmer than here," his father answered. "I was able to go for long walks every day."

"I can tell. You look thinner," Kenny said. "Maybe even too thin."

Elly nodded. "I told him he was losing too much weight. I had to buy new pants for him and a shorter belt."

"So I've lost a few pounds," Carter said with a shrug. "Doesn't mean anything."

"You can't lose weight too fast," Elly said. "That isn't healthy."

"I actually feel better now that I'm lighter. I might even take up jogging."

"Let's not get carried away, Dad," Kenny said smiling. "After all, you're seventy-seven, and that's in people years."

"Bah! I feel like a man in his fifties. Especially after I have my nap."

"I better get home. Emmy texted me and asked what was taking so long."

"Tell her and the kids hi, and we'll come to see them as soon as we're allowed out of the house."

"I will."

They stepped outside and saw Fez walking up to the service door of the carriage house. Kenny waved and he and his father walked toward Fez.

"How are you, Fez?" Kenny asked. "Were you working?"

Fez grinned and asked, "Was it my Darby's shirt that gave it away?"

"That was my first clue." Kenny pointed to the brown paper bag Fez carried.

"It's a burger and fries for my lunch."

Kenny's father asked, "How is the place?"

"It's been quieter than where I was living before, Mr. Colwell. I've been doing a little yard work. Some of the plants are already blooming."

"I appreciate you taking care of the place while we were gone," Carter said.

"Not a problem," Fez said.

Kenny pointed to the brown bag. "Dad, we should let Fez eat his lunch before it gets cold. I'll talk to you later."

Fez headed inside, and Kenny walked with his father back to the house.

"You better start eating more, or else Emmy will get after you," Kenny said.

"It won't hurt me to lose a few pounds."

"A few pounds. Not thirty or forty."

"Say hi to Emmy and the kids for us." Mr. Colwell then turned and went inside.

Kenny hurried home and found Emmy taking inventory in the pantry. "I'm back. What's up?"

"The governor closed schools for the rest of the year. Can you believe it?" She turned two cans of soup so the labels faced the front.

"I guess. I suppose he figured it would be better to announce it now, so schools can figure out how to handle it."

"I can't believe he did that. Kevin was thrilled, but the girls are upset."

"Why?"

"Graduation. They were looking forward to graduating with their friends. Now they can't have a ceremony." She counted eight cans of diced chilies and four cans of various flavors of refried beans and added them to the list.

"I didn't think they cared about it."

"I think they're sad because they might not see some of those kids again. They could all end up in different high schools."

"I didn't think of that. Maybe by June we will be able to have a party, and they can invite all their friends."

"We'll see."

Chapter Twenty-One

"Emmy, that was the clinic on the phone," Kenny said then stopped.

"What did they say? You look like you're about to faint."

"You're fine, but I have the virus," he said then sat back down on the couch.

"What? That can't be right. Don't tease me."

He shook his head. "I'm not joking."

"You haven't had any symptoms. I'm the one who had a cold and sore throat." She started to sit beside him but he motioned her away. "Are you sure they didn't screw up the test? Can you call them back? There has to be a mistake somewhere. You can't be sick. I won't let you," she said then wiped away her tears.

"They asked if anyone I've had contact with in the last two weeks has gotten sick. I couldn't think of anyone. Dad was in the hospital, but he's doing better."

"Could someone be infected simply by being around you?"

"I guess so, but the clinics and doctors are probably being extra cautious."

"What does this mean? Do you have to go to St. Bart's? Will they admit you?"

"No, not unless I get really sick. Whoever I talked to gave me a website to check. I guess there's a list of precautions and things to do once you're confirmed as positive." He shook his head, sighed and said, "I have no clue where I could have picked this up or who from. It could be anyone, or anywhere."

"What do we have to do now? Do the kids and I have to wear masks around you? Are you supposed to wear a mask?"

"Let me read the email."

They read it together.

"You're kidding, right?" Emmy pointed to the screen. "You seriously have to stay locked up in the bedroom for two weeks. No way! We've been together all week. If you were contagious, we've all been exposed."

"You have to sleep in another room," he said with a grin. "Think you can handle it?"

"Like that's gonna happen," she answered.

"It has to happen unless you want to get infected."

They spent the next hour calling friends and family.

"Do we have to get tested?" Diane asked.

"Not unless someone gets sick. You know headaches, sore throat. You've read about the symptoms, right?"

"Yeah, but no one I know is sick. What about the guys in the band?"

"Kenny called and told them, but no one is feeling sick."

"Hopefully, no one else will catch it."

"I need to call Pastor Tyler and Liz. I'm concerned about the kids."

"Call me if you need anything, Em."

Emmy called Liz and told her the results.

"How could he have the virus if you're the one who had the symptoms?"

Emmy shrugged and said, "Don't have a clue, but this means me and the kids can't leave the house for two weeks."

"Can we help with anything?" Liz asked.

"No, but we have to be extra careful about washing our hands and stuff. I have to clean the whole house."

"Your house is spotless," Liz said with a laugh. "I've been in hospitals that weren't as clean."

"I have to disinfect surfaces and things, and that's not the worst part."

"What's the worse part?"

"I have to sleep in the nanny suite. He's got to stay in our bedroom by himself."

"Heaven forbid!" Liz exclaimed.

"That will be the hardest part. I can deal with making all his meals and taking them up to him like he's ordering room service in a fancy hotel, but the sleeping part." Emmy sighed. "That's not going to last."

"You will survive. You would be apart on tour for longer than two weeks."

"Yeah, but he wasn't with me. Now he's upstairs, and I can't even go in the room."

130

"What about your clothes?"

"I packed a suitcase, and moved all my makeup and toiletries to the nanny suite."

Liz laughed again. "I'm sorry for laughing, but you have to trust God for the strength to survive two weeks."

"I'll be okay, but it's hard to sleep alone."

"Have you talked to everyone?"

"I called Kristen, Tony, Andy and everyone in Bristol Ridge. I need to call Rory and Rochelle."

"I'll let you go so you can make your calls. We will be praying for you."

Emmy called Rory's cell phone and left a message.

"Are you serious?" he asked later. "I thought you were the one who was sick."

Emmy shook her head. "Wasn't me. I'm glad you guys haven't been around lately."

"Really? Don't you like us anymore?"

"No, I meant you weren't here, so you couldn't have picked up the virus. You know what I mean, Rory."

"I know."

"How are things at Mercy? Are you getting a lot of patients with the virus?"

"We have two floors of COVID-19 patients, and all the routine procedures have been canceled. I'm not doing anything but paperwork."

"Paperwork?"

"It's not on paper anymore. Computer stuff."

"Oh, I get it. Are the virus patients allowed to have visitors?"

"No way! The nurses and staff have to gown up and take extra precautions."

"Do they have to wear hazmat suits?"

"Close."

"Kevin would love it. Can you get him one?"

Rory laughed and answered, "Sorry, Em, but I can't do that."

"Not even if I say pretty please?"

"Nope."

"Party pooper. I better go. Make sure you guys stay safe, okay?"

"We will use every precaution known to man. Let me know if he starts feeling worse. Sometimes people think they're getting better, but then they feel worse. It's like the symptoms come and go."

"I'll keep an eye on him."

"Have you told his parents?"

"He called them. I think his father should be tested."

"Has he been sick?"

"Kinda, sorta. They recently returned from Florida, and he was in the hospital down there."

"They probably tested him then, Em. If he starts feeling sick again, make him go to the ER."

"I'll try but he's stubborn."

"Like someone else I know, huh?" he teased.

"I am not stubborn."

"If you say so."

"Have you watched any of the church services on Facebook?"

"I did. We did. You must miss not being able to see people."

"It's rough. I hope this is over soon."

"Don't hold your breath."

"Is that on the record as a health official?"

He laughed and said, "No, just my opinion."

Chapter Twenty-Two

"Mom! YouTube froze up again," Kevin hollered from the family room.

"Switch to the Facebook page," Emmy said. "Pastor Tyler must be having technical issues with the livestream."

"How?" Kevin asked.

"I'll do it," Heather said. "Pastor Tyler was doing the announcements, and he froze. I could hear him talking, but his image wouldn't move."

Emmy walked down the hall from the kitchen to the family room. "There are so many people using YouTube now. The system can't handle it."

"Facebook is working. Liz and Mr. and Mrs. Collins are moving into position to sing," Isabella said. "How long will it be before Pastor Rebecca comes back?"

"A couple weeks at least," Emmy answered.

Kevin pointed to the TV. "What is Mr. Robby sitting on? You told me but I forgot."

"It's a cajon. He's using that instead of real drums."

"Please join us now as we sing," Liz said into the camera.

"It's working again," Kevin said.

Emmy joined the kids in the family room, and they watched the service together.

"Today I am going to use John 14, and we are going to learn about peace. Specifically the peace that only comes from God."

"Why does it keep freezing?" Kevin asked.

"I'm not sure, Kevin, but maybe Pastor Jonah can figure it out."

Toward the end of the message Tyler paused, looked into the camera and said softly, "This morning I received news that one of our church members has tested positive for the virus..."

"Mom, did you tell him about Daddy?" Isabella asked.

"I called him early this morning. I thought he needed to know since I've been to the church in the last couple weeks. I would die if anyone caught the virus because of us."

"I still don't see how Daddy could have it, and not you or us," Heather said. "He wasn't the one who was sick."

"I don't understand either, sweetie. It is going to be a hard two weeks, but we have to remember God is in control and our peace comes through Him."

"Pastor Tyler talked about stress and anxiety today. He said God gives us peace over stuff even if it all doesn't go away," Isabella said.

"Do I have to wash my hands every time I touch something?" Kevin asked. "Do I have to use those special wipes every time I pee?"

Heather shook her head and muttered, "You are so gross."

"Let's record the service instead of doing it live," Tyler decided Saturday morning. "We are having too many issues with the livestream, and Jonah can't figure out why. He thinks it's because so many people are trying to stream all at once, and the systems can't handle it. If we record it, he can add the lyrics to the songs and they'll show up on the screen. We won't need the TV at all."

"Have you called Regina or Robby? Rebecca and Ryan won't be here because of the baby, and Emmy certainly can't leave her house."

"I thought it would have to be the two of us this week. I can play the piano, and you can sing. I can record the message later. Then Jonah and I can edit it. I got a video from Ann Williams' daughter this morning. Her mother turned 100 today."

"Do I know her?" Liz asked.

"Maybe not. She's been housebound for years. I didn't meet her until recently. She attended here in the sixties and early seventies."

"Did you get enough videos from people talking about a favorite verse? Are you going to include the one from Mrs. Williams in the service?"

"I thought I should. It's not every day one of our members turns 100. The only other one I know was Elmer Burrington. He turned 100 back in 2014, but passed away a week later."

"What about the Bible videos? How many did you receive?"

"I have close to twenty. I thought we could spread them throughout the service," Tyler replied.

"Did Emmy send one?"

"Yeah, it's her and the kids in the house somewhere. It was nice."

"It's time for church," Emmy said to the kids. "Let's sit in the family room to watch."

"Is Daddy going to watch?" Isabella asked.

"He has his laptop, so he can watch with us. Kinda. In the bedroom."

"We know what you mean, Mom," Kevin said. "He's still in prison and can't come out."

They waited for the video to become available on Facebook and listened as Phoebe Hammond recited her favorite verse.

"She's still so cute," Emmy said, "and smart for her age. Smarter than some other children I know."

"When will our video be on?" Kevin asked.

"I don't know, son. Pastor Tyler put the service together."

Tyler and Liz sang and the Bible verse videos were interspersed between the songs.

"Who is that lady?" Kevin asked. "She looks pretty old."

"I think she looks pretty good for her age," Emmy said.

"Is she really 100 years old?" Heather asked.

"According to the video, she turned 100 yesterday," Emmy answered.

The video Emmy and the kids recorded appeared after the message.

"That was pretty awesome, Mom," Kevin said. He jumped up as the intercom buzzed. "It's Dad!"

"When did you guys record that?" Kenny asked.

"We did it yesterday, and Mom sent it to Pastor Tyler. Did you like it?" Kevin asked.

"I did. It was so good it made me cry," he admitted. "Are you behaving for your mother?"

135

"Yeah, and we're helping her clean everything. I've been washing my hands..." he looked at Heather, grinned and said, "every time I pee."

Heather and Isabella ignored him.

"Mom's going to make meatloaf and cheesy potatoes for lunch. Are you hungry?"

"I am but I'm getting thirsty. I'm down to three bottles of water in our little fridge."

"I'll make sure I bring you more when we deliver lunch."

"Thank you, Kevin. I miss you guys so much. I wish I could give you big hugs."

"We miss you, too, Daddy," Kevin said with more emotion than he wanted to let his sisters hear.

"I'll talk to you later. Be good and give your mother a hug for me."

"I will." Kevin ran to the kitchen and brought back the wipes they used for disinfecting the house. He wiped down the intercom.

"What are you doing?" Heather asked.

"I don't want to catch the virus germs."

"They can't go through the intercom, you twerp," Heather said.

"I'm just being safe."

Emmy looked at the kids, sighed and said, "That's it! I'm sick and tired of all this nonsense."

The kids stared at her.

"What are you going to do, Mom?" Isabella asked.

"I'm going upstairs and releasing the prisoner from jail. None of us are sick, and I don't think he's still contagious."

"What did the guy on TV say?" Kevin asked.

"I don't give a rat's... tail," she said. "The people on TV and the Internet and YouTube don't have a clue. They are all blowing smoke for the attention."

She dashed up the stairs, threw open the bedroom door and caught Kenny wiping his eyes.

"Em, what are you doing? You're not supposed to be in here."

136

"I've had enough of this crap. You can come downstairs. I can't believe any of us will get sick after all this time. The kids need to see you."

"But what about the..."

"Don't even go there. None of these government officials know anything. You are leaving this room, and I am sleeping with you tonight."

"But..."

"Try and stop me if you dare."

He followed her out of the room.

"Is Daddy coming downstairs?" Kevin asked as he and his sisters waited at the bottom of the stairs.

"Yes, he is on parole," Emmy said.

Kevin raced up the stairs and hugged his father.

"I don't care if I get the corona. I missed you so much."

"I missed you guys more," he said.

When he got to the bottom of the stairs, he held out his arms for the twins. "Are you afraid to hug me? It's okay if you are."

Isabella hugged him first. "I'm not afraid."

He looked at Heather and saw her tears flowing. "It's okay, sweetie."

"Are you sure you should be in bed with me?" Kenny asked that night.

"Yes, but if it will make you feel safer, you could wear a mask."

"How can I kiss you if I'm wearing one?"

She shrugged and whispered, "I will have to do all the kissing."

Chapter Twenty-Three

"Does Daddy have to stay inside?" Isabella asked Monday before lunch.

"He should stay in the house," Emmy replied.

"Can he eat with us, or does he still have to eat alone?" Heather asked.

Kevin grinned and asked, "Does he have to eat spinach and stuff, or can he eat food that tastes good?"

"I have to talk to his doctor," Emmy answered. She shrugged and said, "I don't have all the answers."

"You could call Uncle Rory. He should know," Kevin suggested.

"That's a good idea. I'll call him after we eat."

Emmy called Rory, asked her questions and waited for an answer.

"Let me ask Rochelle. She knows more than me."

Rochelle got on the phone a minute later. "Has it been two weeks from when he first went to the clinic?"

"Yes. It's been two weeks since we got tested."

"Then you may release the prisoner," Rochelle said with a laugh.

"Good, because I released him yesterday. I couldn't stand it any longer."

"I don't blame you," Rochelle said.

"I was so frustrated because no one really knows what they're talking about. The government officials are turning this into a political war, and that's wrong."

"I agree. The doctors and administration at Mercy are as clueless as anyone. There is a small percentage of false positive tests. Maybe Kenny's test was one of those."

"Thanks, Rochelle. I've missed him."

Kenny walked up from the basement and stood by the island. "I kinda feel like we're getting away with something and the quarantine police will come and arrest me."

"It's like we're breaking the law," Kevin said.

"Don't tell anyone we let him out," Emmy said.

"Eat lunch with us. You can eat real food and not just healthy crap," Kevin said.

He asked Emmy, "Do you remember me?"

She turned to face him, grinned, but then put a hand to her lips. "You kinda look familiar, but I don't know."

"Mom!" Kevin said. "It's Dad. We let him out of jail yesterday, remember?"

Heather and Isabella giggled.

"Are you sure? I didn't think your father had a scruffy beard like this person."

"I haven't shaved for two weeks."

"Did you take a shower?" Emmy asked.

Kevin laughed at this.

"I took one earlier, and I even put on clean underwear."

"Have you brushed your teeth?"

"Give me a kiss and you'll know."

"Kiss him, Mom," Isabella said.

"Should I?" Emmy asked walking closer to Kenny.

"Yes!"

Kenny pulled her into his arms and kissed her until they ran out of breath.

She backed away and looked at the girls. "You better never kiss a boy like that until you're married."

She made a ham salad sandwich for Kenny, and they sat in the breakfast nook to talk.

"Have you heard of anyone we know getting sick?" he asked between bites.

"No, and everyone who was tested has been negative."

"Thank God," he whispered. He tried to hide the tears but couldn't.

"Emmy, I want to come over," Kristen said two hours later. "I am going bonkers. Zach and Grace are driving me and Wyatt nuts, but at least he can go to the church. Are you busy?"

"I'm not sure you should come over here because of the baby, Krissy. You don't need any more complications added to the ones a woman your age already faces."

"I have to do something. Wyatt does all the shopping."

"Aren't you seeing your doctor?" Emmy asked.

"Yes, but that doesn't count. I need to talk to my friends in person. I am so sick of Facetime."

"I can come over there tomorrow, and we can go for a walk around the neighborhood."

"Okay, but we have to do it even if it's raining."

"I decided to come over anyway," Tony said walking into the kitchen with Kevin. "I didn't tell Sloane or anyone you let him out of prison."

"Kevin Michael, did you let this person in the house?" Emmy asked. "He could be contagious or insane or something."

"It's not a crazy person, Mom. It's Uncle Tony. He's wearing a mask."

"Exactly," Emmy said. "He might be a burglar."

"Where is he? Can I see him if I stand six feet away?" Tony asked.

"He's in the family room, and you should always stand six feet away from me regardless of this virus thing," Emmy teased.

"Trust me. I always try to," Tony answered. "Can I take this thing off? I feel weird wearing it."

"You're weird whether you're wearing it or not." She made a face at him. "You can take it off."

Kenny heard Tony and walked into the kitchen. He stood on the opposite side of the island.

"Is she giving you a hard time?" Kenny asked.

"She's trying, but I don't pay any attention to her. How are you?"

"I feel fine. The only thing that felt different was the fatigue. Some days were better than others, but I never felt bad enough to go to the doctor or anything."

"Any headaches or pain in your joints?"

Emmy stared at Tony then asked, "Are you his doctor? What do you know about the virus?"

"I've done tons of research, and I stayed in a Holiday Inn a few years ago."

140

Kenny laughed and said, "I slept more than normal, but no joint pain."

Tony pointed at Emmy. "Even without her snoring next to you?"

"I don't snore!" Emmy insisted.

"Does she?" Tony asked Kenny.

"Not really."

"Sloane does, and sometimes it keeps me awake, but if she's not there I can't sleep because I miss the snoring. Strange, huh?"

"That describes you to a T," Emmy said.

"Who asked you, brat. Just to be safe, I think you should continue to maintain separate bedrooms," Tony said.

Emmy grinned and said, "Too late."

"That's my medical advice."

"And I will accept it for all it's worth," Emmy said. "Which is exactly nothing. No way I'm going to sleep in the nanny suite ever again."

Kenny grinned and the kids giggled.

"I better go. I'm glad to see you're all right." Tony bumped fists with Kenny before leaving.

"Come back again soon, Uncle Tony," Kevin said. "We can wear masks and pretend to be bank robbers."

"I think everyone has joined," Pastor Tyler said. "Jim Rosek still can't figure out how to use his iPad, so he will be listening on his phone. I will call this board meeting to order at 3:04."

"Before we get started, I want to ask how Doris is doing?" LaShae Mabry asked. "Sorry to interrupt, but I haven't heard anything for a couple days."

Carol Wisnewski, the church board secretary, whispered into her laptop, "Doris passed away late last night."

LaShae put a hand to her mouth.

"I am sorry, LaShae. I thought everyone knew," Tyler said. "In case anyone else hasn't heard, Doris passed away late yesterday."

"I didn't know."

"Ron and her sons did see her during the day, but she was in a coma. While we are talking about bad news, I learned two other members have passed because of the virus. Rosa Cartwright and Blanche Burrington. Mrs. Burrington was three months away from her hundredth birthday. She was hoping to make it because her husband did."

"Are the families going to be allowed to hold funerals at the church?" Roger Goldman asked.

"Mrs. Cartwright was living in Florida and Mrs. Burrington lived in Arkansas, so their funerals wouldn't be here anyway. As for Doris, it's too early to tell. I will have to seek guidance on that issue," Tyler said.

"If they do, will the services be restricted to less than ten people?" Marley Menconi asked.

"At this point, I don't know. It would be speculation if I answered your questions now."

Dylan Michaelis waited until there was a break and said, "There's no use asking questions no one can answer. I say we get on with the church business. I don't mean to sound callous, but it does no good to dwell on these tragic events."

"I agree," Roger Goldman said.

Tyler steered the meeting back to the agenda.

"Do we have a motion to accept these reports?" Tyler asked ten minutes later.

"So moved," Tony Bertucci said.

"Any discussion?" Tyler asked.

The motion was seconded and passed.

"Unless anyone has something more, that's all I have. We obviously can't talk about the summer calendar since it's all a mystery."

No one had anything else to add. Tyler closed the meeting with a prayer for the families that suffered the loss of a loved one.

"Let me remind you all to be safe, use common sense and hopefully we will be back together soon. It won't be in May, but beyond that is anyone's guess."

"Before we get started with our study, I want to tell you something," Emmy said. "Kenny tested positive for the virus, but he's gone through his quarantine period, and as far as we know, no one has gotten sick because of him. I didn't mean to keep this a secret, but Pastor Tyler felt it necessary."

After several seconds of silence and stunned expressions, Jared Brodie asked, "How have you kept the media from learning about this? I would have thought the media would be all over a celebrity testing positive."

Emmy chuckled and answered, "They don't pester him because he's the dorkiest celebrity around. He's as boring as a Sunday School teacher, so they know he's not newsworthy."

"Why do you always tease him?" Julia Weishar asked. "He's known all over the world."

"The world may know he's a member of Fridays At Five, but most people wouldn't recognize him in the checkout line at the grocery store. He looks too normal. Except for his ears."

"I've noticed the band doesn't put their pictures on the cover. Is that to protect their identity?" Ryan Deighton asked.

Emmy giggled and said, "No, it's because they are ugly, old men. Sorry, I couldn't let it pass. I don't really think he's ugly. His ears look funny, but the rest of him is okay."

"Pastor Tyler knew he was positive, right?" Shaun Runyon asked.

"Yes, our closest friends and neighbors all knew. Bobby knew because he lives in the guesthouse, and we couldn't keep it from him and Shay and the baby."

"Just so you know, Tyler and I didn't lie to anyone about this," Liz said. "We would have told the truth, but no one asked us who was positive. I think they understood the family needed privacy."

"I think the media has blown this whole thing way out of proportion. It's all you hear on the news and all you read about online," Robby Collins said. "Sure, it's hard on people and everything, but this isn't the first time the country has gone through a pandemic. Plenty of people died from the Spanish flu back in 1920 or whatever year it was."

"How are you and Regina dealing with the school closing?" Emmy asked.

"She can use the Internet for her English classes, but it's harder to teach music online."

"Some public schools were not prepared to teach online," Jared Brodie said. "My kids attend Linden Avenue Elementary and it took them two weeks to get organized."

"Our school was prepared," Liz said. "We have a smaller enrollment, so that helps."

"Let's get started. I want to thank everyone for taking the time to join us tonight..."

"What are you doing, Em? Do you still have to use bleach on everything?" Kenny asked Tuesday morning.

"I guess not, but I got in the habit, and I don't want you to have a relapse."

"I don't think I will catch it again, Em. You shouldn't work so hard. I don't want you to get sick."

"Are you telling me I'm getting too old to take care of my house? Mama turned seventy-six the day you got the test results."

"Really? How can you remember stuff like that?"

"I remember because I forgot to send her a card. I had to call her Sunday and apologize."

"I bet Mama doesn't work as hard as she used to."

"Yeah, but I'm not even forty yet. I can still clean my house."

"I think there's a difference between cleaning it and making it a germ free room like in a hospital, Em."

She wiped the sweat from her forehead. "Maybe so, but I'm not taking any chances. I don't want anyone to come over here and get sick, and you need to call your father."

"Why? Is he sick again?"

"Not that I know of, but he is still your father."

Chapter Twenty-Four

"Has anyone heard from Emmy in the last couple days?" Rebecca asked. She lifted baby Hannah from the car carrier and calmed her down.

Liz chased Isaiah out of the hallway and into the music suite. Tyler adjusted some of the lights in the production room. Ryan scooped up his son and carried him over his shoulder.

"Sorry, Rebecca, what did you say?" Liz asked.

"Have you talked to Emmy? How are they doing?"

"We talked earlier. She sends her apologies for not being here, but she's still afraid to be around other people."

"Are they all right?" Ryan asked. He tossed Isaiah into the air and caught him.

"Kenny is finished with his quarantine, and no one else is sick. Are you sure you want to be here?" Liz asked. "Hannah is only three weeks old. I would be afraid to bring such a young baby out."

"I wouldn't bring her to a normal service, but it's just the four of us," Rebecca replied.

"Thanks for helping us, Jonah. We weren't sure who we could ask to watch the kids," Tyler said. "We know Mary loves kids and was a nanny for a few years."

"Not a problem. She should be here in a second. She stopped to wash her hands."

"Who's watching your kids?" Liz asked.

"They're spending the afternoon with her parents. They haven't seen them much lately."

Rebecca asked, "How is Mary feeling? Is she comfortable watching Isaiah and Hannah?"

"I am doing fine," Mary answered as she walked into the room. "I may be expecting, but I can still chase little boys around the room and Hannah will probably fall asleep."

"I was going to nurse her before we start," Rebecca said.

"Where's Phoebe and David?" Jonah asked. "I saw Natalie and Grayson in the foyer as we arrived. They waved and went back to their books."

"My parents are in town," Liz answered. "They had been in Tennessee to see Maggie and decided to stop for a quick visit."

"How are they allowed to travel?" Ryan asked. "Aren't they afraid of being stopped."

Liz grinned and said, "They're doctors. They can claim they're making house calls."

Rebecca fed Hannah in the nursery as everyone else went over the songs for the week.

"Which one should we run through first?" Liz asked.

Everyone took their positions. Rebecca stood behind the keyboard. Tyler sat on a stool with his acoustic guitar. Ryan sat on his cajon, and Liz took her seat.

"Liz, could you scoot in a bit? You're a little out of the picture," Jonah said.

Liz moved and Jonah gave her a thumbs up.

"We should do them in order in case we add any dialogue to introduce the next song. It would save time for Jonah and me when we edit this," Tyler said.

"We've got all the songs recorded," Jonah said later. "When are you going to record your message?"

"I'll do it after our Family Night Zoom meeting unless I'm too tired."

"Will you need any help? I can run back after dinner."

Tyler waved a hand. "No need. I can handle it on my own, but I could use your expertise editing the video. That takes longer than anything."

"I could meet you here in the morning. Say ten or so."

"I'll be here. Come on over when you can."

Jonah arrived shortly before ten the next morning. He saw Tyler in his office with his head in his hands."

"Are you okay? You sounded like you were groaning or something."

Tyler looked up. "I can't get the lyrics right, and forget about the Bible verse videos. The sound quality is all over the place."

"Let me see what I can do," Jonah said. "This is why I get paid the big bucks."

"I thought we paid you to supervise the athletic programs." Tyler smiled and added, "Oh, wait. We've canceled the sports programs."

"That too, but my primary focus is on technology."

Two hours later the video was ready.

"Thanks, Jonah. It looks and sounds so much better than I could have managed on my own."

"Glad to be of service."

"Did I tell you the church is getting views from all over?"

"All over where?"

Tyler chuckled and answered, "The globe. I can see where the hits are happening, and we're getting views on the website, Facebook and YouTube from Europe, Australia and even South America. Someone in South Korea checked us out."

"That's good, right?"

"Yes, but I can't tell how long they listen. It could be seconds, or they could be watching the whole service. I have no way of knowing."

"Then we have to trust God to do the work," Jonah said with a grin. He paused, tapped his jaw, tilted his head back and forth and added, "I heard a preacher tell that to his congregation once. Several times actually."

Tyler laughed and said, "Thanks for reminding me. I preach at myself more than anyone."

"Thanks for allowing us to do this," Gary Smith told Pastor Tyler. He started to shake hands, but then drew it back quickly. "I know there are restrictions, and there will only be five of us here. Tim and his wife, Sue, are bringing Dad. Janice came with me. I had to tell Mom's sister they couldn't be here. She doesn't understand the situation."

"I'm sorry I couldn't see your mother in the last days," Tyler said.

"I understand. We were only allowed to see her from the doorway, and that took some doing."

147

"She was loved by everyone in the church," Tyler said. "Emmy Colwell always referred to her as the gum lady."

Gary ran a hand through his heavy gray beard and chuckled. "She loved passing out gum to the kids."

"Some of the adults liked the gum, too."

"Have you ever held a funeral without the body?"

"I have, actually, but it was always because the person was cremated."

"The funeral home suggested we bury Mom right away. Since we were all here, we followed their advice."

"You live in Oregon, right?"

"Yes, and Tim recently moved to Arizona."

"Some people are waiting to hold memorial services after this has passed."

"We talked about doing that because I'm sure there are people in the church who want to pay their respects."

"We will do whatever you wish. I plan to record the service today and will post it for people to see."

"We appreciate it."

Tim helped his father into his wheelchair and pushed him into the building. Tyler spoke to Ron for a moment and led everyone into the classroom decorated with flowers to look similar to the funeral chapel. He recorded the short ceremony and talked about how God was still in control even in these trying times.

"Thank you, Pastor Tyler," Tim said later. "I'm not sure if Dad understands everything, but he knows Mom is gone."

"I did talk to him about your mother." Tyler looked closely at Tim. "You definitely remind me of your father. Your brother looks more like your mother."

Tim laughed and said, "People tell me I look more like Dad the older I get."

"I had been visiting him until the nursing homes were closed to visitors."

"He talked about your daughter coming to see him."

"Sometimes I would bring Phoebe with me. She likes it, and the people love to see her. She likes to sing to them."

"Did Gary talk to you about a later service?"

148

"Yes, he did."

"We will have to wait until the government allows larger gatherings, and Gary and I can arrange to fly back."

"I have a feeling large church gatherings might be a thing of the past. We will certainly have to adjust our ways."

Tyler added a short recording about Mrs. Smith to the prerecorded Sunday morning service. He included several photos of her family.

"Doris and Ron have been a part of our church for over fifty years. During that time she served as a Sunday School teacher, started a card ministry as well as serving in other capacities. I've been told Ron served as the church treasurer for more than thirty years, and he sang with a quartet many years ago. His health hasn't allowed him to be here in person in a year or more, but he still talks about the church to everyone in the Astoria Estates Care Center. The family does wish to hold a memorial service when it is allowed."

"Mom, is he talking about the lady who used to pass out gum?" Kevin asked.

"Yes, he is. She passed away a week ago."

"Did she die from the virus?" he asked.

"I think it was partly the virus, but she had other health complications."

Kevin stared at the last photo on the screen and asked, "Did you know her when you were our age?"

"I was a bit older when I met her. I was in high school, but she always treated me like a daughter. We will miss her." Emmy turned away and wiped her eyes.

"Mom," Kevin placed a hand on her back and whispered tenderly, "Would a stick of gum help you feel better?"

Chapter Twenty-Five

"Good afternoon, everyone," Kenny greeted the viewers. "Before we get started I want to inform you that two weeks ago I tested positive for COVID-19. I spent two weeks in quarantine, and if you're wondering, I feel fine. The only symptoms I had were a slight cough and at times I felt fatigued. I consider myself fortunate. My family is fine, and no one I was in contact with over the last month has tested positive. That's why we haven't done a livestream since April 11th. The month layoff has actually helped the tech guys. This show should be better than the last one, and thank you for all the comments both positive and negative."

"There were only a few negative comments," Jeff said. "Some people can't be pleased." He laughed and added, "A couple of the comments complained about the lack of pyrotechnics. To satisfy as many fans as possible, today we will blow up Kenny's basement."

Kenny turned and stared at Jeff. "Really? Did Emmy say it was okay?"

Emmy hit the talkback button on the mixing console, shook her head and said, "Stop being a dork. Kevin and Ben suggested it. It's not going to happen."

"Enough talk!" Dave shouted from behind the drums. "Let's play some tunes." He smacked his sticks together and the band kicked into gear.

Later between songs, Kenny said, "I see there are some comments asking Emmy to join us. How about it, Em?" He smiled at her, and the other guys nodded.

"No, this is your show, and I am retired," she answered. "I'm not going to sing."

The band played two more songs and again Kenny asked Emmy to sing.

"But, Em, there are a lot of fans asking for you. One song at least," Kenny pleaded.

"I can't. I'm not dressed to face the camera."

Will and Stuart looked at her as she sat between them at the mixing desk.

"I mean I am dressed, but I'm wearing scruffy clothes."

"You look normal, Emmy," Jeff said. "An old t-shirt and faded jeans. Come on! One song for the fans."

She thought about it and answered, "I will do one song if you get fifty comments asking for it in the next minute."

"Deal!" Jeff said pointing a finger at her. "Okay, fans, now it's up to you."

The fifty requests happened within less than a minute.

"Fine!" Emmy said rolling her eyes. She joined the guys in the studio. "What song are we doing?"

"Aren't you going to say hello to everyone?" Kenny asked pointing at the camera directly in front of him.

"Okay, but I feel silly."

"You have to pretend there are people watching." Kenny looked at the guys and asked, "What song of Emmy's do we know?"

"I think we could muddle through 'Inadequate Ordinary People,'" Jeremy said.

The rest of the guys agreed, and they started the intro.

"Which mic do I use?" Emmy asked.

Kenny pointed to his.

She lowered the stand and sang the song.

"Now that wasn't too difficult, was it?" Kenny asked.

"No, I guess not," she answered and started to walk away.

Kenny and the guys began playing the intro to 'Gideon's Heart' and waited for Emmy to respond.

"You said one song."

"This will be the last one. I promise," Kenny replied.

She made a face at him, but sang the song.

"Thank you, Em," Kenny said as the last chords faded out.

"Can I leave now?"

"Yes, Em, you can say goodbye to all your fans."

She smiled, waved in the direction of the cameras and walked out.

"We will now resume the Fridays At Five show if any viewers are still watching," Kenny said.

Jeff looked at Will and Stuart. "What are you saying?"

151

Will used the talkback mic. "Fans want to hear some stories about the early days of the band."

"Really?" Kenny asked.

Will nodded.

Kenny looked at the guys. "Anyone got a funny story to tell?"

"How about the time we got lost in the arena in... was it Seattle?" Jeff asked.

"Portland, I think," Jeremy said.

"Yeah! Portland. The green room was almost in another building or something. I remember Ralph and Frankie leading us through these hallways trying to find a way up to the stage. We were like five minutes late."

"That's a great story, guys, but I think the fans want something interesting," Will said.

"How about the time we got caught in a blizzard and almost didn't make it to the gig?" Kenny asked.

"Boring!" Dave hollered from behind his drums.

"How about the story behind 'Street Corner Preacher?' That's the next song on the set list," Stuart mentioned. "Or any of the songs from that CD."

"I wrote the lyrics to that," Kenny said. He looked at Jeremy. "Didn't you come up with the hook in the intro?"

"This one?" Jeremy played the intro on his keyboard.

"Yeah," Jeff said adding the bass line.

"Wasn't it about the guy we saw in Las Vegas who would go up and down the Strip preaching to whoever would listen?" Adam asked.

"I thought he was a homeless guy from New York City," P.J. said.

Kenny shrugged. "It was a long time ago. I think we sat on that song for five years before we recorded it."

"Are those the best stories you got?" Emmy asked.

The guys shrugged.

"You are the lamest rock stars ever," Emmy said rolling her eyes.

"Do you have better stories, Em?" Kenny asked.

152

She laughed and answered, "Of course, but I'd have to kill you if I told you."

"Why, Emmy? Are they stories about sex on the road?" Adam asked.

"Not in my band," she replied.

"Then what?" Kenny asked. "Do you mean the water balloon fights?"

"Those were fun," she said.

"How about the time you were swimming..."

"Let's cut to a commercial," Emmy said.

Jeff looked at Kenny. "Do we have commercials?"

Kenny shook his head. "I think she's trying to change the subject because something embarrassing must have happened."

"Did not," Emmy insisted. "Sing the next song."

The band played two songs from *Street Corner Preacher* and five more before ending the show.

"How did it sound?" Kenny asked Will and Stuart.

"Sounded even better than last time, but you should see the comments. Emmy got almost as many as you guys."

"Maybe it was a mistake to let her sing," Jeff said. "Now we know she's more popular than us."

"We can wait a few minutes to see if anyone else is going to join," Rebecca said Thursday evening. "How is everyone doing?" She looked at the faces on her computer. "Anyone?"

"We are doing fine," Regina Collins said. "Has anyone seen or heard from Emmy?"

Bobby O'Connor responded," I saw them earlier today. They were working in the yard and appeared okay. Why?"

Regina waved a hand at her iPad. "No reason. Just haven't heard anything more about how Kenny's doing."

Gradually, more members of the team joined the meeting.

"I'm sorry I'm late," Emmy said. "I was busy on my laptop and lost track of time. Did I miss much?"

"We've been taking prayers requests," Rebecca said. "Do you have any to add? Regina wondered how you and Kenny were doing."

"We're fine," Emmy answered, "Kenny's father and my brother have been struggling. They're okay and don't have the virus as far as we know, but they could use our prayers."

"We will add them to the list. I will begin and Ryan will close. Please pray as you feel led."

Several minutes later Rebecca asked, "Are we ready to start tonight's study?"

"I have a question," Jared Brodie said a few minutes into the discussion. "I wasn't raised in the church like many of you, and I haven't read much of the Old Testament. It kinda confuses me because God used all these old people like Abraham to do stuff. There must have been younger people around."

"Old? He was only ninety-nine," Emmy said. "That was young back in those days."

"How was it possible for people to live hundreds of years like the guy with the weird name?" Jared asked.

"Anyone have an answer for Jared?" Rebecca asked.

"Years were shorter then," Armon Perez, one of the singers from the teen group, said. "Anyway, that's what my grandmother told me."

"Why did God ask people like Moses to do things when there were other people around with more skills and abilities?"

Rebecca smiled and responded, "Emmy, I think this is one you should answer."

"Jared, I believe it is more important to be willing to follow wherever and do whatever God wants us to do. He will give us the ability, wisdom or strength to do whatever He calls us to accomplish. He can turn an ordinary, inadequate man, or woman, into the perfect person to accomplish His will and further His kingdom. Does that make any sense? I'm not a teacher like Richard Cornejo."

"But your lyrics explained it so well," Rebecca said.

"I have lots of time to work on my lyrics. It isn't always easy to know the right words to say in real time."

Rebecca grinned and asked, "Are you saying God gives you the words to explain the inadequate ordinary people He uses?"

She shrugged and whispered, "Maybe."

154

Later, Rebecca prayed to end the meeting. "I want to thank everyone for making time to be a part of our discussion tonight. Please contact me or Emmy if you have any needs or requests during the week. We are all in this together. See you next week."

"How does it sound?" Jonah asked Pastor Tyler. They were in the production room editing the recorded video for Sunday. "It's difficult to adjust the level on everyone's video."

"Play the one from Mrs. Millner again."

Jonah brought up the video from the retired, longtime church secretary. "That's the best I can do with it."

Tyler listened to most of the clip. "It is what it is. It's a little difficult to understand, but I think everyone will be glad to see she's doing well."

An hour later the video was ready to be uploaded.

"I can do it if you've got other things to do," Jonah offered.

Tyler shook his head. "Thanks, but you should get back to Mary and the family. It will take five to six hours for this to upload. It's a huge file. How is she feeling?"

"Everything is progressing great. Erin and Ewan keep suggesting names for the baby."

"Are you going to come up with another name beginning with E?"

Jonah shook his head. "We can't think of another name for a boy other than Edward, and Mary nixed it right away. Emmy's twins want a job as the baby's nanny," Jonah said.

"They will be old enough to babysit soon," Tyler said. "What about Elliot?"

"I'll suggest it to Mary. The twins are already babysitting for one of the families in Bristol Ridge. Or they were before the virus pandemic shut everything down."

"Natalie wants to get paid for watching Phoebe and David, but I told her she's too young."

"How did she take it?" Jonah asked.

Tyler shrugged and replied, "She wants to start babysitting as soon as the virus scare is over."

"Dad, why do I have to watch in here with you?" Kevin asked. "It's bad enough I have to go to church in the family room, but why can't I watch on my own laptop like everyone else? Even Mom is watching on her own computer."

"You have to watch with me because you were spending too much time chatting with your friends when you were supposed to be doing schoolwork."

"But I was done with all my work," he explained.

"Not according to your mother."

"Fine. I'll watch, but can I text Ben?"

"Make it quick. You need to listen to Tyler."

Emmy walked into the family room later and saw Kevin texting Ben.

"Kenny! Did you fall asleep?"

He opened his eyes with a start. "I am awake. Why?"

"Because your son has been texting Ben and not listening to Tyler's message."

"I was listening, Mom," Kevin said setting down his phone.

"What was the message about?"

"The usual stuff."

"Could you be a little more specific?"

"He was talking about going to church and the benefits of doing that."

"Can you remember what scripture he was using?"

"Mom!"

"You should know if you were paying attention."

"He used 1 Peter 2:1-10. Satisfied?"

"Okay, but you shouldn't text during church."

Chapter Twenty-Six

"Did you hear what President Rhodes said?" George Trotter, another of the church's senior members, asked.

Tyler stared at his cell phone and answered, "I did, and I will send an email as soon as I talk to Dr. Schofield."

"I'm sorry to bother you. You are probably getting bombarded with texts and calls."

"You are number fifty or so to inform me of the President's decision," Tyler said with a chuckle.

"I won't bother you anymore."

"It's not a bother, Mr. Trotter."

Tyler read a dozen more texts and answered five calls before reaching Dr. Schofield. They talked for several minutes.

"Thank you, Dr. Schofield. I will send an email out now. Maybe that will slow down the calls and texts."

"I will release a statement tomorrow afternoon detailing the District's stance. We need to use caution and not make a rash decision."

"Emmy, did you read Pastor Tyler's email about opening the church?" Kenny asked.

She walked up behind him as he sat in his recliner in the family room. "No. When did he send it?"

Kenny checked. "Last night, I guess."

"What did he say? We aren't having church tomorrow, are we?" She sat on the arm of the recliner and looked at his laptop.

"He urges caution and doesn't want to rush and open the church up to the possibility of people getting sick."

"He's probably getting tons of texts and calls."

"I think so. He wants everyone to pray and forget about the politics of all this chaos."

"I agree the politicians need to make wise decisions, too."

"Our governor doesn't agree with President Rhodes. He's going to follow his own plan," Kenny said then looked at Emmy.

"Don't look at me. I didn't vote for the guy."

"Thank you for joining us today," Pastor Tyler said to start the Zoom meeting. "I want to wait a couple minutes because Mrs. Menconi and Genna Ademilola were planning to join us. How is everyone doing?"

Jim Rosek chuckled and said, "Fine as frog's hair, but this social distancing is getting real old."

"I'm glad you finally figured out how to join us, Jim. Unfortunately, I think it's here for at least another month," Tyler said.

"It could be much longer before churches as large as ours are allowed to meet again," Roger Goldman said. "It's sad, but smaller churches are looking like the future."

"I see Genna is here. Good afternoon, Genna. Are you still at work?" Tyler asked.

"Can anyone hear me?"

"Yes, Genna, we hear you."

"I can't see myself."

Carol Wisnewski explained how to open the video.

"Now I can see myself and everybody else." She waved and smiled. "I may have to go back to work, but I am here for now."

Tyler prayed, officially opened the meeting and the board listened to the finance report.

Roger set his copy down and smiled at his laptop. "Because our expenses have been greatly reduced, we are holding steady. Actually, we have more in the bank this month than at this time in April. Mrs. Burns doesn't see any issues for the time being."

After discussing this issue for several minutes, Tyler brought up a proposal from the buildings and grounds chairperson.

"Should I tell everyone, or would you like to?" Tyler asked.

"You can go ahead," Mr. Griffith said.

"Bill has come up with a design for the platform, and would like to use this time to work on it. Since no one is in the building, I think it's a great time to get this done. Let me explain the plan in simple terms," Tyler said. "Bill would like to add some depth to the back wall by building triangular shapes running from the floor to the ceiling."

"Do you have a budget for this work?" Dylan Michaelis asked.

"I have an estimate, but it could be lower if I can reuse the material already in place," Bill replied. "Unfortunately, I won't know until I start ripping apart the back wall."

"Where is Emmy?" Tanya Paduchik asked. "Shouldn't she be here since this concerns the worship team?"

"Emmy is not on the board," Mrs. Wisnewski explained. "Technically, she isn't on the staff either. Pastor Rebecca is on the staff, and none of the other staff members are on the board."

"I'm sorry," Tanya said.

"We could use this time to paint certain areas of the education building," Tyler said.

"Excuse me!" Tanya waved her hand. "Excuse me!"

"Yes, Tanya," Tyler said. "Do you have a question?"

"The plaque in the hallway says the name of the building is the Dr. Dave Behren Hall. Does anyone ever call it that anymore?"

"Some people call it Behren Hall, but most simply refer to it as the school," Tyler answered.

"I didn't attend this church when he was the pastor, so I never really knew him. He is still alive, right?"

Jim Rosek laughed and said, "He was alive when I talked to him last week."

"What does he do now?" Ms. Mabry asked. "Is he still a pastor somewhere?"

"He is the president of his alma mater, Bellchester College, in Bellchester, Indiana," Tyler explained. "He actually hired me as an intern in 2005."

"Has it been that long?" Tony Bertucci asked.

After approving the plans, Tyler brought up an email from Dr. Schofield, the district superintendent. "This article was written by two people at the college, I believe. It raises concerns about how the church of the future might function. Of course, we don't know when we might be allowed to open our doors again, but I'm convinced it will be sooner than some of the experts predict. However, I can see where the church will be changed. Possibly for several years."

159

"You are referring to the article in the email from the district, right?" Jim Rosek asked.

"I am, Jim," Tyler answered.

"All righty then," he replied with a chuckle. "I read that one."

"It is very likely there will be many changes when we are allowed to reopen. We can no longer take for granted we will be able to have church services the same way we have for generations."

"Could you give us some examples?" Tony Bertucci asked.

"We might have to rethink the way we serve the Lord's Supper or do baptisms. Even simple things like taking the offering might need to be changed."

"What about things like Vacation Bible School?" Mrs. Wisnewski asked. "I already have the curriculum for this summer. Do I need to cancel it?"

"Let's not cancel it yet, but maybe we could work on a way to have an online VBS," Tyler suggested.

"What about summer camps?" Lenore Toth asked. "A few of the children are asking. They enjoy the camps so much."

"I talked to Dr. Schofield about camps. As of now, they haven't canceled them, but I expect it to happen. It actually costs the Michigan District money to run the camps."

"They lose money even with how much it costs to send children to camp?" Dolores Hoffman asked. "When I sent my children to camp, it didn't cost more than twenty dollars."

Carol laughed and said, "Times have changed since the sixties, Dolores."

Russell Otto, one of the newest members of the board, raised a hand.

"I think Mr. Otto would like to say something," Tyler said.

Mr. Otto unmuted his computer and said, "One thing we need to consider is the cleaning of the church. I work in a lab, and we have stepped up our cleaning schedule. I don't know how much we spend on cleaning staff and supplies now, but it wouldn't surprise me if that number doubles."

"Good point," Roger said.

"Will we be allowed to serve coffee?" Martin Stackhouse asked. "I love my coffee."

"Will we even be allowed to greet people at the door?" Mike Fisker asked.

Tyler muted the entire group and said, "Before we get carried away, let me say we don't know the answers yet. I do know God is still in control, and we have to trust in Him." He unmuted everyone and waited for a response.

"I understand, but it doesn't make this... whatever we want to call it... any easier," Jim said.

"I have one more item on the agenda. The Wednesday night Zoom meeting. With the exception of five or six people, everyone involved on Wednesday nights is also in another small group meeting. We have Zoom meetings every night except Saturday. I want to hear your thoughts about suspending Wednesday nights until we get back to meeting at the church."

"Is part of this because of the hours it takes to produce the Sunday service?" Dylan Michaelis asked.

"Yes, it is. Jonah and I are spending more hours editing the recording than it took to do the livestream."

"My son-in-law did mention the extra hours," Dylan said. "I don't see a problem with letting that meeting slide temporarily."

The board voted to permit Tyler to temporarily suspend the Wednesday Zoom meeting.

"Thank you, and my family thanks you," Tyler replied. He closed the meeting and encouraged everyone to stay positive.

"Did you have one of those Zoom meetings?" Emmy asked Tony over the phone.

"Tyler had a board meeting. Why?" Tony asked.

"Did you guys talk about Mr. Griffith's plan?"

"I'm sorry, Emmy, but I cannot discuss anything about the board meeting to a civilian."

"So I'm a civilian now, huh? I could call Mr. Michaelis and ask him."

"Yeah, we approved the remodel plan," Tony said.

"It's not a major undertaking," Emmy replied.

161

"I wonder if people will even notice the difference if we ever get back to having church in the sanctuary."

"It will happen one of these days. You have to be positive," she said. "Do you ever talk at these meetings?"

"Why wouldn't I?"

"Because you don't have a brain," she teased.

"Is that all?"

"Did Pastor Tyler mention if anyone else has tested positive?"

Tony rolled his shoulders to get rid of a kink. "No one else has died, but there have been several more positive tests in three of the local nursing homes. He can't even visit them now."

"Not even if he wears a mask?"

"Nope! No visitors whatsoever."

"That's sad. I'm glad I'm not living in a nursing home."

"I think you've got a few years before Kenny puts you in a home for the aged."

"Can you see me sticking out my tongue and making a face at you?" she asked.

"Anything else you want to know?" he asked. "I need to work in the yard."

"Did you guys cancel Wednesday night Zooms?"

"Yes, because of all the other Zoom meetings. It was the same people who are involved in other groups."

"I can see his point. Liz told me how many hours it takes for Tyler and Jonah to edit the recording."

"Talk to you later, brat."

After fidgeting on the couch while watching the prerecorded church service, Kevin said, "This sucks! When are we going to go back to having church like normal? I miss my friends. I never get to see anyone except Ben, Taylor and Coby. I want to see the new zombie movie."

"We have to be patient," Emmy said. "There are still people getting sick from this virus."

"Daddy had it and he didn't get sick. Why can't we go to school and church like normal?"

162

"You want to go to school?" Heather asked. "I'm perfectly content to stay home and do those silly online assignments. They are so boring and simple."

"Did you even listen to Pastor Tyler?" Emmy asked. "What was he saying about the church?"

"He said the church isn't the building where we go," Isabella answered.

"And what does that mean in practical terms?"

"We don't need a big building to have church," Kevin said. "Are we going to sell it?"

Emmy shook her head. "I don't think it will come to that, but what if it did? Would the church go away?"

"No, because people would start doing church in their homes," Isabella said. "I read that's what people do in China and Africa and other parts of the world."

"We are very fortunate to live in America where we don't face persecution because of our faith."

"Mom, I just listened to Pastor Tyler preach. Do I have to listen to you now?"

"We can discuss the message. We should discuss it otherwise we won't remember what he said."

"Can we do it after lunch?" Kevin asked. "God is telling me my belly needs something to eat. Maybe baked beans?"

"It's too hot to use the oven today," Emmy said. "How about something on the grill?"

"Hot dogs!" Kevin yelled.

"We're out of propane," Kenny said. "I forgot to get some the last time I was out."

"Daddy, is everyone wearing masks all the time now?" Isabella asked. "Should we wear masks if we go outside?"

"Everyone I saw at the store was wearing one," Kenny answered. "Wait! I did see one man without any face covering. People were looking at him like he was weird. What a difference from a couple months ago."

Chapter Twenty-Seven

"Dad, I'm sweating like a pig. I might have to take five showers today," Kevin complained. He opened the fridge as much to feel the cold air as to find something to eat.

"It is rather humid," Kenny replied. He looked at Emmy. "How can you drink coffee when it's this hot?"

"Because it's better for you than pop. Why?" She drained her cup as she leaned against the island. "Kevin! Close the door. You're letting the cold air escape."

"That's why I opened it. Can we turn on the AC?"

Emmy looked at Kenny. "It's already in the eighties and supposed to reach the nineties later. I think it's time to bite the bullet and fire up the AC units."

"You make me sound cheap," Kenny said. "I did have Chris Franklin come out to check them last week."

"Daddy, will you turn on the air?" Isabella asked. "You can cut my allowance in half if you need to pay for the utilities."

Kenny looked at Heather. "What do you have to say about the heat and humidity?"

"Nothing."

"Heather! Doesn't it bother you?" Kevin asked.

"Not anymore. I flipped the thermostat switches. The AC should kick on..." she listened, "just about now."

"Thank God!" Kevin said. He put his face on the register to feel the cool air.

"Am I in trouble?" Heather asked as she grabbed a bottle of water from the fridge. "Why do we keep buying bottled water? The fridge does dispense water and crushed ice."

"Good question," Emmy said. "You aren't in trouble, but please don't adjust the thermostats. They're programmed to save energy and reduce expenses."

Kevin stood up, looked out the window and pointed. "When can we go swimming? That would save on AC. We could stay cool in the pool."

Everyone looked at Kenny.

He held up a finger and finished his Dr Pepper.

"Do I have to call the pool company?" Heather asked.

"I called them Saturday. They are booked until Monday. I guess this heat wave caught them off guard."

"I will melt if I have to wait a week," Kevin said.

"You could run through a sprinkler like you used to," Heather suggested.

"Very funny, Heather. You probably did it, too, when you were younger."

Emmy put her cup in the sink and watched two robins hopping along the deck railing. "I might turn on a sprinkler."

"Could we go to a hotel and use their pool?" Kevin asked.

Emmy shook her head. "I think their pools are closed because of the virus."

"Could you find out?"

"We are not going to a hotel," Kenny said. "It's already cooler in the house."

"Who was on the phone, Mom?" Heather asked. "Was it about our graduation ceremony?"

"It was Mrs. Crawford. She's helping coordinate the schedule. I got another email this morning with instructions."

"What time do we have to film our walk down the aisle?" Heather asked while walking slowly away down the hall. She turned and faced Emmy. "Was that formal enough?"

"You only have to walk a few feet in your cap and gown. Pastor Jonah will be filming you," Emmy said, "You need to be in the old sanctuary by 2:15. You will have a few minutes to get ready and you will need to clear everything out of your lockers if you haven't already."

"Will Mary be there? We want to see how big she is. We haven't seen Erin or Ewan in forever. Jonah would bring them to school occasionally."

"I doubt if she or the kids are there."

"When will we get to watch the *ceremony*?" Heather asked using air quotes.

"I don't know. Pastor Jonah and whoever else knows how to edit video will put it all together and someone will inform us."

Emmy drove the girls to the church, and forty-five minutes later they climbed into the Odyssey to head home.

"That wasn't too bad, was it?" Emmy asked.

Heather rolled her eyes.

"Did you notice the diplomas on the table?" Isabella asked.

"Yeah," Heather answered. "What was that about? Why didn't Mrs. Toth give us our diploma?"

"It was because the filming wasn't in alphabetical order," Emmy said. "Normally graduates line up in order and the amount of diplomas is reduced..."

"I get it, Mom. It would look funny if Tal Zbikowski was the first to film his thing and the table was covered in diplomas."

"It would have been too difficult for the school officials to count how many diplomas would be on the table after each student received a diploma," Emmy explained.

"I was ready to crack up when I walked across the platform," Heather said. "I expected music and Kevin to yell something childish."

"Kenny, did you see this?" Emmy carried her laptop into the den.

He pivoted in his desk chair. "See what, Em?"

"There's a video of a man... it's awful." She handed the laptop to Kenny and wiped away a tear.

He watched then asked, "Is that real?"

"Unfortunately, it is," she whispered.

"I have good news," Emmy said as Kevin finally made his way downstairs.

"What?" Kevin asked. "Is there anything to eat?"

"I made breakfast for your father three hours ago. If you want lunch, you can make a sandwich. That's the price you pay for sleeping until almost eleven."

"I was tired. What's the good news?"

"Look outside," she said then pointed.

He yawned and looked. "What am I supposed to see?"

"The two guys working by the pool for starters."

166

He looked again. "Is the pool going to be ready to use?"

"Within an hour I would guess. It might be cool, but you can go swimming."

"All right!" he hollered racing out of the kitchen and stampeding up the stairs. He pounded on his sisters' doors. "Get up! The pool's almost ready to use." He disappeared into his room.

Heather and Isabella opened their doors a moment later.

"Did you hear what Kevin said?" Heather asked. "I was in the bathroom."

"I think he said the pool was open. Let's ask him."

Isabella knocked on his door.

"What?" he yelled.

"Can we come in?" Isabella asked.

"Give me a second. I'm changing." He put on his swimming trunks and hollered, "You can come in."

"Did you say something about the pool? Why are you wearing those hideous trunks?"

He looked at his neon orange trunks. "I like pineapples."

"No, you twerp. It's the color. Never mind. The pool?"

He pointed to the window. "See for yourself."

The girls rushed to look.

"The pool company is here!" Heather squealed, "Look, Isa. We can go swimming."

"Mom said in about an hour," Kevin said.

"Isa, come on let's wear our new bikinis," Heather said.

They rushed out of Kevin's room and into their own to change.

Kevin looked out the window again. "I can't wait until Ben and Taylor can come over to use the pool." He sighed and mumbled, "I suppose I will have to share it with my sisters for now."

The pool company left thirty minutes later.

"Now?" Kevin asked.

Kenny nodded. "It will take a while to heat up, but it's safe to use." He shook his head as Kevin raced outside. He looked at the twins. "Are you going swimming, too?"

"Yes," Isabella answered.

"Hang on one minute, young ladies! Why do you look guilty? What's going on?"

"Nothing," Heather said.

Emmy walked into the room and laughed. "They're hiding something."

Kenny grinned at Emmy. "I like your bikini. Is it new?"

"I ordered this one when the girls bought theirs. Does it look okay? Is it too skimpy?"

"You couldn't wear it to church, but it's okay for here."

Heather used this opportunity to remove her large beach towel. "How about mine?"

Kenny turned, saw Heather's suit and shook his head. "No way! That shows too much." He pointed up. "Back upstairs. Change into one more modest. Now!"

"Like what?" Heather asked.

"Wear what you did last year," he suggested.

"They don't fit anymore," Heather said.

"Why not?" Kenny asked.

Emmy grinned and answered, "Because they've grown up since last summer."

"No they haven't. They aren't much taller."

"I'm not talking about being taller," Emmy said. "Girls, go outside while I explain a few things to your father."

Heather and Isabella dashed out of the room.

"I knew Daddy would freak," Heather said. "He's probably going to tell us we can't have any boys in the pool."

Emmy put her hands on her hips and faced Kenny.

"What?" he asked then pointed. "Did you see what they're wearing? I could see... part of their... chests."

"They aren't babies. You used to like seeing me in a bikini."

"That's different! And you weren't twelve."

"They are fourteen, and would you care to explain the difference?"

"They are babies. They need suits that don't show... anything."

"Should they dress like women did in the Victorian Age?"

"If that's when they didn't wear bikinis showing their legs and bellies, then yes."

Emmy sighed and turned around. "You can join us if you're ready to act like a sensible father."

"I am being sensible!"

"Yes, you are, but you aren't accepting they are teenagers."

"Do I have to accept it?"

"Yes, if you want to watch me swim."

He looked at her. "You are blackmailing me."

She giggled and looked over her shoulder. "Yes, I am."

Kenny took a deep breath. "Fine! But they can't have any boys over here."

"Tell that to Kevin."

"I don't mean Ben and Taylor and... you know what I meant. No boys who aren't related."

"I will let you explain it to them. I could use a good laugh." She headed outside to join the kids.

"Mom, the water's freezing but it's great," Kevin hollered as he cannonballed into the pool.

"Watch out for your sisters," Emmy warned.

Kenny watched from the kitchen. He turned when he heard a knock on the door. "Come in."

Father James entered and asked, "Is it safe to come in? I'm not wearing a mask."

"I'm not either," Kenny answered. "It's safe. Everyone's outside except me."

"Aren't you allowed to leave the house yet? I thought you finished the quarantine thing."

"I did, and I was getting ready to head to the pool. Care to join me?"

"Why not? It's warm and sunny."

They walked out to the deck.

"Uncle James!" Kevin hollered. "The pool's open."

"We could sit by the pool. Are you thirsty?" Kenny asked.

"Thanks, but I'm good."

Father James waved at Kevin, and he and Kenny joined Emmy at one of the round, glass tables.

"I didn't know you were coming," she said. "Have you been keeping busy? Can you even go to St. Bart's?"

"I haven't done a thing lately," he answered with a shrug. "I can't go to the nursing homes. St. Bart's and Mercy are off limits. I have been going for walks since the weather's better."

"I thought we were going to have to start building an ark," Kenny said. "If the power had gone out, the basement would have flooded."

"Really?" Emmy asked. "We have a backup system."

"Oh, right." Kenny watched as Heather got out of the pool and dried off. "Heather! Fix your suit."

She turned to face him. "What?"

He twirled a finger. "Turn around."

She did.

"No, don't turn around."

Emmy laughed. "Heather, your father is trying to tell you to fix your bottom."

Heather adjusted her bikini bottom.

Kenny groaned and looked away. "Don't do that while we're... ah... never mind. Emmy, you have to return those bathing suits."

She shrugged and said, "No can do. Once they've been worn, they are ours to keep."

 Father James shook his head. "You are sailing in troubled seas, Kenny."

"He is embarrassed because the girls have new bikinis. He wants them to wear... What do you call the uniforms nuns wear?"

"Habits."

Emmy grinned and said, "He wants them to wear habits everywhere."

"Do not."

"He won't allow any boys to use the pool."

Heather overheard her mother and walked up to the table. "Why not? Am I correct you don't mean our cousins? Uncle Tony won't put in a pool because they use ours."

"I meant other boys. Like Ian Plant and whoever else lives here." Kenny waved to include everything to the north and west.

170

Heather stared at her father for a few seconds. "Is this because of the virus and social distancing?"

He pointed at her and said, "Yes! That's it exactly."

"Don't lie to me, Daddy. You don't want boys to see us in our bathing suits."

Emmy grinned and said, "She's got you there."

Kenny turned to Father James.

He shrugged and said, "Don't look at me. I don't know a thing about raising teenagers."

"You're a big help," Kenny said. "Isn't there something in the Bible or the church manual, Emmy?"

"I remember the story about Abraham having a son with one of his servants."

Kenny leaned forward and put his hands to his temples. "It was easier to be quarantined in my room."

"Doesn't it suck to have to wear masks when you're working?" Kevin asked one of the landscaping crew Friday morning. "How can you breathe?"

"I'm used to it. Should you be talking to us? We are supposed to keep our distance."

Kevin looked at the ground. "We're more than six feet away. I'm Kevin. I live here."

"I am Rodrigo Quezada. Nice to meet you."

Kevin pointed to the trailer. "Do you own the company?"

"No, it belongs to my father and my uncle."

"Why is it called Two Bears Landscaping? That's kinda weird."

Rodrigo shrugged. "I am not sure where the name came from. I could call my father and ask."

"That's okay. I'll let you get back to work. Thanks for mowing the yard. It means I won't have to when I get older." Kevin picked up a small tree branch and added it to the pile then walked away. He saw his mother on the deck and headed that way. "Hey, Mom!" he hollered taking the steps two at a time.

"What's on your mind, son?" she asked checking her email. "I need a new laptop. This thing takes forever to boot up."

"I was talking to one of the guys doing the yard. I told him the name was weird, and asked him why it's called Two Bears. He didn't know. Do you?"

Emmy laughed. "You really think it's weird, huh?"

"Yeah. There aren't any bears in SoHam."

"Your uncle Tony and Zach's father started the company when they were still playing football. Does that explain it?"

He scratched his ear. "They played for the Bears, right?"

"Yes."

"They should have come up with a better name."

"They sold the company to the Quezada brothers. I thought they would change the name, but they never did. Now it's too late. There are Two Bears trucks all over the county."

"The guy I talked to was named Rodrigo Quezada."

"He's one of the sons, but I don't remember which brother."

"I told him thanks for doing a good job."

"That was thoughtful."

"Yeah, I figured as long as they're doing the work, I won't have to when I get older. See you later. I'm going to explore the woods."

"Who was on the phone?" Liz asked. "Should I even ask?"

"Mrs. Duffin."

Liz tilted her head. "Do I know her? The name's not familiar."

"You might recognize her. She's probably in her seventies. She uses a cane and... she... uh... she used to come to Pastor Milhuff's Bible study for seniors."

"Doesn't help." Liz shrugged and said, "You were going to say something else."

Tyler chuckled and said, "She has an annoying laugh and a screechy voice."

Liz grinned.

"Remember her now?"

"Yes. She was friends with Mrs. Thompkins. One of the complainers."

"She has strong opinions," Tyler said.

172

"How can you be so nice when you're getting so many emails, texts and calls telling you what to do? Everyone thinks they have the best solution to the virus pandemic. Some of them don't even know what social distancing means. I get so frustrated."

"It can be frustrating, but I try to listen with an open mind."

"Ha! Some of those people have minds so open nothing sticks in their brains." Liz picked up her cell phone and punched it.

"Are you angry at your phone?"

"No, but I'm going to call Emmy and vent. She's a good listener."

"You won't tell her what I said, will you?"

"No."

Emmy saw it was Liz calling. "Hi. I was thinking about you guys. How are things? I'm guessing Tyler is getting blasted with calls and stuff."

"You have no idea," Liz said. She explained the situation for several minutes. "I'm sorry for dumping on you."

"It's all right. I've never been a pastor's wife, but I remember how busy Kenny would be in the early days of the band. He would have to talk to every DJ and reporter and answer the same dull question over and over. I would have gotten annoyed, but he let it slide off his back."

"Have you talked to Tony about anything?"

"I'm assuming you mean church business, right?"

"Yes."

"I ask him about stuff, but he's kinda secretive. I know the board and staff have to come up with a plan for when the church is allowed to open. Things will be different."

"It might be easier for the small churches to open, but there's no way we can distance everyone if we even have several hundred people in the sanctuary."

Emmy giggled and said, "We might have to rent SoHam Memorial Stadium."

"That might not be a bad idea, Em. I'll tell Tyler."

"I was joking," Emmy said.

Chapter Twenty-Eight

"Were you here when the pool company came back?" Kenny asked as he and Emmy stepped off the deck and headed around the northwest corner of the house.

"I was upstairs cleaning. Why?" she asked looking at the top of the house.

"It looked strange to see them working in shorts and no shirts but wearing masks. It's like this whole virus thing is a joke."

"Too bad we couldn't open the pool before Memorial Day." She pointed to the gutters. "Have you thought anymore about adding the master bedroom suite to the first floor, and if we do add it, what will happen to the gutter and those windows?"

Kenny shielded his eyes as he looked up. "I'm not an architect, but I think in the original plans the window in the middle wasn't there. The ones on the end can stay, I think."

"How will the roof go? Will it match the garage?"

"Maybe. Should we make an appointment to see Mr. Tomanek and have him explain it?"

"Didn't he retire?" Emmy asked. She turned around and checked the area. "Would we lose these trees?"

"I think he still works on a few projects." He walked over to the closest tree. "We would have to cut this one down. If the wind knocked it over, it might land on the roof." He listened to the leaves fluttering in the cool breeze. "Are you seriously wanting to add it now?"

"I'm thinking about our future. One of these years we won't want to climb stairs. It would be nice to have a first floor master."

"We could always add an elevator."

"Where?" she asked with a laugh.

He tapped his jaw. "We could replace the half-bath."

"We need a bathroom on the first floor."

Kenny picked up a branch and tossed it into the treeline. "We would still have the one by the library."

"That's too far from the kitchen. I wouldn't want to walk so far when I get old and gray."

"You could use a wheelchair," he teased.

She poked his arm. "Do you think I'm silly for even thinking about adding on. Once the kids are grown, we will have way too much room."

"We could turn it into a bed and breakfast and move into the guesthouse. I doubt if Bobby and Shay will live there forever."

"We could if we hire someone to do the cooking and cleaning. I'm not going to work that hard when I get old, but the income might come in handy."

"Why are you concerned about our income? Our investments are solid."

"Even with the recent stock market crash?"

He put an arm around her shoulders. "The market didn't exactly crash."

"It certainly didn't go up."

"We are safe."

She looked at the house again and sighed.

"I know that sigh, Em," he said. He moved his arm around her waist.

"When we first moved here, I would see this house and think it belonged to someone else. I would think how wonderful it must be to live in a mansion."

They walked to the front, and Emmy stared at the house for a moment. "If we don't add the master suite, we could turn the den and library into our bedroom. That would be easier and cheaper."

"Where would we put our books? Where would you write your stories?" he asked. "You use the den more than me."

"I could use the family room, and we could move the library to the basement. There would be room right underneath where it is now."

Emmy walked to the front porch and sat on the steps. Kenny joined her a couple minutes later.

She pointed to the east. "It's difficult to see Tony's house in the winter, but now I can't see it at all. I can't see Kristen's house even in winter. We might as well be in the middle of a wilderness."

They paused because they heard a siren.

Kenny laughed. "Not many wilderness areas have fire trucks racing down the road."

"How can you tell it's a fire truck and not an ambulance?"

"Kevin taught me the difference."

She stood up and tugged on his hand. "Come on! Something's happened."

They used the kids' mountain bikes because they were outside by the garage.

"I told them to put these away yesterday," Emmy said as she sped down the driveway.

"Hang on a sec, Emmy! This is too small for me. I look like a circus clown riding a toy bike."

She glanced over her shoulder, laughed and rode away. She waited at the gate as another fire truck raced past.

"Can you tell where they're going?" Kenny asked.

She rode into the street and stood up on the bike. "It might be Mr. Robertson's house. I can see smoke."

They rode around the curve and stopped in front of the entrance to Bill and Mona's estate.

She pointed. "It's not the house. It might be his big garage."

They rode up the drive and took a footpath to get to the side of the yard. She stopped and waved.

"What is it?" Kenny asked.

"Tony's fifth wheel. It doesn't look like there's much left."

Within a few minutes the fire was out and the fifth wheel reduced to a smoking mass of charred walls and warped metal.

"I don't think we should move closer, Em," Kenny said.

"That's okay. Tony's coming this way." She waved and hollered, "Are you all right? What happened?"

"I'm fine, but the fifth wheel caught fire."

"Yeah, we can see. How did it start? Do you know? Were you working on it?" she asked in rapid-fire fashion.

"I came over to check on it because we wanted to use it as soon as people are allowed to travel..."

"So what happened?" Emmy interrupted.

"I'm not a fire inspector, but if I had to guess, I would say faulty wiring. It's a total loss no matter how it started."

"Could it have been started by kids messing around?" Kenny asked.

176

Tony rubbed his smudged chin. "I suppose it could have been, but none of the boys have been over here."

"Kevin's been in the pool all day," Emmy said.

"I'm sure if it was kids, they weren't local," Tony said.

"Is there any damage to Mr. Robertson's building?" Emmy asked.

"Maybe some smoke damage on the exterior wall, but nothing more. Don't worry, Em. The cars are safe."

"He loves those old cars," Emmy replied.

They watched a while longer then Emmy said, "I'm glad no one was hurt, and I'm sorry about your fifth wheel. I know how much you liked it."

"I did, but it's only a toy. It can be replaced."

"Thanks for meeting me, Inspector Harmon. I was surprised by your quick call," Tony said.

"Some investigations take much longer, but this was one of the easiest I've ever solved."

"Do you know who started it?"

"No, but it was most likely teenage boys."

"Can you tell me how it started?"

They walked closer to the remains of the trailer.

"They broke in using a lever. It could have been a screwdriver. Those locks are not real secure."

"I was going to add a deadbolt. I guess I shouldn't have waited," Tony said staring at what remained of his trailer.

"The fire started on the couch. We found remnants of magazines, cigarettes and beer cans."

"Do I need to ask if you could identify the magazines?"

Inspector Harmon chuckled. "Use your imagination. I didn't know they printed those anymore with everything available online. Anyway, I would speculate cigarettes caught the magazines on fire. They might have been asleep, woke up because of the smoke and panicked. The fire could have been easily extinguished when it started." He shrugged and said, "In a case such as this, the police might find the kids if they continue setting fires, but it's a long shot. Sorry."

"I appreciate how quickly the trucks arrived. I assume they came from the new station on Hough Street."

Inspector Harmon nodded then pointed to Mr. Robertson's building. "Have you been inside?"

"Yes, many times. I stored the fifth wheel inside over the winter."

"I don't know Mr. Robertson personally, but I know of him."

"Are you a car buff? I have the keys and know the code if you'd like to see his collection."

"Would you mind if I took a quick look?"

"Not at all. I called Mr. Robertson yesterday. He and his wife are in Idaho. He owns a large spread north of the Sawtooth Mountains. Among other homes."

Tony opened the building for Inspector Harmon and showed him the cars.

"I have a '67 Sting Ray. I'm in the process of restoring it, but only as a hobby." He looked at the walls.

"Pretty amazing, huh?" Tony said.

"Mr. Robertson was smart. This is about as close to a fireproof building as you can get." He pointed to the sprinkler system. "They would have gone off if the smoke got in here. Good thing it's not water. That would damage the cars."

Tony looked up. "Oh, I assumed it was a water sprinkler."

Inspector Harmon shook his head. "No, it's a high tech chemical foam. Smothers the fire without damaging the interior."

"I never knew such a system existed," Tony said.

"It's costly, but effective. Thanks for the tour. I will send my report to the authorities and someone will follow up."

"Am I allowed to remove it now?" Tony asked.

"A salvage company should be able to haul what's left out of here. You did call your insurance, right?"

"Yesterday, and I sent pictures."

"Sorry, for the loss," Inspector Harmon said then walked back to his vehicle.

Chapter Twenty-Nine

"I apologize for the extremely late notice," Pastor Tyler said to the board members gathered in the largest classroom in Becker Hall. "But circumstances are changing almost hourly, and I felt it urgent we meet tonight." He glanced at the members in attendance then checked his laptop. "A few members are joining via Zoom. I hope we can communicate efficiently. Let me pray to open the meeting, and I promise to move through the material quickly." He prayed then said, "Before we get sidetracked into the political aspects of the whole COVID-19 situation, I would request we refrain from pointing fingers at the politicians and civil servants. Everyone of you has an opinion, and while I respect that, it will accomplish nothing if we turn this into a debate about who did what or who was responsible for whatever." He looked at each person present. "Do I have your support?"

Most people nodded. A few raised a hand. Some verbally agreed.

"How about the Zoomers?" Tyler asked. "I think I created a new word."

"I agree," Genna Ademilola said. "I'm at work, but on my lunch break."

"Thank you for joining us, Genna. Martin, are you there?"

Martin Stackhouse's face appeared. "I'm here. It took a minute to figure out how to join."

"Did you hear my request?"

"I'm sorry, but I did not."

Tyler explained it briefly.

"Yes, I agree. I don't follow politics as closely as my wife."

"Let's get started. This is the plan put together by Gathering Point in Morrison Harbor, California. They are currently the largest single campus Nazarene church in the country." Tyler handed out the document. "They are opening this Sunday, and have formulated a plan to comply with California requirements, which are even crazier than the ones in Illinois."

"Is that possible?" Jim Rosek asked. He raised a hand and said, "I apologize. That was my political opinion. I will zip it."

179

"Please pass the document along, and I will go over the plan starting with this page." He held up the front page. "Does everyone have a copy?"

"We do now," Carol Wisnewski said.

"This is the plan for meeting outdoors." Tyler waved. "Before you bombard me with questions, the state and the district are recommending outdoor gatherings to start. It will be much easier to follow the guidelines."

Forty-five minutes later the board understood the steps needed to resume meeting physically.

"Obviously this will take a tremendous number of volunteers. Let's begin by determining the various positions required."

The list of positions filled the whiteboard.

"Carol, could you make a list of these, please?"

"Already done," she said as she finished typing.

"We need a list of volunteers." Tyler erased the list, but the whiteboard did not fill again.

"As you see there are many more positions than board and staff people to fill them." He circled the names. "I would like to form a committee to meet every few days to track our progress and supervise the volunteers."

Six people volunteered.

"Okay, now we can move on..."

"I have something to say." Dolores Hoffman raised a hand. She glanced at the other people in the room. "I'm confident I am the oldest person here, and I want to know if you are telling senior citizens to stay home. Are you?"

"Not in so many words," Tyler replied. "It has to be a personal choice. I do not want to be known as the pastor of a church which cares more about numbers and dollars than the health and safety of the community. Does that make sense?"

Roger Goldman said, "Mrs. Hoffman, with all due respect I don't think the wording is telling our more seasoned members to stay home."

"I disagree." She held up the document. "I feel this is telling us to stay home because we are old."

180

Tyler took a deep breath. "Before this escalates, the language can be changed. We do not intend to deny anyone the opportunity to worship. Our intention is to protect those who are at greater risk. Doesn't it make sense to stay home if you are sick and exhibiting symptoms of the virus. I agree we cannot force people to stay home anymore than we can force everyone to wear a mask."

"I would like to see the language changed," Mrs. Hoffman said. "I want to come back as much as anyone, and I don't want to feel excluded because of age."

"You should not feel excluded," Terry Marjai replied via Zoom. "I work at Mercy in the ER, and I see people of all ages testing positive. But I agree with Pastor Tyler. The elderly are far more susceptible to... to phrase it bluntly... dying from the virus. Would you want our church to suffer because we rush into opening without regard for the health of our congregation and community? Personally, if I felt like a threat to anyone's well-being, I would stay home."

Russell Otto removed his mask and asked, "May I speak frankly?"

"You may," Tyler said with a chuckle.

"We should always speak frankly," Roger said.

"I have MS, so I am at greater risk then most of you. I made a decision to be here tonight." He held up his mask. "If I am able to attend our reopening, I will wear my mask. I would hope people respect my right to do so. I respect those who feel they are unable to wear one, however, I will stay far enough away from them to be comfortable about my safety."

"Well put, Russell," Jim Rosek said.

Fifteen minutes later, Tyler sighed and said, "Wow! This has been the most contentious meeting in my memory. Are we all in one accord now?"

Everyone in the room and on the Zoom meeting agreed.

"Thank you all for coming, and I will send out an email tomorrow or Friday to everyone on our list to inform them of the plan and date."

"Don't forget the time change," Carol Wisnewski said.

"Thanks for reminding me. We will start with two services. One at nine and the second at ten thirty."

"No Sunday School, right?" Robby Collins asked.

"No small groups and no nursery available."

Sloane handed her phone to Tony as he walked in from the garage. "It's Emmy. You should talk to her."

Tony leaned against the counter and said, "You know I can't divulge anything we discussed, right?"

"Don't give me that crap. I know better. How did it go?" Emmy asked.

"We avoided World War III."

"That serious, huh?"

"You could say that."

"I bet I know who was upset."

Tony paused while Ben and Taylor grabbed snacks, then said, "You can guess all you want."

"It was probably Mrs. Hoffman or Mr. Stackhouse."

Tony didn't respond.

"So, you can't tell me who raised the biggest fuss, huh?"

"You've always been so smart, brat."

"Fine. Don't tell me," she said with a sigh. "Is Pastor Tyler okay?"

"He handled the situation with finesse and diplomacy."

Chapter Thirty

"Do we have to watch it now?" Kevin asked. "It's going to be on Facebook later. I want to use the pool."

Kenny pointed to a chair. "You are going to watch your sisters graduate. It's an important event in the life of a young person..."

"Daddy! It was junior high," Heather interrupted. "It will be important when we graduate from college."

"How many students graduated?" Kenny asked at the end of the thirty minute ceremony.

"I counted thirty-two," Emmy answered. "I thought Jonah and his team did a fantastic job editing it. It was seamless and the background music was tasteful."

"I'm glad Noemi had to make a speech instead of me," Isabella said. "I would have been too nervous even though no one was there."

"Can I go swimming now?" Kevin asked.

Emmy pointed outside. "Go! Don't come back until your attitude has changed."

"Do we even have a say in this?" Heather asked. "You know I don't want to go to the Barclay Academy."

"You have made it perfectly clear," Emmy said.

"Why don't you want to go to the Academy?" Kenny asked. "Dotty likes it there. She will be a junior this fall."

"Isa, what do you have to say about this? I can't see you and Heather going to different high schools," Emmy said.

Isabella shrugged. "I'm confused. Carson loved going to St. Raymond's, and Dotty has said Barclay isn't as bad as she thought it would be. It's not a Christian school, but it is a private one. You and Daddy went to Roosevelt, so I know a little about it."

Kenny shook his head. "You wouldn't be attending Roosevelt. We are in the Ronald Reagan district. When the city opened that school, it changed the boundaries."

"Couldn't we go to Roosevelt if we want to?" Heather asked.

"SoHam is not like Chicago where you can go to any high school you want," Emmy said.

"Why didn't the church start a high school?" Isabella asked. "I thought they were going to."

"There was talk about it, and they did research the possibility, but right now it isn't feasible. It might be in a few years," Kenny answered.

"Great! As soon as we're in college Crest Ridge will have a high school," Heather said as she leaned back on the couch with her arms over her chest.

"Why did the city build a new school?" Kevin asked. "Is it because Roosevelt is so old?"

"It is old, but that's not the only reason. Let me tell you about the schools in SoHam," Kenny said.

Heather, Isabella and Kevin looked at each other and rolled their eyes.

"The first school in SoHam was started before the city was even incorporated. It was built of wood and all kids attended there no matter what grade they were in. It lasted about twenty years and then burned to the ground. The city then built a new school a few blocks from Roosevelt. Roosevelt wasn't there at the time, but the new school was built close to where Roosevelt stands today. Do you follow?"

"I follow, Dad," Kevin said.

"It was called South Hampshire High School and was open from around 1875 until it finally closed in 1943 during the second world war. Their sports teams were called the Steelmen because of the steel mills on the east side of town."

Heather, Isabella and Emmy groaned. Emmy threw a pillow at Kenny but missed.

"Then in 1927 the board of education wanted to build a new, bigger school. The city passed a resolution, and started building it. That was Theodore Roosevelt High and it opened in 1930.

Heather pretended to yawn.

Isabella closed her eyes, leaned against Emmy and asked, "How much longer?"

184

"He can't have much more useless information. Let him finish."

"Just a few years later they built another high school..."

"Let me guess," Kevin said. "The new one was named Abraham Lincoln after the president because he was from Illinois."

"Right you are!" Kenny raised a hand for a high-five, but Kevin was too far away.

"When was St. Raymond's started?" Isabella asked.

"Isa! Don't encourage him," Heather said.

"Actually, St. Raymond's was founded years before Roosevelt or Lincoln. The Carmelite Brothers started the school back in 1895 as a school for boys of all ages." He raised a hand. "But the Franciscan Sisters actually started a school for girls even earlier. Back in 1869, I think."

"Were you around then?" Emmy asked with a grin.

"No, but my great-grandfather was, or maybe it was his grandfather. Anyway, one of my ancestors lived in SoHam at that time. The girls' school was called St. Francis, and it was part of an old college that no longer exists."

"I have to pee," Heather said. She stood up and started to walk out.

"I'm almost finished," Kenny replied.

Heather plopped back onto the couch.

"The boys' school was called LaSalle School for Boys and then later changed to St. Raymond's in the thirties."

"Isn't there a new school on the east side somewhere?" Kevin asked.

"That would be South Hampshire East and it is set to open in August. Of course, with the virus thing that could change, but the building is there."

"Is it possible we might be stuck having online school again?" Isabella asked.

"Maybe. I don't know." He shrugged.

"If there's only one high school in Crest Ridge, why is it called Central?" Kevin asked.

"Good question, son."

"I just wet my pants," Heather whispered.

"Hush. You did not," Emmy said.

"At one time Crest Ridge was growing faster than SoHam, but then things changed and now SoHam almost surrounds Crest Ridge. There is one in New Linden called New Linden High School, and Melrose Grove opened a second one in 2016 called Britton River High School. Their mascot in a Bengal tiger."

Emmy, Heather and Isabella got up and marched out of the family room.

"Hey! I'm not finished. I didn't mention any of the junior highs, or middle schools as some are now called."

"I'm still here, Dad," Kevin said.

"Do you want to hear about the middle schools?"

Kevin shrugged and answered, "To be honest, Dad. You kinda lost me at Steelmen."

"Mom, I got the mail and guess what?" Kevin asked.

"What?" Emmy replied. She poured the dressing over the taco salad and grabbed the slotted spoon. "Are you hungry?"

"Yes." He held out the mail. "There are two letters or whatever from school. They're thicker than report cards."

"Let me see them."

He handed the envelopes to his mother then tried to grab a bite of taco salad.

She swatted his hand away. "Use a spoon and a bowl. She opened the packages. "Girls! Come here."

The twins raced from the family room to the kitchen.

"What? Did Kevin do something to lunch?" Heather asked.

"No," she answered. "Your diplomas came in today's mail. You are officially eighth grade graduates."

Heather's shoulders slumped. "Great! A piece of mail and we're finished, huh?"

"There is a letter explaining the reasoning. There will not be another ceremony later. School is officially over for the year."

"I understand why they have to do it this way, but it still kinda sucks, Mom," Isabella said.

"I know, and I would feel the same way. Think of the people who are graduating from high school or college."

"Why?" Heather asked.

"They have put more years into school than you and may not have a formal ceremony either."

"I suppose we should be happy we didn't have to march across the platform in front of everyone," Heather said.

"Kenny, I heard from Liz," Emmy said as she got ready for bed.

He walked out of his bathroom and joined her in bed. "What about?"

"Andrew Truman passed away today."

"Tyler's pastor friend?"

"Yeah. He battled brain cancer for almost three years." She replied to Liz then set her phone on the nightstand. "I remember when he came to speak at our church."

"Aren't his parents missionaries in South America?"

"No, his wife's parents are missionaries. They've got two young children."

"That will be tough. I wonder how Tyler's taking this."

"You know he doesn't always show his emotions," Emmy answered. "Do I get a cuddle before we go to sleep?"

"One cuddle," he replied with a grin.

"Emmy, you aren't supposed to leave the house," Brady said as he opened the door for her.

"Our prison sentence is over. Thank God. We are actually allowed to leave solitary confinement and go outside," she answered.

"Prison, huh?"

"We can even leave the neighborhood without checking with our parole officer. Where's the high school graduate?"

"We're in the family room, Aunt Emmy," Connor said. He took her hand. "You can sit with Lily and me on the floor."

Diane heard him and said, "Aunt Emmy is too old to sit on the floor. She's almost forty."

"I heard that, Diane." Emmy sat next to Lily. "Forty's not too old to sit on the floor."

"Maybe, but will you be able to stand up?"

"I'll help her up," Caden said. "Thanks for the card and cash. Mom wanted me to write a thank you note, but I ran out."

"It's okay, Caden. I don't need a card, and you're welcome for the dough. Don't let your mother borrow it. She'll never give it back." Emmy stuck out her tongue then swiveled to face the TV.

"Can we start it?" Carson asked. "It's over an hour long."

"Give your father a chance to get comfortable," Diane said.

"I'm good," Brady replied after shifting his weight in his recliner.

"Okay, this is the auditorium, and the guy speaking first is Dr. Waikus. He's the principal. He's okay, but he always looks like his underwear's too tight."

"Carson! Don't say that," Diane warned.

"I think Carson's right," Emmy said with a giggle. "Look at his face. It would shatter if he cracked a smile."

They listened to Dr. Waikus for five minutes.

"Not too boring," Carson said.

"Who's the guy with the funny hat?" Connor asked.

"Bishop Ragusa. He's in charge of St. Raymond's and half the kids are afraid of him and the other half makes fun of him for being a lush."

Diane frowned at Brady. "Do something."

Brady shrugged. "It's true. Bennett knows him and he said it."

"When do we get to the good part?" Caden asked ten minutes later.

"Be patient," Diane said.

"First, Tarrell Barnett has to give his speech. He's cool. He's a jock, but isn't stuck up like most of them."

"That was quick," Emmy said. "What was it? Like five minutes tops."

Carson laughed and said, "Wait till you hear Stacey Behlendorf's speech."

"Why?" Caden asked. "Does she make a mistake?"

"She's the student council president and a total bore. She comes from a rich family and is the biggest snob in the school."

As they listened to Stacey's speech, Carson kept looking at the clock.

"How long?" Emmy asked when the speech ended.

"Eleven minutes or so," Carson answered.

"Why did she always talk about herself like she's an old lady?" Lily asked. "Isn't she your age, Carson?"

Carson motioned for his little sister to sit next to him on the couch. "She is, but she thinks she knows everything about life. She will probably end up having a baby soon."

"Carson!" Diane exclaimed. "Don't listen to him, Lily."

After another speech by Dr. Waikus, the video cut away to a photo of one of the graduates.

"This is the boring part," Carson said. "There are over three hundred kids in my class. Do we have to watch the whole thing, or can I fast forward?"

"I want to see the other students," Diane said.

Carson shrugged and slumped back against the couch.

Pictures appeared on the right half of the screen as each graduate's name was read by an off-screen voice. The left half contained a list of that person's accomplishments.

"Who is reading the names?" Emmy asked. "They butchered Arambasich. I went to Roosevelt with a boy with the same name."

"I remember him. He's this kid's father," Diane said. "He's a police detective."

The names continued.

Carson pointed to a photo. "That kid stinks! He refused to shower after gym class. Some of the guys called him Cheese."

"Why?" Lily asked.

Carson laughed and explained, "His last name is Blue and blue cheese smells weird."

"What about that kid?" Caden asked. "What does he do that's weird?"

"He used to pick his nose in class."

Connor and Caden laughed and pretended to pick their noses.

"Stop that," Diane scolded.

189

Carson continued his commentary of most students.

"Who is she?" Emmy asked.

"That's another one I don't know," he said as a photo of a heavy girl appeared.

"That one!" Connor pointed.

Carson laughed and to grab Connor. "That photo is from eighth grade. He sent it in as a joke, but they had to use whatever photograph you sent."

"There's Carson!" Connor shouted.

Emmy smiled and high-fived Carson. "Great job."

Lily hugged him. "I made a card for you, but I left it in my room."

"That's okay. You can give it to me later," Carson replied.

"What are you going to study at North Park?" Emmy asked after the video finished.

"I want to be a teacher if we still have schools. By then everyone might have to be homeschooled."

"I hope not," Emmy said. "I wouldn't know how to teach high school."

Chapter Thirty-One

"Thank you for making time to be here," Pastor Tyler said as he mentally tallied how many people were in the foyer. "There is much work to accomplish, but many hands make the work easier. Something like that," he said then chuckled. "I printed a list of cleaning tasks for the new sanctuary. The rest of the space will be closed when we gather again. There will not be any small group meetings."

"What about the nursery?" Genna Ademilola asked.

"Unfortunately, the nursery will not be available. All children will remain with their families."

"Even the babies?" LaShae Mabry asked. "Several of my friends have given birth in the last couple months."

"I'm sorry, but we need to follow the guidelines set by the Department of Health," Tyler said. "Before this turns into a question and answer session, I will send an email to the entire church once we have our plan completed."

"I will bring my kids to help clean Friday. I don't have to work, and they need something to occupy their time," Genna said. "We can clean the bathrooms."

"That will be a big help."

"Is the remodeling finished?" Regina Collins asked.

"They finished yesterday. We need to vacuum the carpet and probably the chairs close to the platform."

"Are we going to need to clean the rest of the building before we move inside even if we don't use the space?" Tanya Paduchik asked. "That could take several days if not an entire week."

"More like a month," Regina said.

"I don't expect anyone to clean every item in storage. We have stuff that hasn't been used in years."

"Now might be the perfect time to get a dumpster and do some serious housecleaning," Robby suggested.

"We tried a couple years ago, but I caught a lot of pushback from the older crowd. They don't like to see anything thrown away."

"I understand, but we aren't a warehouse. I was looking for a whiteboard in the gym closet a few weeks ago, and I came across a Styrofoam cross we haven't used for years.

"We could use it again," LaShae said.

"Maybe, be it had the year 2000 carved into the foam," Robby answered. "I doubt if it will ever be used again."

"Okay, I see your point. I hope you threw it away," LaShae said with a laugh.

"The coffee shop will be closed when we come inside," Tyler said. "No coffee. No donuts. People will need to make sacrifices."

"We can bring our own coffee, right?" Regina asked. "I do not function well unless I've had my morning caffeine."

"You may bring your own. The idea is to eliminate areas where people congregate and touch common surfaces."

Emmy, Rebecca, Ryan and Shaun met in the music suite in the evening to discuss the music for the coming week.

"We won't sing the usual number of songs," Rebecca said. "Since we will be outdoors, there won't be lyrics on the screens for the congregation."

"We can't hand out lyrics either," Emmy said. "No bulletins or any handouts of any kind. No offering. Not the regular way, I mean."

"I have a question," Shaun Runyon said. "Are we going to be on the grass? Will it be totally acoustic?"

"No," Emmy answered. "Reed Shafer and Mr. Griffith are building a stage with a canopy. It won't protect us from rain, but it will provide shade."

"What will we do about a PA system?" Rebecca asked. "We can't sing loud enough to be heard all over the property."

Emmy grinned, raised a hand and said, "Lucky for us, I have some connections. Kenny's tech guys have volunteered to put together a small system for us."

"A small system?" Ryan asked.

"Maybe bigger than a small system. We won't blast the neighborhood, but it will allow us to be heard."

"Are there going to be cables all over?" Ryan asked. "Should I use real drums or the cajon?"

"I know the speakers are Bluetooth capable, so they won't need cables. We have wireless mics for everyone," Emmy said. "It's up to you whether you want to use a full kit or not. Unless Rebecca has an objection."

"I don't have any objection, but will we have monitors?"

"We will use the wireless in-ears. Those are easy to set up."

"Do we really expect people not to sing?" Shaun asked as he read the guidelines. "I can't see that happening unless we use brand new songs." He looked at Emmy, grinned and said, "Can you write three or four new songs in the next hour?"

"I can do all things with the help of Jesus," she said with a smile. "But they might not be any good."

"I don't see a way to prevent people from singing," Rebecca said. "The guidelines say to expand the distance between groups if there will be singing or recitations."

"I agree," Emmy said. "There isn't a way to keep certain people from singing, and others won't sing at all."

Pastor Jonah stepped out of his car while rubbing his eyes then yawning. "I made it, but I might not be completely awake."

"Thanks for getting here so early," Pastor Tyler said. "Not everyone gets out of bed before the sun rises.

"I'm usually up by this time because the kids get up. Once they're up, we're up. Last night was chaotic."

"Same with me. I try to wake up before them, but it doesn't always happen."

"Are we really going to draw circles in the grass and expect people to stay in them?"

Tyler shook his head. "I have a better idea." He pointed to a box. "I found this in the storage closet by the kitchen. I don't remember why we have them, but we can use them now." He pulled a red flag from the box. "They're similar to the flags JULIE uses to mark utilities except these are red, white and blue."

"We probably used them for the Fourth of July," Jonah said. "Duh! I guess they wouldn't be for Thanksgiving."

"This is my plan..." Tyler explained his idea.

Later they stood back and admired the result.

"So, the white flags are for couples or singles. Blue is for families with children, and the red ones are for seniors who might be at risk."

"In a perfect world, everyone will follow the plan."

"We might have to adjust the numbers depending on who actually comes," Jonah said.

Tyler chuckled and said, "If I've learned one thing over the years, it's to be flexible."

"Tyler, have you seen what's happening on Facebook?" Liz asked entering the family room.

"No, I've been working on the cleaning list. More volunteers are coming tomorrow. Why?"

"Rebecca posted a request for prayers for SoHam because there's a protest going on."

"Where?"

"Police were called to break up a demonstration at the intersection of Raynor and Commercial. One officer was injured and several people arrested. The police dispersed the crowd, but they moved to the area around the mall. According to the accounts being posted the whole area surrounding the mall has been blocked off."

"I did hear some sirens earlier."

"There are reports of looting and fights breaking out. Protesters shattered windows at the business next to Darby's."

Tyler shook his head. "Crazy. This must be because of the man killed in Minnesota."

"Plus people are tired of the whole virus thing."

Phoebe and David scurried into the room.

"You are supposed to be in bed," Liz said.

"I heard more sirens and something like fireworks," Phoebe said. "It's not a holiday. Why would people be setting off fireworks?"

"I'm not sure, but you need to go back to bed," Liz said. She glanced at Tyler. "Maybe we should lock the doors tonight."

Chapter Thirty-Two

"Why are you calling so early?" Emmy asked. "The party doesn't start until later."

"Have you heard about the curfew?" Tony asked. "Will this affect the pool party?"

"What curfew, and who says you're invited? I invited Sloane, Mama and the kids." She tapped her chin. "I don't recall inviting you."

"Doesn't matter. I'm coming to act as a lifeguard. Anyway, the mayor of SoHam has issued a curfew for eight o'clock tonight. Everyone is supposed to be inside at home by then."

"Really? Why did he issue a curfew?"

"Apparently, it's because of the rioting last night. You did hear about it, right?" Tony asked.

"I did. Liz said they could hear sirens going off, and there were squad cars cruising up and down Canton Lane. The mall's only half a mile away. Too close for comfort. Fez told Kenny's father the rioters were going up and down Campbell busting windows and looting, but they left Darby's alone. Thank God they used some common sense."

"I don't understand what people hope to accomplish by rioting and looting. It's insanity if you ask me."

Emmy laughed and said, "You would know about insanity."

"You're the one to talk. What time is the party starting?"

"Noonish. I'm making sandwiches. Your mother is making potato salad. We're not having a lot of food. It's a party for the graduates."

"At least we can use the pool for real."

"Oh, didn't I mention."

"What? I can tell you have a smart answer."

"We filled the pool with virtual water. You can walk around the pool and pretend you're swimming," she said then giggled.

"Why do I bother listening to you?"

195

"Mom! Watch how long I can swim underwater," Kevin hollered. He made sure she was watching then pushed off from the other end.

"Why aren't you in the pool, brat?" Tony asked as he stood behind Emmy. "I took a quick dip."

"I might use it later, but the kids are enjoying themselves now," Emmy answered. She sat on the edge of the shallow end with her feet in the water. "Can you believe they will be starting high school in the fall."

"Assuming school opens on time."

"They will be in high school whether it's online or in person. Personally, I don't see how the officials can keep schools closed in the fall."

Tony sat beside her. "I have faith the schools will open. Changes will be made, but schools will open."

She watched Kevin and Ben racing each other. "With everything going on these days, I don't discount anything."

"At least we can have a party," Tony said. He caught a beach ball and tossed it back to Taylor.

"Do you remember Kristen's and Derrick's graduation parties?"

"High school or college?"

"High school. We were dating, and you couldn't come to the parties because of football."

"I do vaguely remember playing football, but I took plenty of hits to the head. Could you explain what you mean?"

"You're a doofus. I wanted you to come to the parties with me. Though, looking back, I'm not sure why I wanted to be seen with you," she teased.

"Did we even know each other when Derrick graduated?"

Emmy shifted her head back and forth. She tucked a curl behind her ear then looked at Tony. "I guess not. Kristen didn't introduce us until the fall."

"You and Derrick dated your junior year. If you want to call whatever you guys did dating."

"They weren't what I would call dates now. We were never romantically involved. We did things together as friends."

196

"What about the times we went out? I remember kissing you once or twice," he teased.

"Please!" she said slowly. "I'm trying to erase those images from my memory."

Tony watched Kevin dunk Grace under the water. She popped up and tried to climb out, but lost her grip and tumbled into the pool.

"Are you okay, Gracie?" Kevin asked assisting her out of the pool. "I didn't mean to scare you."

"I'm okay, but don't do it again."

Tony looked at Emmy. "Was Kristen's party the time you asked... was it Scott something... to the party?"

"Yes. Scott Simmons. He was older, and I thought if he brought me to the party, I would look older."

Tony laughed and she elbowed his side.

"Sounds illogical now."

She said, "I was seventeen and looked younger. He didn't want to bring me, but I convinced him after mentioning free food. He left early and I got a ride home with Barry Newton if memory serves right."

"You were upset with me."

"Yeah, but I got over it."

Tony pushed off the ledge and stood in front of her. "I think you should cool off." He grabbed her ankles and pulled her into the water.

She landed on her feet and splashed him. "Creep!"

"Mom, are you going swimming now?" Kevin asked. "Ben and I are racing each other. I beat him every time."

"He's bigger and has more mass to move through the water," she explained.

Tony splashed her then frowned. "Are you saying my son is fat?"

"No, but he is heavier than Kevin."

Tony picked her up by the waist. "You will pay for that, brat."

"What are you doing? Put me down this instant," Emmy shouted.

"I intend to put you down." He grinned and tossed her toward the middle of the pool.

"Do me, Uncle Tony," Heather said. "Throw me like you did Mom."

Emmy swam to the side and watched as several kids asked to be tossed into the air. "Serves you right for almost drowning me."

Tony shook his head as the kids encircled him clamoring for another turn. "No more. I'm not as young as I used to be." He swam to the side, hopped out and sat on the edge.

Emmy sat beside him and said, "It happens to all of us eventually."

Tony looked at her and laughed. "Someone is turning forty in less than a month. Should Kenny buy you a wheelchair?"

"You might need one if you keep it up."

"You look lost in thought, Em," Kenny said. He rubbed her back and sat beside her on the deck steps. "Did you have fun at the party? Can you believe they will be in high school next year?"

"Not really. You must be getting old."

"Why do you have your laptop out here?"

"I was checking my Facebook page and going through my list of friends."

"You have friends?" he teased.

"A few, but I don't even know most of these people."

"You could start a page for your band."

"We have one, but I don't need a band page anymore. I'm retired from singing other than at church."

"You could make it an author page. You plan to keep writing books, right?"

"Yes, I really enjoy writing, and I don't need to leave home."

"Then do that and start a page for family and friends."

"How would I keep it private?"

"Use another name."

She grinned, leaned into him and said, "I could use Olivia Porter. I used it on the road a few times."

"Do that and only tell a few close friends. That way you could keep it private."

She got an email at that moment and opened it.

"This is from Scott Simmons."

Kenny listened to the birds singing and watched two squirrels chase each other up and around a tree. "Do I know him?"

"Maybe not. I barely remember him. I met him at church a long time ago. Anyway, he moved to Texas, got married and I haven't seen him in years."

"Why would he email you out of the blue?"

"He didn't. I was going through my list of Facebook friends, saw his name and sent him an email." She read through the brief reply. "He's still married, has three kids and is on the staff of Dripping Springs Nazarene."

"That's a unique name." Kenny laughed and asked, "Where is it?"

Emmy read more of the email. "Outside of Austin, Texas. If I remember right, his parents were missionaries in Africa or somewhere."

"Would you consider him a friend of Olivia Porter?"

"What do you mean?"

"If you start a new page under that name, would you send him a friend request?"

She thought about it. "Probably not. He's someone I once knew, but he's not a friend like Kristen or Rory or Bobby." She pointed to the pool. "He's teaching Karissa how to swim. I hope he doesn't drown her."

"Karissa is probably a better swimmer than Bobby, and Shay is watching her," Kenny said.

"Did I tell you I started an outline for a new book?"

"Maybe. Another Claire and Ruby book?"

"No, but I should do that soon. This is a book about the two weeks you were quarantined. I thought people might like to read about what fun that was."

"Fun, huh?"

"Not at the time, but looking back, there were some humorous moments."

"Oh, there were, huh?"

"Yeah, like the time you tried to escape out the window."

He pulled her onto his lap and tickled her side. She yelled loud enough for Bobby to hear.

He stood by the pool fence and hollered, "Get a room! There's a young lady out here."

Emmy squirmed away from Kenny and ran to the pool. "Do you mean Shay or Karissa?"

"Both," Bobby answered. "Should we go home so you guys can use the pool for your fun?"

"No need. I was telling him about an idea for a book, and he started tickling me. It wasn't anything more than that."

"Yeah, sure, Emmy."

"If you're hungry, we have leftovers in the house."

"Any desserts left?"

"There's a cherry pie no one touched. Would you like some?"

"Maybe after I get out of the pool." He turned, ran and jumped into the pool.

Emmy laughed and turned around just as Kenny grabbed her and picked her up.

"Put me down!"

"In a minute."

"Where are you taking me?" she asked with a giggle.

"I thought you might like to go for a swim." Kenny carried her around the fence to the gate.

"I would, but not in my dress."

"I heard that," Bobby said.

Kenny set her down by one of the round tables with an umbrella. "I wasn't going to throw you in the pool, Em. Tony would but not me."

They sat and Emmy smiled at Shay and Karissa. "She's so cute. I'm glad she looks like you and not him." She pointed at Bobby.

"Are you saying I'm not handsome and irresistible to the opposite sex?"

"That's not what I meant."

"Better not be."

"Shay finds you attractive for some reason."

Bobby scooped his seven-month-old daughter from her mother and held her high above his head. Karissa giggled at her father and kicked her legs. He saw Emmy looking at him.

"What?"

"Nothing, I was thinking about when I first met you."

"Can you remember that far back?" Bobby asked.

"Barely. You were such a punk and look at you now. You're a real father."

"As opposed to a fake one or what?"

"Not all men who have children are real fathers," Emmy said.

"Do you love your daddy?" Bobby asked as he made weird noises blowing on Karissa's belly.

She laughed and jabbered at her father.

"See! She said Dada."

"Doesn't mean anything," Emmy said. "It's easy for babies to say."

"She knows what she's saying. Don't you, sweetie pie?"

Emmy looked at Shay and they grinned.

"Are you ready to record the next CD?" Bobby asked Kenny.

"I think we will start next month. While I was quarantined, I wrote lyrics for several new tunes," Kenny answered. "It's too late to organize a tour for this year, so we might as well record."

"Do you have an idea for the title yet?" Emmy asked.

"Maybe. I was thinking of calling it *The Year of the Virus*.

Emmy stuck a finger in her mouth and gagged. "Please don't. That is so lame."

"Some of the new lyrics refer to the virus."

"Karissa, what do you think of Kenny's title?" Emmy asked.

Karissa chose that moment to spit up.

"There's your answer," Emmy said.

Chapter Thirty-Three

"I'm leaving, Kenny. Make sure you bring lawn chairs and sunscreen. You will be sitting in the sun." Emmy kissed his cheek, stood up and checked herself in the mirror. "Church starts at ten, so don't forget."

He turned onto his side and asked, "Where is my mask?"

"There is a box of masks on the kitchen desk. Kevin needs to wear one, and he has to sit with us. Don't let him tell you he can't breath because he will use any excuse not to wear one. Families need to stay in a group. It's one of the guidelines."

"I can't imagine how families with small children will keep them from running all over."

Emmy grinned and said, "They need to be inventive. Maybe they can use ropes or leashes."

She listened to the songs for the service on her way to the church. *I know this is an older song, but it fits what's going on today. I wonder who wrote it.* She parked in her usual area, walked inside the new building and saw Pastor Tyler.

"Good morning, Emmy. You're early. I haven't seen anyone else from the worship team."

"Good morning. Should I wear my mask?"

He chuckled and said, "I'm not wearing mine until I go outside and people begin arriving."

"Do we have enough volunteers to handle the crowd when they arrive?"

He shrugged and answered, "We will see. Wyatt, Jonah and Daryl are in charge, and they have a team to show everyone where to go."

"I saw an old Western a couple days ago. There was a cattle drive," she said then grinned. "Hopefully, we won't have to herd our people to the backyard using cowboys."

"Yeah, I hope so, too. I don't know if Wyatt's ever been on a horse."

"You are so funny," Emmy said while grinning.

"Then why don't people ever laugh at my jokes during the message?"

"Maybe they are too complicated," she said. "Or else they're simply not funny."

"We're ready," Will Consoli said. He waited for a reaction from Emmy. "Emmy, can you hear me?" He asked. When she didn't respond he waved.

She pulled her earbuds out and looked at them. She replaced them and grabbed her wireless mic. "Will, I'm not getting anything in my ears." She looked at Rebecca. "Are you getting any sound?"

Rebecca pulled out one earbud, shook her head and said, "I don't hear anything."

"Give us a minute, Emmy. We need to check it out. It was working earlier."

Several minutes later Will grinned and used the talkback mic. "Someone pulled the plug, but we should be good to go now."

Emmy replaced her earbuds and said, "Check one. Check two. Can you hear me?"

Rebecca, Ryan and Shaun gave her a thumbs up and the soundcheck proceeded.

"Good morning, church," Pastor Tyler said shortly after ten. "It's good to see you, and I'm glad the weather is cooperating." He shielded his eyes from the sun. "I ask this every Sunday, but it's good to be able to see your faces this time. Have you come to worship?" He waited for a response and heard murmuring from the crowd. He turned to Emmy and asked, "Did you hear anything?"

"It was rather weak."

"Let's try again and remember we are outside. Let's make sure the neighbors hear us. Are you ready to worship this morning?"

This time the response echoed from the building across the property.

"Why do we worship?"

"Because Jesus is alive," the people shouted.

"Let me pray to get us started."

"Did anyone count how many people were here?" Wyatt asked after the service. "I know we don't have to report any numbers to the district, but I'm curious."

"Liz did a quick head count and thought there were over two hundred."

Kristen walked up with Zach and Grace and heard part of the conversation. "She told me most families sat together and about half the people wore masks."

"I noticed many of them wore a mask until they got to their seating area. We can't force them to keep it on, but I feel confidant we are informing them of the guidelines."

"What will we do if it rains next Sunday?" Grace asked.

"It might be fun to sit in the rain. Maybe you could set up a slip 'n slide," Zach said.

Tyler chuckled and said, "I can't see that happening, but I hope we can move inside before we have to deal with the weather."

"If we have church outside in July, can we wear shorts?" Zach asked.

Kristen shook her head. "No one knows when we will be allowed to worship inside. The rules change every day."

"This is all of us. Pastor Milhuff is still in Florida," Tyler said the next morning. "This will be a short staff meeting because I need to meet with the SDMI board to discuss Vacation Bible School at ten."

"Do you think we will have VBS this year?" Wade Dickinson, the children's pastor, asked. "If we do, it will out of necessity have a different feel."

"Unless things change rapidly, I feel we might be forced to either cancel or do it online, but we will discuss it later." Tyler glanced at the financial report. "Have you heard any feedback from yesterday? It's early, but if the more seasoned members are displeased about something, they react quickly." He looked around the table.

Wyatt said, "Everything I heard was positive."

"Same here," Wade said.

Wyatt added, "Everyone was happy to see each other no matter if they had to wear masks and maintain the proper social distance."

"I was pleasantly surprised families sat together and the younger children didn't run around. They were better behaved than in the past," Wade said.

"I saw several teens waving to each other and hugging themselves. I suppose it's their way of bypassing the guidelines," Tyler said.

"I did see a few teens hug each other," Daryl said.

"I checked the state website for the latest updates to the guidelines," Jonah said. "I think we should plan for at least one more Sunday outside. Depending on the weather, of course."

"I agree," Tyler said.

"Hi, Emmy, it's Rebecca. I'm sorry to bother you this early, but I need to let you know Ryan has been called to active duty."

"Oh no! When did this happen?" Emmy asked. "He was at church Sunday."

"He was called to Peoria Heights yesterday morning. His group is going to Rockport to assist with COVID-19 testing."

"Do you have any idea how long he will be gone?"

"All he knows is it will be a minimum of two weeks, but could be as long as forty-five days."

"Can he come home on the weekends?" Emmy waved to Heather and Isabella and motioned for them to join her on the deck.

"What's up, Mom?" Heather asked.

"I'm talking to Pastor Rebecca. She is going to need help watching her babies."

"I'll help," Isabella said.

"I'm sorry, but I was talking to the girls. What did you say about the weekends?"

"He won't be allowed to come home. He's staying at a hotel. He has a credit card to use for whatever he needs. Food. Laundry. Other stuff, I suppose."

"Did his entire unit get called up?" Emmy asked.

"I think so, but I'm not totally sure. He did tell me a few weeks ago he volunteered for something like this."

"I hope he's not gone for a month. That would be terrible."

Rebecca groaned and said, "Tell me. He mentioned being quarantined for two weeks after his time is over. I'm not sure if it means quarantined at home, or if he will be locked in a hotel room, or what." She shrugged. "I don't know, and neither does he."

"We need to come up with a schedule of volunteers to help you. Isaiah is running all over the place, and Hannah needs your attention. What about Ryan's job?"

"His company has to give him back his job when he returns. That's the law. He's not worried about that, but he is concerned about us. Me and the babies."

"I'm assuming your family and his already know about this, right?"

"Yes, and my mother-in-law is coming tomorrow to help. My parents are willing to watch them for a few hours at a time, but Dad is still working. Mom's retired, but she doesn't always have a car."

"I will help and the girls will do their part."

"I can pay them," Rebecca offered.

Emmy laughed and said, "They would love it, but that won't be necessary. It will do them good to help out without doing it for the money."

"Liz promised to do whatever she can, too. My sister told me she could come for a weekend once or twice a month. I'm sure God will provide our needs."

"We're going to add Bobby on drums to replace Ryan, and Mason Williams is willing to play bass," Emmy said. "I don't want to add anymore musicians because of the stage size."

"I agree," Pastor Tyler said. "I can fill in on guitar if Shaun doesn't get back in time."

"Where did he go?" Rebecca asked.

Tyler answered, "His fiancee lives in South Dakota. She's a pastor at a small church. Shaun goes up there a couple times a month."

Emmy grinned and said, "We're going to lose him sooner or later. He's in love, and will probably propose within a month or two. Maybe sooner."

"Is there a chance she will move here?" Rebecca asked.

Tyler shook his head. "Not according to Shaun."

Bobby O'Connor and Mason Williams walked up to the portable platform together.

"About time you got here, punk," Emmy said to Bobby. "What's your excuse today? Did you get lost in Bristol Ridge?"

"No, I had to pick up Mason, and I didn't know we were rehearsing outside."

"It's okay. I probably forgot to include it in my email," Emmy said. "Hi, Mason. Thanks for helping out."

"Not a problem, Ms. Colasanti."

Emmy stared at the guys. "Did Bobby tell you to call me that?"

Bobby threw his hands into the air. "Why do you always assume I did whatever. Maybe Mason is being respectful to his elders."

Emmy looked at Mason. "Are you being respectful?"

"In a way, but Bobby told me it would get a rise out of you, and I wanted to see your reaction."

"I'm doubling your rent, punk," Emmy said making a face.

Twenty minutes into the rehearsal, the wind picked up drastically. The stage shook and the canopy flapped violently.

"I think we need to shut down and move inside," Tyler said. "We could be in for a thunderstorm."

Ten minutes later the ground was covered by pebble-sized hailstones.

Emmy looked outside, saw the ice and said, "I remember going outside to gather hailstones on my twentieth birthday. Tony and Kristen threw a surprise party for me. It stormed and I ran into the yard to collect the stones. Ice. Whatever. I got soaked and had to wear one of Tony's old sweatshirts."

Tyler looked at Emmy and shook his head.

"What?" she asked.

"And I thought my stories were lame."

Chapter Thirty-Four

"I hope it's not as windy as Thursday," Rebecca said.

Emmy looked at the canopy over the stage. "Good. It's been fixed. I don't think it will be too windy this morning. It's not supposed to be as hot, either." She waited until everyone was in position. "I will pray then we can start rehearsal."

"Is it too early for rehearsal?" Mason asked.

"Why? We're all here," Emmy replied.

Tyler checked the time and said, "He is thinking it might be too early for the neighbors. We do get rather loud."

"I can keep the house sound low, and you could rehearse. Stuart and I can use headphones for now," Will said.

"That will work," Rebecca said. "Everyone is using in-ears."

Emmy grinned at Pastor Rebecca. "I know you don't like them, but you will become accustomed, and realize you can hear everything much clearer."

"Once we go indoors, we can use our iPads and iPhones to control our own mixes," Bobby said. "Technology is amazing."

The rehearsal went smoothly and thirty minutes later, they were finished.

"That was one of the fastest rehearsals I can remember," Bobby said.

"We're only doing four songs, doofus, and they're old ones everyone knows," Emmy teased.

"Still, it flew past. I didn't break a sweat."

"I think there are more people here than last week," Emmy said as the worship team moved into position to start the service. "I'm glad we don't have to do this twice."

"Do you think the church will go back to two services after everything settles down?" Rebecca asked.

"I don't have a clue," Emmy said with a shrug.

Pastor Tyler opened the service then the band took over. Fifteen minutes later, they left the stage and joined the congregation in the lawn.

"Did we sound okay?" Emmy asked Kenny. "I lost my in-ears during the third song."

"I saw you take them out. Was it a battery issue?"

"Probably. I forgot to check the batteries after rehearsal. It wasn't Will or Stuart's fault."

"You sounded good, Mom," Kevin said. "It was like a short set by an opening band and now Pastor Tyler is the headliner."

"Listen to Pastor Tyler," Heather said. "He's starting."

"I want to thank you all for coming out on this beautiful morning. But I have bad news," he waited as part of the crowd groaned. "This will be our final service outdoors."

More groaning from everyone.

Tyler grinned and waved. "Before you fire me, next Sunday we will be moving indoors. There will be guidelines, but we will worship inside."

He waited for the clapping to stop.

"All righty then," Jim Rosek shouted.

Tyler chuckled and prayed for the service.

"Are we really going inside?" Isabella asked.

"Yes," Emmy answered.

"How many people will be on the platform? Will it be a full band like before?"

"We need to discuss it. Are you anxious to start singing again?"

"I miss it. I like singing with the teen band. We would play every Wednesday night, and once a month for the Sunday services."

"That went smoother than the previous week," Will told Stuart after they shut everything down. "If we add an extra six feet to that stage, the guys could use it for an outdoor gig."

"It needs more room and a riser for the drums," Stuart Lederer replied. "Are they talking about doing one?"

"They might do a livestream for the Fourth of July. They can't actually play anywhere yet, but there would be room in Kenny's back yard. Or on the side by the garage. We could figure out a place to set up. People could sit in the grass and listen."

"We could record the whole event."

"True. They won't make any money, but at least they would get to play live," Will said.

"There's got to be tons of artists without any income now. CD sales are in the tank. Live performances are the only way many artists generate any income at all."

"This is my plan for the coming week," Reed Shafer told Pastor Tyler Monday morning. He handed the paper over and sat in front of the desk.

Tyler took the time to thoroughly read the document. "Do we have enough time and man-hours to accomplish it?"

"If we have a few volunteers to supplement my crew, it can be done. I want to go over the sanctuary first. Then we can tackle the bathrooms. Am I correct in assuming there won't be anyone using the education building?"

"Yes. You are correct. There won't be any grow groups meeting. That will have to figured out down the road. I'm grateful we can move indoors. There were times yesterday when the sun was baking me, and others when the breeze would chill me."

"No one got sunburned around me," Reed said. "They came better prepared this week."

"Let me know how much help you need, and I'll send out an email."

"Will do." Reed took back his list and headed to the maintenance office.

"Are four cameras enough to cover the sanctuary?" Pastor Jonah asked.

Josh Morrissey, who had recently been hired to head the production team, glanced at the empty space. "It will do for a start."

Tyler chuckled and said, "I'm glad Mr. Tomanek made sure there was a large production room for the tech team. Since we're live streaming everything, we need a dedicated broadcast studio. Room. Whatever."

"We will make use of it," Josh said.

210

"We have trained volunteers to staff every position," Jonah said. "Josh knows more about the technical stuff than any of us."

"Except for the guys from Steward Music and the Fridays At Five organization. Those guys are pros," Tyler said.

"Josh convinced Nolan Carpenter to do the broadcast mix. He works for Channel Eleven and knows how to use all our gear."

Tyler turned to Josh. "I will let you work your magic. I don't have a clue how some of this works. Let me know if you need anything."

"I will, Pastor Tyler. We have all the gear needed to put on a first-class livestream."

"Keep in mind this is a church service," Jonah said.

Josh nodded. "I grew up in this church. I remember what it was like when my father programmed the lights. He had to curb his enthusiasm at times."

Tyler saw Reed Shafer in the hallway Friday morning. "How's it going? Are we ready for Sunday?"

"The volunteers will clean the bathrooms again tomorrow evening. The sanctuary chairs are situated as best as we could place them. We don't know how many large families will be here."

"We can always make adjustments, right?"

"Yes, I have a group of ushers who know what to do and how to keep everyone from congregating together. How serious will we enforce the mask guideline?"

"I'm not going to throw anyone out for not wearing a mask. We have tons of free ones to offer them. But if they absolutely refuse, perhaps we could suggest they sit in a section of like-minded people."

"My volunteers will be wearing masks."

"So will the staff unless they are speaking on the platform."

"Do you think many people will notice the changes the guys made to the back wall and elsewhere?"

"It's been so long since they were in the sanctuary, they might not remember. Most of the changes were subtle anyway. It's not like we turned the platform into a movie set from Ancient Egypt or anything."

211

Reed stared at Tyler.

Tyler chuckled and said, "Someone actually suggested we create an image of the Great Pyramids on the stage."

"I'm glad saner minds prevailed."

"Kenny, are you going to Men's Bible study this morning?" Emmy asked.

"Yeah, but I'm not sure which group I should join. Tyler and Wyatt are both leading one."

"Do you know what each group will be studying?"

Kenny shook his head. "I think we're going to meet as one group first to decide what to do."

"Kristen called earlier. Wyatt's car wouldn't start. Could you give him a ride?"

"No problem. I was picking up Tony, too."

"Why does he need a ride? Did he break his new truck?"

"No, Sloane needs it because Peter is using the van to practice driving," Kenny answered. "Did I hear right? Did Carson finally get his driver's license?"

"Diane said he did, and he wants to buy a used car."

"Why a used one? Brady could buy him a new one with all the new safety systems."

"I suppose. When the girls are old enough to drive will you buy them new cars?" Emmy asked.

"Will people still be driving cars in thirty years?" Kenny asked with a grin.

"You're such a dork. Tony should buy Peter a car. His monster truck is too big for Peter or Sloane to drive."

"You've driven it, Em."

"Yeah, but I know how to handle a huge vehicle."

"What kind of car would you suggest for Peter or Carson?"

Emmy tapped a finger against her chin. "I would suggest one of the new Corvettes or possibly an older Ferrari."

Kenny shook his head. "I'll see you later. Does Wyatt know I'm coming?"

"I'll text Kristen." She kissed Kenny and grabbed her phone.

"Thanks for the ride, Kenny. I don't know what happened to my car. It worked fine yesterday."

"Emmy told me to ask if you put gas in it," Kenny said after Wyatt buckled in.

"Gas! I never thought of it. That has to be the issue."

"I ran out of gas once in high school, and she rode me about it for years. I hope she runs out sometime."

"She's smart enough to call roadside assistance, and they'll take care of her. You won't ever know."

Kenny turned into Tony's driveway and saw him waiting by the garage.

Tony hopped in the rear of Kenny's Jeep. "Thanks for the lift. I need to buy a car for Peter soon."

Kenny pulled onto the street and said, "Emmy thinks you should buy him a Corvette or a Ferrari."

Tony laughed and said, "Tell the brat she has to buy her own sports car. I'm going to look for something safe that gets good gas mileage."

"She will be so disappointed."

Kenny parked in the front lot of the church, and the men gathered in the foyer to start.

"It's good to see such a fine turnout. If we grow much larger, we might need three groups," Tyler said. "Let me pray to open."

The men followed the social distancing guidelines and about half wore masks.

"I've had several suggestions about what to study for the coming weeks. The most frequent requests were to study one of the Gospels, but almost as many would like to study one of the books I mentioned in March."

"I wouldn't mind leading a study of the Gospels," Wyatt said.

"How many are interested in Robert Galt's book? Raise a hand," Tyler said.

The group was evenly divided, so they broke off into two groups.

213

"How did it go?" Emmy asked later. "I'm making sandwiches for lunch."

"Pretty good. There were more men than anyone expected."

He explained how Tyler divided the group.

"Which group are you in?"

"I wanted to join Tyler's group because I heard that book was pretty good, but I decided to go with Wyatt's group. It will be a way to get to know him better. He is a neighbor now."

"Kristen said he feels uncomfortable at times living here because he doesn't make anywhere close to what the other men earn."

"He shouldn't feel like that. Everyone in the neighborhood, who knows him, respects what he does."

"I doubt if the Ramels do."

"Why would you sat that?"

"Because they're Buddhists or Hindus or something."

Kenny sat at the island and shook his head.

"They should still respect Wyatt. Maybe they do, but some of the other families in that part of Bristol Ridge don't have any church affiliation whatsoever."

"That reflects poorly on us. We should invite them to church," Kenny said.

Emmy rolled her eyes. "We have. Numerous times. Some people are clearly not interested in going to a church."

"Maybe they would be interested in the livestream, huh?"

"Good thinking. I'm friends with almost everyone who lives here. I'll make sure I post something about the livestream on Facebook."

"As Olivia, or as Emmy?"

"Probably as Emmy."

Chapter Thirty-Five

"Hey, punk, would you like a ride to church this morning?" Emmy asked. "We both need to be there by nine thirty for rehearsal."

"I don't know, Ms. Colasanti. Would I have to put up with your verbal abuse the entire ride?"

"Fine. I'll stop teasing you. You want a ride or not?" Emmy grabbed her keys and purse.

"Sure. I'm ready now. Do I have to walk to your house, or will you drive all the way here?"

She laughed and said, "Start walking, and I'll try to run you over."

"You wouldn't leave my daughter fatherless, would you?"

"No, but only because she's not old enough to know you're a punk." Emmy kissed Kenny who was sitting at the island. "I'm picking up Bobby."

Emmy and Bobby arrived at the church a few minutes before the scheduled time for rehearsal. She parked next to Rebecca's Prius.

"Why did you park next to her? Bobby asked waving at the empty spaces. "You have a whole parking lot. You should park six spots away."

"You better hope Shay and Karissa are here later to take you home. I'd make you walk." She shut off her SUV, and they got out. "Hey! What is that? Listen. It sounds like Rebecca's car is running."

"It is. I wonder if she was using it in electric mode and forgot to turn it off."

"Can you shut it off?" Emmy asked.

"I can if it's not locked." He tried her door. "It's open."

Emmy rolled her eyes. "Turn it off before she runs out of gas."

"That would take a long time. These cars get great fuel economy."

"Just shut it off, Bobby," Emmy said rolling her eyes.

He did and they walked inside. They saw Rebecca talking to Pastor Tyler.

"Rebecca, did you leave your car on?" Emmy asked. "I parked next to it, and we got out and it started running."

Tyler chuckled and said, "I've done that before. I forget it's electric and don't turn it off because it's so quiet."

"I'll turn it off. Be right back," Rebecca said.

"No need. I shut it down, but I didn't lock it. I didn't know if you had the keys," Bobby said.

Rebecca pulled her keys from her purse, pointed the fob at the car and locked it. "Thank you."

Within a few minutes everyone on the worship team had arrived. By the time they finished rehearsing, a few people were in the building.

"We thought the service was starting at ten," Mrs. Boothe said.

Emmy explained, "We started at ten while we were outdoors to avoid the heat, but now we're starting at ten forty-five. You can go inside and find a seat if you'd like."

Mrs. Boothe looked around the foyer. "Where are the tables for the coffee shop? I usually get my coffee here."

"I'm sorry, but we aren't serving coffee or donuts because of the pandemic guidelines."

"I didn't know," Mrs. Boothe said.

"Do you get the emails from Pastor Tyler?"

"My grandson bought me a computer, but I don't like to use it."

"Do you have a cell phone? Tyler sends texts to people without computers."

Mrs. Boothe smiled and pulled her phone from her extra large purse. "I have a phone, but I don't know how to text."

Emmy guided her to a couple chairs inside the sanctuary. "If you'd like, I can show you how to use your phone."

Ten minutes later, Mrs. Boothe could read her texts and answer her phone though Emmy doubted she would remember for long.

"Thank you, child. I should use it more often."

"If you need help again, please ask someone at the church. We will help you."

"I thought the attendance would be higher," Wyatt said to Tyler after the service as he waited by the church office with Kristen, Zach and Grace.

Tyler read the report from Mrs. Burns, the church treasurer, and grabbed his check. "I'm pleased some of the older folks were here. I wasn't sure they would feel comfortable being inside. I noticed a few new faces, too." He chuckled and said, "Though it wasn't easy to recognize everyone because of the masks."

"I talked to one of the ladies," Kristen said. "She found our livestream and decided to check us out in person. She lives close and brought three of her children."

"Did you get her information?" Wyatt asked.

"No, because I couldn't find anything to write on."

"We removed all the connect cards and aren't doing any handouts for the time being," Tyler said. "I guess we will have hope they return."

"What are we having for lunch," Kevin asked as soon as he walked into the house. "I'm so hungry I could eat liver and onions."

"Please, don't tell him that's what we're having, Mom," Heather said. She walked straight to the fridge and pulled out a cheese stick.

Emmy checked a text on her phone. "James is coming for lunch and requests taco salad."

"Do we have everything you need?" Kenny asked. "I can help put it together."

Emmy checked the pantry. "I need to thaw the hamburger, but I think we have everything.

The landline rang and Isabella answered. "Mom, it's Uncle James. He wants to know if you got his text."

"Let me talk to him."

"Hang on. Mom wants to talk to you." Isabella handed the phone to her mother.

"Why are you calling to see if I got your text? Why didn't you call and save the trouble of texting?"

"I sent the text an hour ago, but you didn't respond."

"*I* was at church," she said. "Where were you?"

"In between masses. Aren't you allowed to use your phone during church?"

"Right! That would look great. I'm in the middle of a song and stop the band to say 'Excuse me, but I need to answer a text.' Sounds like the perfect plan to me."

"Whatever. Can you honor my request, or should I stop at Darby's?"

"Darby's or taco salad?" Emmy asked the kids.

"Both," Kevin said.

"You don't need both," Emmy said. "I can make taco salad, but if you want to pick up fries, I won't argue."

"Will do," Father James said. "See you soon."

He arrived thirty minutes later and set two bags from Darby's on the island.

"What did you bring, Uncle James?" Kevin asked.

"Fries and three hot dogs with the works. You can share with your sisters."

"I'll wait for the taco salad," Isabella said.

"I can eat two," Kevin said.

"You will wait until I finish the taco salad," Emmy said. "It's taking longer because I had to thaw the hamburger, but it's almost ready. I have to add the chips and dressing."

Emmy offered the mealtime prayer a few minutes later.

"Does anyone mind if I eat two hot dogs?" Kevin asked.

"I don't mind," Heather said.

Kenny smiled. "I'll take one."

"What have you been doing, Uncle James?" Isabella asked. "We haven't seen you in ages."

"I was here a month ago, but your mother hasn't invited me back."

"Since when do you need an invitation?" Emmy asked.

"I hate to show up unannounced or uninvited," he said spooning taco salad into his bowl.

"Did you have church today?" Kevin asked. "Our service was inside even though the weather was perfect."

"We did have mass." He added salsa to his salad. "We had to wait until we could have church inside. Mass is sacred and not a picnic."

Emmy rolled her eyes.

By one thirty the kids were in the pool. Emmy, Father James and Kenny sat at one of the tables and watched.

"Mom, can I see if Ben and Taylor can come over?" Kevin asked.

"Go ahead," she answered.

"All right," he hollered and grabbed the landline from the table.

"See if Peter wants to swim," Heather said.

Kenny looked at Emmy.

"It's okay if Tony's boys swim over here," Emmy said.

"I know that, but why does Heather want Peter to come over?"

"Why shouldn't she? Kevin, tell whoever answers everyone is invited."

"Even Uncle Tony?"

"Yes, even him," Emmy answered.

"Peter will be seventeen in a couple weeks," Kenny said.

"You've always been so good at math, dear."

"The girls are twelve."

"We are fourteen, Daddy," Heather shouted. "Don't pretend you don't know how old we are."

"I see where you're going, but do I have to explain it again?" Emmy asked.

"It was different with us." Kenny looked at Father James then shook his head. "Yeah, I know. You don't know how to deal with teenage girls."

"Why are you worried about Peter. The girls treat him like a cousin."

Kenny raised a finger. "Aha! They aren't cousins. They aren't related at all."

219

"And your point is?" Emmy asked.

"Carson is their cousin, and they aren't asking him to come over and see them in those skimpy bathing suits." He looked at Heather and hollered, "Find a pair of shorts to wear over your bikini bottom."

"Daddy!"

Kevin handed the phone to Emmy. "They will be here soon." He grinned at Heather and said, "Peter is coming, too. He can't wait to see you in your bikini."

"I'm going to murder you, Kevin Michael," she shouted. "You better not say anything to him."

"Can't I talk to him? He's my cousin, too."

"He's not really our cousin," Heather said. "We're not technically related."

"Shorts, Heather," Kenny said. He looked at Emmy for support.

"Did you notice anything different about the taco salad today?" Emmy asked her half-brother.

"It tasted a little sweeter," he answered.

Kevin pushed Heather from behind. "Mom calls Uncle Tony her long lost cousin, so we are related."

She turned around and pushed him back. "No, we aren't, and don't push me."

"What was different?" Father James asked.

"Shorts!" Kenny hollered.

"I used a mixture of dressings because I didn't have enough of the Western."

"I can push you if I want," Kevin said.

"Try it again, and you will pay dearly," Heather hissed.

Isabella floated on an inflatable raft and sang one of Emmy's songs about peace and love.

"I'm not afraid of you, Heather," Kevin said taking a step back.

"You should be. You have to sleep at night." She turned her back to him.

"Shorts," Kenny said with less authority. He looked at Emmy. "A little help, please."

220

"What was the other dressing," Father James asked.

"Russian," she answered with a grin.

"Emmy!" Kenny hollered.

She and Father James looked at him.

"What? We're talking."

Kenny pointed to Heather.

"Yes, that is our daughter. One of them," Emmy said. "Should I introduce you sometime?"

"She's wearing a *bikini*," he said as if that explained everything.

Father James turned to watch a deer walking through the woods and began whistling.

"The girls have been wearing two-piece bathing suits for years. You just now noticed?" Emmy asked.

"I can see part of her..."

"Thanks for inviting us to use the pool," Ben hollered as he sprinted past.

"Yeah, thanks, Aunt Emmy," Taylor said as he followed his brother.

Emmy looked over her shoulder and saw Tony and Coby coming.

Kevin, Ben and Taylor jumped into the pool, which flipped Isabella into the water.

"Watch out for Isa," Kenny hollered. "Shorts, Heather."

Everyone ignored him.

A car pulled up to the garage, and Peter got out with Dotty and Noemi.

"Check out my cool ride," Peter hollered holding up the keys.

"You bought him a car?" Emmy asked as Tony opened the gate and walked in.

"Sure. Why not? He promised to chauffeur Mama when needed. She doesn't like to drive if she can avoid it."

"What is it?" Emmy asked. "All cars look so much alike now."

"It's a 2020 Hyundai Elantra," Tony answered. "Great gas mileage and warranty. It's loaded with safety features, too."

221

"Does he know it?" Emmy asked.

Tony shrugged and headed for the pool.

Peter opened the gate for his sisters and then walked up to Emmy.

"Congratulations, Peter," she said.

"Thanks," he said jangling the keys. "I'm not supposed to use it unless there's a good reason."

"That's a good idea, Peter," Father James said.

"Thanks for letting us use the pool."

"You're welcome anytime, Peter," Emmy said then looked at Kenny.

"No one listens to me," Kenny said.

Tony got out of the pool, walked over to Emmy and dripped water on her.

"Stop it, creep. If I wanted to get wet, I would be wearing a bathing suit."

"So why aren't you? It's a perfect day for it."

She pointed to the pool. "I thought I'd go later after the kids are tired."

Tony laughed and said, "They never get tired. You'll have to chase them away at some point."

Kenny watched as Peter, Dotty and Noemi talked to Heather and Isabella at the other end of the pool.

"What do you think they're talking about?" Kenny asked.

Tony pulled a chair over from another table and sat across from Emmy. "Don't know, but maybe Dotty will tell us."

Dotty walked up to Tony and asked, "Would it be all right if we, and I mean the older kids, order a pizza? Maybe two if you want some."

"I don't see why not," Tony said. He looked at Emmy. "Do you mind?"

"I think it's a good idea, Dotty, but we might need more than two."

After a short discussion, Emmy used an app to order the pizza from Kerry Lynn's Pizza and Pasta.

"They should be here in an hour," Emmy said. "I paid online and added a tip."

Dotty joined the other teens at a table as far away from the adults as possible. The younger boys continued to swim.

Kenny leaned close to Emmy and whispered, "Dotty isn't wearing a bikini."

"Hush. I'm not telling the girls to change. If you want to be one of those fathers who locks their daughters in a closet until they're thirty, go ahead. I'm sure they will appreciate it."

"That's not what I mean, and you know it."

"What are you guys whispering about?" Tony asked.

Father James shook his head and mouthed, "Don't go there."

Emmy looked at Kenny, then the teens sitting at the other end of the pool before answering, "Kenny doesn't like Heather's bikini because he thinks it's too skimpy."

Tony turned to look at the teens. "I didn't notice Heather's or Isa's suits, but I got after Noemi and Dotty. Sloane thought I was being too strict, but I made them change."

Kenny looked at Emmy. "See. I told you so."

Emmy rolled her eyes and looked at Father James.

He began whistling again.

Chapter Thirty-Six

"I talked to the person in the mayor's office. I can't remember her name, but she's in charge of the fireworks display," Andy Walker said as he met with the guys from Fridays At Five in the conference room next to his office.

"What time are they starting their show?" Kenny asked.

"Nine. There won't be an audience in the stadium, but people are going to be allowed to park nearby. Even in the stadium lots unless I heard incorrectly," Andy said.

"So, we need to finish by nine, right?" Jeff said.

"We're starting at seven, so a two-hour show should be long enough," Jeremy said.

"Is there a limit to how many people can watch us in person?" P.J. asked.

Kenny thought about it. "The yard's big enough to hold all our families and maybe a few extra."

They counted how many people might be there.

"We have some chairs, but it would help if your families brought a few," Kenny said. "We have pop and water in the garage, but if you want snacks, I suggest bringing your own."

Adam Vicini said, "I don't think Juliana will be coming. Alex has been out of sorts."

"I'm sorry to hear it," Jeff said. "I love watching him walk. He's like Frankenstein."

"He's been running now, too. I might bring Kinsey if someone could keep an eye on her," Adam said.

"She could play with Lily and Conor," Kenny said. "I'm pretty sure Diane and Brady are coming over."

The Fridays At Five road crew arrived at two and set up the stage and all the gear needed for the livestream.

"It may not be exactly a live Fourth of July show like in the past, but it's the best we can do for now," Jeff said.

The tech team was ready for a soundcheck by five thirty.

"Let's give it a shot," Jeff said. He wiggled his fingers back and forth. "I think I remember how to play."

The band moved into position and warmed up for close to an hour while the production team made adjustments.

"I think we're good here," Will said on his talkback mic.

Emmy brought the guys bottles of water and clean, fresh towels. "You guys are all sweaty. I hope no one can smell through the livestream," she teased.

"We weren't sweating that much, Emmy," Kenny said. He checked his shirt. "Do I have time to change?"

"Em, aren't you going to sing one song with us?" Dave asked. "It won't be a Fourth of July show without you. Please?" he begged.

"One song, Em," Jeremy said.

P.J. held up one finger.

She put her hands on Dave's shoulders, looked up and said, "It's time for Fridays At Five to stand on your own two feet. Twelve feet. Whatever. You've relied on me to pull in the crowds for too long. If you're ever going to become a decent band, you have to sever the apron strings." She made a snipping motion. "It's time to cut the umbilical cord."

"So, is that a no?" Kenny asked.

She rolled her eyes and walked away.

"We're live in ten seconds," Will said into the guys' in-ears.

Kenny watched for Ty Dalicandro to count down the last five seconds.

"Good evening, SoHam!" He stretched the name for several seconds...

Emmy watched from the side of the driveway with the kids and rolled her eyes.

"Has Dad always been so dorky?" Kevin asked.

"Your father is a dork, but we love him, right?"

Isabella smiled and said, "I still think it's cool to have a famous father."

"Are you ready to rock?" Kenny asked. "This isn't our usual Fourth of July show, but we are still going to have fun. There are some people scattered about, and I hope they yell loud enough for everyone to hear."

Will Consoli, the Belanger brothers and Bruce Sutherland controlled the live audio. Stuart Lederer mixed the audio on the fly for the broadcast stream. Randy Lemmert and Phil Barnes handled the video production under the guidance of Nolan Carpenter.

"We are going to play until nine. Stephanie is monitoring our website and Facebook... whatever... to see the comments. Let us know if you have requests, and we will try to fit in a few." He looked at Dave.

Dave counted off the first song, and the show began.

"Are the lights working?" Kevin asked his mother. "It's hard to tell."

"It's not dark enough, but they are working. They aren't using as many and only a few moving ones. Hopefully by eight thirty it will be dark enough for the finale."

"Are they going to set off the pyrotechnics?"

"They have something lined up," Emmy said.

The band played one final song and finished seconds before nine o'clock.

"Thank you to everyone who is watching, and if you stay tuned, the SoHam fireworks show should start real soon. Thank you again for all your love and support over the years. Next year we hope to be playing at the stadium again. Good night." He waved to the camera and the feed switched to the stadium.

Kevin and Ben raced to the stage as the guys were walking off.

"Dad, I thought you were going to blow something up like at a real show," Kevin said.

"We set off the flashpots."

"Yeah, but nothing really exploded."

Jeff laughed and ruffled Kevin's hair. "There's always next year, buddy."

"Come on, Ben. Let's go inside and watch the fireworks on TV."

The crew began the job of packing the gear.

Emmy walked up to Kenny and asked, "Are the guys mad because I wouldn't sing?"

226

He grinned and answered, "Not a bit. They are tired of you always stealing the spotlight. You are such a diva."

She made a face and then smiled. "I can write about the band in one of my books."

"Okay."

"I write fiction, so I can make believe the band is famous, and you guys are real rock stars..."

Kenny picked her up, held her over his shoulder and headed to the pool.

"Put me down before I start screaming," she hollered.

"Go ahead, Em. Everyone is watching and using their phones to make a video."

"They better not," she hollered. She tried to escape but couldn't. "Are they really watching us?"

He checked and answered, "People are following us. They want to see what I'm going to do with you."

"I suppose we should give them a show, huh?"

"That's my plan, Em."

He carried her all the way to the pool's edge before setting her down.

"There you go, Em. I think we have everyone's attention," Kenny said with a serious expression.

"I knew you weren't going to throw me..."

He grinned and pushed at that moment.

Chapter Thirty-Seven

"Let me open with a few announcements," Pastor Tyler said. "There aren't many."

The worship team moved onto the platform a moment later as he prayed. He finished and Emmy nodded at Bobby. He kicked off the song, and the second week of indoor services began.

"It's good to see everyone today," Emmy said. "I hope you all had a great holiday, and I hope you're ready to worship."

Kevin showed his footage of his father pushing his mother into the pool to Ben and Taylor again.

"This has gotten over a million views so far," Ben said.

Kevin nodded and whispered, "It was the best part of the show. Mom tried to pull Dad into the pool but couldn't. Your father was watching and laughing, and he finally pulled her out. She tried to smack him, but lost her balance and fell back into the water."

"It couldn't have been funnier if they practiced it," Taylor said.

"Come on. We better find a seat in the back before we get in trouble," Kevin said.

"I thought we're supposed to sit with our parents," Ben said.

Kevin pointed toward the back. "The teens are sitting together. We can sit in the corner, and no one will see us."

"I didn't get an exact count, but the sanctuary was fuller today," Pastor Tyler said to Liz after the service.

"You're right, but I didn't see some of the regulars. I thought the Hendersons were back from Louisiana."

"I know a few are traveling now since more states have opened or relaxed their guidelines."

"Jim and Stella Rosek are in Mississippi, and the Hoffmans are in Wisconsin," Liz said.

"I don't think we will see everyone coming back for a while," Tyler said as they walked to the door. Tyler set the alarm, they stepped outside and he locked the building.

"Some people might be watching the livestream," Liz said. She saw her children trying to coax a local cat to come closer. "Others we might never see again."

Tyler watched as the cat scampered into the trees. "I didn't mention it before, but I felt the church had reached a plateau before the virus thing hit. I wonder how it will respond when the situation eases."

"If it ever does," Liz added. "How are you going to respond if you get another call from a different church? I know you've been refusing to entertain any thoughts of leaving in the past."

"I will always go where God leads me," he said with his head up.

Pastor Tyler waited until eleven Tuesday morning and joined the group in the foyer of the new sanctuary.

"Why isn't there any coffee?" Arlene Connors asked.

Ellen Boothe sat at one of the tables and asked, "Why are we meeting in here? I like the classroom better."

Tyler sighed and said, "We aren't serving coffee because of the guidelines, and the classroom isn't large enough to accommodate everyone and still practice safe social distancing. Any other questions?"

"I forgot what we were studying. Does anyone remember?" Irene Smalling looked at her husband, Ellis.

"I don't remember." Ellis looked at Jim Rosek. "Do you know?"

"Don't look at me," Jim said with a laugh. "I can't remember what day it is."

Tyler opened his Bible and said, "According to my notes, we are still in Luke. Chapter five."

Because this group of older church members had not been together since March, they spent the first thirty minutes talked about everything except the reason for the meeting.

Finally, Mrs. Thompkins slammed her Bible closed and said, "Enough of this. We need to get started."

Tyler chuckled as he looked away.

Chapter Thirty-Eight

"Mom, why are you still cooking?" Kevin asked. "You should let the caterers bring all the food."

"They are bringing most of it, but I've had a few requests for corn souffle and other dishes the caterers don't make."

"Is corn souffle what Mama makes?" he asked.

"Yes, and there are ladies at the church who make it. They compete to see who has the best recipe."

"Will you be mad if people bring presents?"

"I won't be mad, but I don't expect any gifts."

"People never listen." Kevin grinned and added, "I know someone who bought you something." He didn't elaborate before racing away.

"I suppose it can't be avoided," she said with a sigh.

Kenny walked up to her an hour later. He put his hands on her hips and began swaying. "Are you about ready to come upstairs?"

She did an about-face and looked up. "Soon."

He wiped some of the flour from her cheek and touched the tip of her nose.

She blew her hair from her face and asked, "Are the kids asleep?"

"Maybe. They are in their rooms, and I don't hear any commotion." He raised his eyebrows up and down.

"Don't use that Groucho move on me. I'm too old to fall for it."

He smiled and whispered, "You're not too old, Em. You're still in your thirties."

She looked at the clock on the microwave. "Only for another hour and five minutes."

"Don't take too long," he said then kissed her ear and nibbled on it. "I want to make love to a beautiful thirty something woman one more time."

"Did you have someone in mind?" she asked.

He rubbed his jaw then scratched his ear. "Yeah. Why? What are you asking?"

230

"Most of my friends are either married, or still in their teens," she said with a grin.

"Oh, I get it now. You're playing hard to get, right? That might be fun."

"Have I ever played games in bed?" she asked then added, "Don't answer that. I meant... never mind."

"I have someone in mind. She's pretty sexy and still amazing in bed."

"Do I know her?"

"You could say that," he whispered. He tried to kiss the back of her neck, but she moved away.

"Does this mean once you've had your way with this *older woman*, you're going to look for a younger version?"

"Never. I want to grow old and gray with my older woman."

She turned him around. "Go upstairs. I'll be there in ten minutes."

"I'll be expecting you."

She swatted his butt and grinned as he walked away. "Such a dork. He'll never see my hand print." She grabbed a towel and wiped the flour from her hands.

"Good morning, sweetie," Kenny said. He put a hand on Emmy's back, leaned close, moved her hair and kissed her ear. "I think it's someone's birthday today." He moved his hand lower. "Are you ready for a birthday present?"

She moved his hand, rubbed her eyes and blew some hair off her face. "You gave me your present last night."

"Yes, but it might have been before midnight. Today's your birthday."

"Are you going to keep reminding me all day? Are you sure you want to make love to a forty-year-old woman?" she whispered.

"Yes, and I will still want you when you're fifty, sixty, seventy and eighty."

"What about ninety?" She turned onto her back and grinned at him.

231

"I can't guarantee anything past eighty. I know modern medicine can work wonders, but that might require a miracle," he said then kissed her. "Happy birthday, Em. Should I let you sleep longer?"

"Yes," she answered. "You promised I wouldn't have to do anything for the party."

"All you have to do is come downstairs before one o'clock."

"I'm pretty sure I can manage that."

He kissed her again and touched her stomach. "I can wait until tonight to give you another present."

"Daddy, when is Mom coming downstairs?" Isabella asked. "I want to make breakfast for her. I have Uncle Andy's recipe for blueberry pancakes."

Kenny stood behind Isabella and kissed the top of her head. "She wanted to sleep longer. Could you wait until ten?"

"I want something now," Kevin said. "Could Isa make pancakes for us and make more later for Mom?"

"Yes, but you can't eat all the batter," Isabella said.

"Deal."

"What time is everyone getting here?" Kevin asked. He pulled a carton of orange juice from the fridge, sniffed it and poured a glass. "I told Ben we could use the pool before the party."

"You can use the pool, but when it's time to eat, you have to stop."

"What will we do if it rains?" Heather asked as she set the breakfast nook table.

"We will have to come inside, but spread out. We are still supposed to keep a safe distance from each other."

"It better not rain," Kevin said. "I told the guys we can play in the woods."

"Are you making coffee, Daddy?" Heather asked.

"Your mother's not up, and I don't want any."

Heather finished setting the table and walked to the coffee maker. "I need my caffeine. I know how to use this machine. Can I make some?"

232

He shook his head. "Your grandmother never let me drink coffee at your age."

"What time are Grandma and Grandpa getting here?" Kevin asked.

"Not until noon," Kenny answered. "Why?"

"I want to show Grandpa the ramp we built in the woods. We can jump our bikes across a gully."

Kenny shook his head. "One of these days you will crash and break your bones."

The landline rang and Kenny answered. "What's up?"

"Mama wants your best guesstimate for a count," Tony answered. "She wants to know if she needs to make two batches of potato salad or if one is enough."

"You'd better tell her to make two. Everyone in Bristol Ridge is coming except for the Robertsons. All our close friends and family, I mean. My parents are coming. Tyler, Liz and the kids. I don't know if she heard from Paul and Lynette. Father James is on his way." Kenny tapped his jaw. "Is there any way she could make three?"

"I'll let her know to make enough to feed two armies."

"Tell Uncle Tony to send the guys over right away," Kevin shouted.

"Did you hear that?" Kenny asked.

"Yes, but they're being lazy, and when they do finally get their butts out of bed, I have chores for them. It will be close to noon before they get there."

Kenny passed along the message. Isabella made the pancakes and set aside enough batter for later.

"Anyone home?" Father James asked from the mudroom doorway.

"Come on in," Kenny said. "You just missed breakfast. Isa made blueberry pancakes."

"Thanks, but I ate earlier." He glanced into the kitchen then the living room. "Where's the birthday girl?"

Kenny chuckled. "In bed. I told her she could sleep while we get the house ready for the party."

"I can't believe she's forty. She was only thirty when I met her." He sat on one of the island barstools. "I've aged twenty years since then, but she doesn't look any older."

"She was giggling last night like a little kid," Kevin said. He looked at his father and grinned.

Father James inspected the bananas in the wicker basket.

"You weren't supposed to hear anything," Kenny said.

Heather walked up and poked his side. "You aren't supposed to leave your door open. I had to close it for you."

"We were tickling each other," Kenny said.

"I would drop it before it's too late," Father James muttered.

"Is that what it's called now," Heather asked.

"We weren't..."

Father James tossed a banana at him. "That one's rotten. Do something with it."

Kenny checked it. "It's only starting to get ripe. Isa likes them this way."

"Are you doubting my word as a man of the cloth?" Father James stood up. "I need a beer. Is there anything in the garage?"

"It's pretty early, isn't it?" Kenny asked checking the time.

"I can wait until the party."

Father James winked at Heather and they both whispered, "He's a dork."

Emmy walked into the kitchen only minutes before ten. She rubbed her eyes and stretched her arms over her head.

"Happy birthday," Isabella said. "I can make pancakes for you. Would you like some, too, Uncle James?"

"I'm good," he said while reading his newspaper in the breakfast nook.

Emmy lowered her arms over her chest. "I didn't know you were here."

"Obviously," he said without looking up again.

"I'm dressed," she said.

Isabella shook her head and replied, "You're still in your pajamas, Mom."

Emmy sat at the island. "Where is everyone? Have the caterers arrived?"

"Not yet. It's early," Isabella answered. "Daddy and Kevin ran to the store to pick up water, pop and beer."

"The beer's for me. Not Kevin," Father James said.

"Heather went over to Aunt Diane's to help with something or other," Isabella said. "Maybe she was going to bake a cake."

"What? No way," Emmy said. "She doesn't know how to make a cake."

Isabella shrugged and said, "Maybe she went over to Uncle Tony's house. She's not here."

"You don't have to cover for her, Isa."

Isabella sighed and said, "Peter is showing her his new car. It's not serious, Mom. She likes boys."

"She reminds me of myself too much," Emmy said.

Isabella made the pancakes, and Emmy sat at the island.

"Thank you, sweetie. They were delicious. I better take a shower and get dressed."

"Good idea," Father James said. "Because I heard Tony's truck pull up."

Emmy ran upstairs before Tony walked into the kitchen.

"Morning, Isa. Mama sent me over with the potato salad. Where should I put it?"

"There's room in the garage fridge, or in the basement."

He looked around. "Where's your mother? Is she still in bed?"

"She's in the shower, I think," Isabella said. "Were you going to wish her a happy birthday?"

"I have three months to tease her before I turn forty. I'm going to take advantage of every minute. I'll put the potato salad in the fridge and come back later."

Emmy came downstairs ten minutes later. "Did Tony leave?"

"He will be back later to tease you," Father James said after he closed the fridge. He looked at her and grinned. "You still look like the girls..."

"Thank you."

"Only smaller," he finished. "Nice t-shirt and shorts. Did you borrow them from Isa or Heather?"

"Neither. They're mine."

Kenny and Kevin walked in carrying groceries.

"Your beer's in the fridge, Uncle James. Dad wouldn't let me try any. I gotta shower, so me and Ben and Taylor can go swimming then play combat soldiers in the woods."

Emmy shook her head. "He will be needing another shower before the party."

"He's twelve, Em," Father James said. "He's supposed to smell."

"Who's supposed to smell?" Heather asked as she and Peter walked into the room.

"Your brother. Morning, Peter."

"Happy birthday, Aunt Emmy." He paused and stared at her.

"What?" she asked. "I got dressed."

Father James rolled his eyes and shook his head. "This should be good," he whispered to Heather.

"Everyone is going to tease her all day."

"Is that really you, Aunt Emmy? You sound like her, but you look different."

Emmy finally caught on. "You can tell your father I don't look or feel any different today, and his birthday is coming up."

"He made me promise to tease you. I don't think you look any different than when I was a kid."

"Thank you. Please thank Mama for the potato salad."

"I will."

"We're going downstairs to watch a movie. Call me if you need help," Heather said.

"Okay," Emmy answered without hearing as she sorted through the groceries.

Kenny watched Heather and Peter leave. "Don't you have something for her to do?"

"Who?" She held up a package can of whole black olives. "We need sliced not whole."

236

He grabbed the can and looked. "Sorry, I grabbed the wrong one. I can slice them if you want."

"No, you'll cut off a finger. I'll do it."

The caterers arrived at noon followed by Kenny's parents and some of the Bristol Ridge neighbors and family.

"You're early," Emmy said to Tony. "And you can tease me later when everyone's here."

"What? Me tease you? No way," Tony said.

Mama hugged her and kissed the top of her head. "You don't look any older than yesterday, dear."

"Did Tony tell you to tease me?"

"He's telling everyone, but it's okay. You will have the last laugh in October."

Emmy walked outside and heard the kids playing in the pool. She walked through the gate and stood by the edge. "Make sure you look out for the little ones. Phoebe and David aren't used to this many kids in the pool," she said to the guys sitting at a table.

"We're watching them," Tyler said.

"Where's Liz? I haven't seen her yet." She made a face at Tony and said, "You will get yours later, buddy boy."

"She saw Bobby and Shay with the baby and stopped to talk to them." He pointed to the place where the driveway split off to go to the guesthouse. "Here they come."

"Does she plan on swimming later?"

"Probably not," he answered. "Too many people."

"I understand, but I'm going in the pool later." She looked at Kenny and said, "Without my clothes on this time."

Kenny, Tyler and Father James stared at her.

She realized what she said. "I didn't mean it like that. You are such a dork."

"What did she say?" Dad Colwell asked. "I was listening to the kids."

"She said she wasn't going to wear her clothes when she goes swimming later," Kenny said.

Father James looked at Tyler and they chuckled.

237

"This should be good," Father James whispered.

"Kenneth Travis Robert Colwell, did you hear what you said?" she asked with her hands on her hips.

"Yes, I heard. What did I say?"

"You made it sound like she wasn't going to wear anything when she goes swimming," Tyler explained.

"Oh," he said. "That's not what I meant. Sorry, Em. You can wear your clothes this time."

Everyone laughed.

"What did I miss?" Bobby asked. "All I heard was something about Emmy wearing clothes."

Tony explained.

"Way to embarrass your wife, Kenny."

"I didn't mean to," he said.

"You do it without thinking," Emmy said. "Like last night when you... never mind." She stuck out her tongue and headed inside.

Tony looked at Father James. "What happened?"

"You don't want to know," he answered.

"Are we going to sing after the prayer, or before we eat the cake?" Kenny asked shortly after one.

"We're starving," Kevin hollered. "Let's sing after we eat."

"After we eat is okay with me," Emmy said as she stood beside Kenny. She looked around and asked, "I saw Rory and Rochelle arrive a few minutes ago, but where are Diane and Brady? They should have been here by now. Do you think they got lost, or forgot about it?"

"Carson, Caden and the little ones are here," Kenny said. He pointed to Diane's four kids.

"They better not be fooling around because they're alone in the house," Emmy said.

Emmy's cell phone chirped and she pulled it out of her pocket.

"It's Diane. Hang on while I ream her a new one."

"We can't wait too long, Em. Those boys look ready to attack," Kenny said with a laugh.

238

"Hey, Diane. What's up? Why aren't you here? We're ready to eat."

"Sorry, Emmy, but we aren't going to make it."

"Why not? Are you sick?"

"No, sweetie, but Mona called. Mr. Robertson had a heart attack..."

Emmy dropped her phone.

"Em, what is it?" Kenny asked.

She held up her arms and whispered, "Hold me."

Check out these other titles by the author. Visit the website:
kennethleemcgee.com

The Emmy's Story Series

1. We Were 'posed to Get Married
2. One Of The Guys
3. A New Friend
4. Did You Like the Ravioli Tonight?
5. Completely and Forever: A Wedding
6. It's Time To Go!
7. How Difficult Can It Be?
8. Forever... Isabella... Forever
9. The Forgettable Year
10. Turning Thirty
11. Hello, I'm James
12. Remember The Struggle
13. But God! I Write Songs
14. A Lifelong Dream
15. Gideon's Tree
16. New Priorities
17. Christmas Surprise

The Annie Mercer O'Dell Series

1. Roosevelt High
2. North Park College
3. Smoky Mountain Summer

The Rex Ford & Clay Horn Books

1. The Amazing Adventures Of Rex Ford & Clay Horn

The Stockton Woods Series

1. Sounds Like a Mournful Train Today
2. Sounds Like a Happy Train Today

Stand Alone Books

1. Growing Up In Kinmundy Junction
2. Grandpa, Lions and Kitty Cats: A Collection Of Short Stories For Children Of All Ages
3. The True Stories Of Ol' Melvin, Obadiah, Perkins MacGhee and other Characters

www.ingramcontent.com/pod-product-compliance
Lightning Source LLC
Chambersburg PA
CBHW030252200626
46816CB00002BA/611